WHAT YOU DON'T SEE

Books by Tracy Clark

BROKEN PLACES

BORROWED TIME

WHAT YOU DON'T SEE

Published by Kensington Publishing Corporation

WHAT YOU DON'T SEE

TRACY CLARK

KENSINGTON BOOKS
www.kensingtonbooks.com

KENSINGTON BOOKS are published by

Kensington Publishing Corp.
119 West 40th Street
New York, NY 10018

All Kensington titles, imprints and distributed lines are available at special quantity discounts for bulk purchases for sales promotion, premiums, fund-raising, educational or institutional use.

Special book excerpts or customized printings can also be created to fit specific needs. For details, write or phone the office of the Kensington Special Sales Manager: Kensington Publishing Corp., 119 West 40th Street, New York, NY, 10018. Attn. Special Sales Department. Phone: 1-800-221-2647.

Library of Congress Card Catalogue Number: 2019953572

Kensington and the K logo Reg. U.S. Pat. & TM Off.

ISBN-13: 978-1-4967-1493-0
ISBN-10: 1-4967-1493-8
First Kensington Hardcover Edition: June 2020

eISBN-13: 978-1-4967-1495-4 (ebook)
eISBN-10: 1-4967-1495-4 (ebook)

10 9 8 7 6 5 4 3 2 1

Printed in the United States of America

ACKNOWLEDGMENTS

As always, thank you to my agent Evan Marshall for his enthusiasm and stewardship, and to my editor, John Scognamiglio, at Kensington Publishing, as well as to the entire Kensington family, for going above and beyond. Thanks to family and friends (you know who you are) for their continued support and encouragement. Thanks also to all the talented writers I've met over the last couple of years who have been so gracious with their time, advice, support and attaboys. I'm so honored to be a member of such a welcoming community. And a quick shout-out to Christina St. Joseph. Christina, room 455 made it in. LOL.

Chapter 1

It's time. Long past it, really. She won't be able to ignore me this time. Will she rant or cower? The Great Lady. The Star. The fake. I'll bring her low, make her crawl for help that won't be there. But for now, let her rant . . . please. Only later will it need to be fear; only then will she have to quiver and beg and recognize. I'd kill to see that. Have killed. I tingle when I think of her taking her last breath. Anticipation courses through my veins like a drug, warming me in tender places. Her last breath. Her end. Me standing there. Watching.

Soon she'll hold my letter; my words will be in her head. This time her hands will surely tremble as the full weight of my loathing floods out. On an endless loop, the moment plays. Her hands. My hate. Every frame, every image, a feast to savor one morsel at a time, slow and easy, as I digest each bite in infinite stages, stretching a lifetime between first taste and last.

Now.

Stark white paper, bright red pens lined up like bloody soldiers. What a presentation it makes. The paper feels cool under the reverent sweep of my hand. It's almost a shame to write on it . . . almost.

Just the right words.
A monstrous debt is owed; payment is now due.
Where to begin . . . ?
Ah, yes . . .
>   *Dear Bitch . . .*

"You know that bike cost more than my first car, right?" Ben said as I coasted up to him on the bike path at Promontory Point.

I'd spotted my old partner a half mile out, sitting on the weathered bench under a stand of bur oak, his back to the Museum of Science and Industry. He was hard to miss. His burly-cop body all but dwarfed the resting spot. I dismounted, took my helmet off, smiled. I wasn't surprised to see him. We'd arranged the meet.

"First car and likely your current car, which, pardon my *français*, is a rolling piece of garbage."

"It's only got ninety-six thousand on it. What're you talking about?"

I hooked the helmet onto a handlebar, slipped my towel out of the frame bag, and grabbed my water bottle from the bike's down tube, and drank deep. Ben's bench marked mile twenty-eight on my round-trip trek to tip-top shape and improved mental focus, a trek that hit every high point along Chicago's lakefront, from this spot south all the way north to Lincoln Park Zoo and back. Normally, I didn't stop until I hit the bagel shop around the corner from my apartment a mile or so west, but today Ben came before my whole wheat with raspberry cream cheese.

"Eight thirty on a Sunday morning, most people are still in bed." He had draped his blazer across the back of the bench and had loosened his collar and tie. Cop clothes. He'd just clocked out of a midnight to eight.

"Yeah, but look what 'most people' are missing," I said. "It's a beautiful morning."

And it was. It was a week before Labor Day, the unofficial end of a mild summer, and Lake Michigan shimmered like blue-green glass, slow moving compared to the traffic building behind us on Lake Shore Drive. On the bike and pedestrian paths, the truly committed were on the move, driven by whatever internal spark goosed them along. Ben took a sip of coffee out of a Dunkin' Donuts cup. I plopped down on the bench beside him, slipped off my riding gloves, and stretched my legs out.

"You're sweating," he said.

I slid him a look, amused, then toweled off a bit. "That's what happens when you raise your heart rate. When's the last time you did that, by the way?"

"Vegas. Her name was Sherrie. Damned good memories. How many miles you up to at a pop, you don't mind my asking?"

"Today? Fifteen up, fifteen back. From here, another mile to my shower nozzle. It really wakes you up."

Ben stared at me without enthusiasm. "I can see that. I might get into something like that one of these days."

The man was built like a Bears linebacker, wide, solid, and lead of foot. I doubted his monster feet would even fit on a pair of bike pedals.

"Not a bad idea. One you've had for the whole time I've known you, yet you haven't made it onto a single bike seat yet."

"I'm thinking a Harley-Davidson might make it a little easier on the cartilage," Ben said.

I gulped more water, swallowed, the bottle almost empty. "No doubt. Wouldn't do a thing for your heart rate, though."

He shot me a mischievous grin. "Would if I rode it right."

I needed to refill my bottle. There was a water fountain across the path, but I didn't feel like making a go for it yet. I was tired. I stared at the fountain instead, willing it to come to me.

Ben stretched his arms over his head, yawned. "Sorry I had

to kick your new boyfriend to the curb, but things got awkward. No hard feelings?"

Boyfriend? I chuckled. "Funny, the way he told it, he kicked you, and if I'm not mistaken, I told both of you things were going to get stupid."

He was referring to Detective Eli Weber, his latest ex-partner, my new . . . friend. I had met him a couple months ago while investigating the murder of Father Ray Heaton, my surrogate father. He had been a kind man, a patient man, especially with me. Pop. That's what I'd called him. I was still grieving his loss, missing him.

Ben and Eli had tried partnering, but it had lasted only a few weeks. The closer Eli and I got, the weirder it got for all three of us. It wasn't as if Ben and I had designs on each other. He was a pal, like a brother almost, but what woman wanted her brother working with the guy she was sleeping with? Not a single one.

"It's not like he was giving me a blow-by-blow," Ben said. "But still . . . whatever. Let's talk about something else."

The fountain was playing stubborn. It still refused to budge. I sneered at it. "So, what's up? Why are we sitting here on a bench on a Sunday morning, when I've got a bagel waiting for me?"

He tapped his newspaper against his thigh, eyed the trees. "I asked you here because I have a job for a talented ex-cop turned PI such as yourself. Interested in taking on a little something?"

"Depends on what it is."

He glanced at me, shook his head. "Must be nice. Captain of your own ship, mistress of your own fate. No more having to take whatever croaks or pukes in front of you. You're just out there, footloose and fancy free."

I kicked off my shoes, wiggled my toes around in my sweaty socks. "Yeah, life's sweet. Stop stroking me."

"Patience is a virtue," Ben said.

"So is chastity," I said, "but in for a penny, in for a pound."

Ben breathed in deep, let the breath out slow, a smile on his face. "Weber's one lucky bastard, I tell ya." He tilted his face toward heaven, eyes closed, as if working on a tan. "Vonda Allen."

I groaned. Vonda Allen was a fusspot prima donna, the publisher of her own glitzy magazine, called *Strive*, which leaned heavily toward glitterati puff pieces. Ben worked security for her on his off-hours to pay for some white-guy fishing boat he was mooning over, but that didn't stop him from complaining about the woman's prissy ways.

I waited for more, but apparently, he wasn't in any hurry. He knew the slow approach got under my skin. We'd partnered together for years. He knew I didn't do long and drawn out, which was why he was smiling, messing with me.

"The great Vonda Allen, the woman with her finger on the pulse of urbane and upwardly mobile black folk, the movers and shakers, the stride makers." I was reciting Allen's well-worn hustle, often repeated whenever she showed up anywhere to get her picture taken. I'd skimmed her magazine only once or twice before deciding I wasn't quite urbane enough for what she was laying down. Ben wasn't urbane enough, either, or in any way black, but the money was good, and a side gig was a side gig. I broke first, but only because I had a full-day nap planned. "So?"

"Allen thinks some numnuts has a thing for her. The idiot's been sending her notes filled with not-so-sweet nothings, and now she thinks he might want to cancel her subscription permanently, if you get what I'm saying." Ben reached into his shirt pocket, pulled out a folded piece of paper, and handed it to me. "Flowers, too, and there've been some nuisance calls."

When I unfolded the paper, the words *Dear Bitch*, scrawled in red, leapt out at me. The rest of the page was filled with vile expletives, thrown in to hammer home the writer's obvious disquiet.

I refolded the paper and handed it back. It was a copy, not the original. "He's imaginative."

Ben shrugged. "He overuses the word *fuck*, you ask me. A true sign of a limited vocabulary."

"And Ms. Allen's upset by the crudeness?"

"I figure she's been called bitch a few times. Never, I guess, by mail."

"Just the one?"

"The only one they'd share. Kaye Chandler, her assistant, gatekeeper, whatever you want to call her, made a copy and slipped it to me. Allen ordered her to shred the rest in a show of utter defiance—her words, not mine. Chandler thought I might be able to do something. Convince Allen to take things seriously, if nothing else."

"Define 'the rest.'"

"More than one, less than a dozen. That's as close as I could get. All sent over the past couple months. Allen doesn't want to talk about it, and Chandler doesn't talk about what Allen doesn't want to talk about. Long story short, Allen wants to avoid making a big thing out of this, but she wants her ass covered."

We sat quietly, listening to the leaves rustle overhead.

"She has no idea who's sending them?"

"She says no, but that doesn't necessarily mean no. I've been a cop a long time. I know when I'm being given the business. And, honestly, it could be just about anybody walking. Allen's a real barn burner and doesn't exactly tread lightly."

Two women jogged by. Ben's eyes followed them coming and going until they were well out of sight.

"So, you're going to look into it?" I asked. "Officially?"

"Nope. I'm to stay close. That's it. Allen has less than politely declined my advice to involve the department, and I sure as hell can't force her. So, my job is to just stand there, looking big and tough, and hope Mr. Poison Pen runs out of ink and steps off."

"So where do I fit in?"

Ben pressed his lips to the rim of his cup, found the brew cold, and chucked the liquid over his shoulder onto the grass. The cup, he crushed in a beefy palm as he looked around for a can to toss it in. The can sat next to the water fountain across the way, but it didn't look like Ben wanted to make a go for that, either. "I'm figuring it might be good to double up on this one."

"Since when do you need a co-babysitter?"

"I don't. But you're a woman, and she's a woman. You're black. She's black. See where I'm going with this? Thought you might be able to get something out of her I can't."

I slanted him a look. "Oh, you did, did you?"

"She's got a lot at stake presently. There's talk she's closing in on a deal for her own talk show, and she's got a memoir coming out next week. There's going to be some fancy wine-and-cheese things happening, a couple book signings, some talk or other over at the Harold Washington Library. That's a lot of flesh-pressing, a lot of opportunities for some nut to take a shot. I'm figuring a good look at some high-profile security and he'll wisely find some other way to get his jollies."

"What about your day job?"

Ben tossed his crushed cup into the air and caught it. "Three-week furlough started the minute I clocked out this morning."

I frowned. "Two bodyguards for a few crank letters? Sounds a little heavy handed."

Ben leaned back and crossed his arms against his wide chest. "Maybe. But who am I to tell the not-so-idle rich how to spend her money?"

I drained my water bottle, but my throat was still dry. I sighed, knowing I was going to have to make a move for the fountain. "You say she's difficult."

"Oh, she's difficult, all right."

"Bodyguard for a bitchy magazine peddler . . . ," I muttered. "You run out of cop friends looking for an easy side job?"

"No, but besides the female and black thing, I'd like somebody on this who can't get busted down for telling Allen where to stick her inserts. That wouldn't be a problem with you."

I let a beat pass while I thought it over. "I don't do big and tough, in case you hadn't noticed."

"So, you'll be lean and mean. All she's looking for is a competent buffer."

"I'm not mean."

"You're opinionated and not the least bit bashful. And cocky as the day is long. Also, a little standoffish."

I glared at him.

Ben took a long look at my face. "And you're thorny . . . but sweet on the inside. Like a pineapple. Doesn't mean I don't appreciate your uniqueness. Just letting you know I see you."

Thorny? What? "Bottom line her for me."

"For one thing, she's as aggressive as a feral pit bull. She likes head games—prying, digging, seeing how much she can get away with. All the while she's got zero tolerance for the same kind of treatment. You wouldn't believe the turnover rate in her office." Ben let out an impressive whistle. "I'd say money seems real important to her—who has it, what she has to yank to get at it—and she does all her wheeling and dealing with the sincerest look of insincerity on her face. It's bone chilling, really. I can't completely rule out demonic possession."

I said, "Might explain the 'Dear Bitch.'"

Ben chuckled. "Might at that."

We sat enjoying the breeze, watching the joggers, the lake, the trees. No rush. Ben and I'd ridden in a cop car without killing each other; we could certainly share a bench on a slow Sunday morning without it getting awkward.

"This gig sounds like a real pain."

"Pays five thousand for the week, to start. Open to re-upping, if necessary." Ben nodded at the bike. "More than enough to buy a pretty pink basket for that rolling investment of yours." He stared at me and shook his head. "You know you could look a little impressed. You heard me when I said five Gs?"

"I heard."

You have got to be the only person I know who doesn't jump at the chance to put five grand away just for standing around."

"Seems kind of high."

"Why are you so suspicious? Next time I'm adding *suspicious*."

I turned to face him. "Why's it so high?"

He cleared his throat. "Well, for one thing, there's her personality, which means she's not easy to work for, and then there are the constraints."

"What kind of constraints?"

"You'll have to sign an NDA and take her secrets to the grave."

My brows lifted. "Say what?"

"Nothing gets out of the office. From the kind of shoes she wears, who visits her, to who, or what, she may or may not be sleeping with. She's paying for tight lips, which shouldn't be a problem for you. Never seen anyone hold on to a confidence as tightly as you. You up for it?"

"A week could be a long time."

"Oh, it's going to feel a lot longer than a week. I won't paint you a rosy picture."

"You could try."

"Nope. I've got my pride."

I snapped on my helmet, slipped back into my shoes, eased my fingers back into my gloves, then tucked my towel back in the bag. I reached for Ben's empty cup and took it with me as I trotted, at last, across the path for water. I ditched the cup in the trash can, filled my bottle, took a long drag, and then trotted back.

"One week," I said. "And only because it's you asking. But why do I get the feeling you're luring me into a viper's nest?"

Ben glanced up at me, smiled. "Because you're a suspicious pineapple. Now git along, little dogie. Word of advice? Stop pedaling when you hit the Des Plaines River."

Chapter 2

Vonda Allen held sway from a pricey office suite in the John Hancock building, a sleek, tapered one-hundred-story behemoth sitting smack-dab in the center of the Mag Mile, right next to high-end retail shops that charged forty dollars for a pair of socks and to review-worthy restaurants with too-cool-for-school decor and clientele.

I'd dressed for business in a single-breasted navy suit, the hem of my skirt hitting my leg mid-thigh, a silk tee, nylons, and Italian sling-backs. Ben rose from the couch in Allen's reception area when I walked in, and if his shirt and pants weren't a different color, I'd swear he was wearing the same clothes he'd had on yesterday.

My introduction to Allen was scheduled for ten, and I was early. I was always early. I liked getting a feel for a place. I glanced around at the glass and chrome and high-end paintings, breathing in deep, catching a hint of sandalwood mingled with what I could describe only as unmitigated ego. Allen had a reputation for being haughty, and it showed. I had gone back and looked her up after my bench meeting with Ben and had found several interviews where she talked nonstop about her brand, whatever that meant. As I looked around at all the pretentious trappings, it was obvious to me that whatever her brand was, she was as serious as a heart attack about it.

The receptionist was a young black woman with a flat face and a forced smile. After I gave her my name and stated my purpose, she picked up the phone on her desk and called back to announce me, then hung up. "Ms. Chandler will be right with you," she said before turning back to her computer.

Ben sidled up next to me. "Nice digs, huh?"

"It's a little much."

"You should feel the leather on that couch. It's as smooth as a baby's butt cheeks."

I slid him a look. "What're you doing feeling babies' butt cheeks?"

He frowned. "Cute. You should really think about putting a couch like that in your office in place of that hobo pullout you've got now. Class it up a bit."

"There's nothing wrong with my office."

Ben grinned and then did that Groucho Marx thing with his eyebrows. "You sure about that?"

I turned away from him. He was clowning, and if I didn't stop it, it would go on indefinitely. The best thing to do was just ignore him until he reined himself in. I eyed the copies of all the glossy magazines fanned out on one of the tables, the faces of Chicago celebrities and political VIPs staring up at me with megawatt smiles. Ben caught me looking.

"The police superintendent's in that one," he offered in a stage whisper. "He's no pretty boy, but he's photogenic in a plain sort of way. I wouldn't tell him that to his face, of course. I don't think he'd take it as a compliment."

I slid him a look. "Will you knock it off?"

He glanced past me and his smile disappeared. I turned to see what had prompted the shift, and saw a tall black woman rush into the reception area, a woman I assumed was Kaye Chandler, Allen's right-hand. She moved like she had a purpose, fast, all steam and propulsion, her Louboutins regally kissing the carpet. She headed straight for Ben, zooming right past me.

"Detective Mickerson," she said.

"Ms. Chandler." He glanced over at me. "This is Cassandra Raines, the private investigator I recommended."

She turned to face me and took a moment to check me out. She looked to be in her fifties, dressed neatly in a paisley dress, her dark face well made up, short black hair layered in waves. My first thought was that Allen paid very well, but after taking in Chandler's dull eyes, pursed lips, and the stern set of her prominent jawline, I had a feeling that despite the flash, I was looking into the face of a woman who hadn't had a good time in forever and likely spent her days dancing at the end of puppet strings. For that, I decided, whatever Allen paid, it wasn't nearly enough at all.

"Yes, the private investigator." The way she said it sounded like she was slightly amused, as though Ben had said I was a kiddie magician or circus juggler. "Follow me. Vonda's just about ready for you." She turned to the receptionist. "Pamela, Vonda would like you to hold all calls for twenty minutes. Twenty, not twenty-one or twenty-two." She didn't wait for Pamela's acknowledgment. She'd apparently given the young woman all she felt she needed to know.

Down the hall we went, passing boxlike offices on both sides, each box fronted floor to ceiling by glass. Most of the offices were empty, but not just empty. Vacant. Only a handful of staff occupied the others, men and women sitting glumly at small desks, tapping computer keys or cradling phone receivers between chin and clavicle. As we passed, each of them glanced up to look but then quickly lost interest and went back to what they were doing. None of the offices had privacy drapes or blinds. I felt exposed for them. It was like passing displays in a Museum for the Clinically Morose.

"You're punctual," Chandler said as we moved along. "Vonda insists on punctuality."

I flicked a look at Ben, but he acted like he didn't see me. "Uh-huh." I was a little curious about what else Allen insisted upon, but let it go. "Does the staff know what's been going on?" I asked. It would explain why half the offices were cleared out. Who wanted to work in close proximity to a woman with a target on her back?

"Vonda hasn't authorized me to make a formal announcement. Besides, it's Vonda who's on the receiving end of all this nastiness, not staff."

I let a beat pass, considered my words carefully. "If there's a threat, the office, and those in it, could be at risk. They should at least be made aware, so they can be on alert."

Chandler stopped abruptly, turned, and her eyes held mine. "You're here for Vonda. She'll inform the staff when she feels it's the appropriate time. Security. Protection. That's what she needs. Detective Mickerson has explained this to you?"

I watched her, mesmerized by the intensity, wondering about its source. "He did. But security doesn't get at the source of the problem, does it?"

Ben cleared his throat. His signal to me to shut it. "Anything new since last time I was here?"

Chandler's eyes shifted from mine to Ben's. "Nothing that needs to concern you."

Chandler then shot Ben a cold, off-putting look, which Ben returned in kind. He was a cop, not one to shrink under a withering glare. I smiled slightly, watching the face-off, though I had little doubt who'd win it. And, as I suspected, Chandler blinked first. I waited for Ben to follow up with another question or Chandler to volunteer more information. Neither did, so I jumped in.

"So, no more flowers or letters?"

Chandler gave me the same stare she'd just given Ben. It was obviously her go-to move, but she got the same from me as she'd gotten from him. Her sculpted eyebrows flicked upward, but she didn't answer. Instead, she turned on her heels and walked on. Ben and I shot each other a "What the hell?" look, then quietly followed.

I wondered about the threats, though. Ben had told me Allen and Chandler had thrown evidence of them away, the flowers, the letters, all except the copy Ben had been given on the sneak. It was an opportunity missed. The flowers could have been traced; maybe the letters had had prints on them. Why destroy everything? Chandler was definitely Team Allen, though. Not much evidence of concern, or none at all, for the people around her. That was telling. Maybe it was a disgruntled staffer who was tormenting the boss, or a fan who thought he hadn't gotten enough attention. Or maybe the heat was coming from someone a little closer to home. As for the flowers, flowers weren't threatening, unless they were anonymous, unless they kept coming, unless they were unwanted.

The hall opened up into a small oval sitting area, with a large corner office on the far side. Allen's name was on the door. This office, too, was fronted by glass, but unlike the others, Allen had drapes, which were now drawn. Across the hall sat a similar office with Chandler's name on it. Ben and I stood patiently at Allen's door and listened to a woman's voice, Allen's presumably, escalate in anger. It sounded like she was giving someone a lot to think about. Chandler's face showed little emotion as she rapped lightly on the door, and then melted quietly away. She'd obviously become inured to these kinds of exchanges. Inside, a man fought to get a word in edgewise but was quickly shouted down.

"Wow. She's got some lungs on her," I said.

Ben grinned. "Yep."

I strained to get the gist of what she was saying, but couldn't make out much; the door was too thick. "Does it sound like we'll be standing here awhile?"

"Hope not," he said. "I feel like a frickin' idiot. You?"

"Friend of a frickin' idiot."

Allen yelled the word *bastard* loud enough for us to hear it distinctly. The meeting didn't sound like it was winding down, so we continued to wait.

"Maybe all this is freaking her out," I said.

"Vonda Allen doesn't freak out. Wait. You'll see. Bright spot in all this is building security's more than decent. I had to practically give up a kidney to get up here, and I'm police."

"That stops the invader at the gate, maybe." I kept my voice low. "But it doesn't do much for someone who badges their way up here and then sits in one of those zoo-cage offices, waiting for a chance to go to town on her with a stapler or a letter opener."

Ben slid me a look, shook his head. "Zoo-cage offices? Stapler?"

"Yeah, I said it. You were thinking it, don't lie, and yeah, a stapler, or something worse. What kind of flowers, anyway? Roses?"

"You'd think, but nah. Last ones, the way Chandler described them, sounded like marigolds. Lovesick fan, likely."

I pulled a face. "Dear Bitch? Nuh-uh." But it got me thinking about the flowers. *Marigolds. Who sends a rich, prominent woman used to the finer things a bunch of marigolds? Go big or go home, right?*

We'd both had cases in which flowers and words of love had given way to bruises, fat lips, and shots fired. Frustration levels escalated when someone thought they hadn't gotten the response they felt they deserved. *I love you. Why don't you love me? If I can't have you, nobody can. She made me kill her! I told her I loved her!* A lot of pain and agony had been meted out in the name of love, or whatever.

"Letters, flowers, calls. That's a campaign," I said. "An assault."

"Just protection," Ben said. "If she wants more, she knows where to go to get it. Till then, simple, easy, low key."

"Dumb, shortsighted, dangerous. They could have tried tracking the flowers. Was there a florist's name on any of the deliveries? The name of a delivery service? We'll never know. Why? Because they tossed the flowers away. I know this is bothering you, too. We weren't trained to just shoo people away like flies."

Ben inhaled deep, then let the air hiss out slow. "I'm committed to maintaining the safety bubble."

"Safety bubble? Jeez. You are literally killing me by degrees here."

"Less Wonder Woman, more statue, all right?"

I sneered at him, but stood there quietly, waiting on the door. I peered down the now empty hall, as if the one who had sent the flowers, the one who had written the notes, would be standing there, waving his hands, waiting to be apprehended.

"This is stupid."

"Breathe," Ben said.

"I'm breathing, but you knew who I was when you asked me to do this. And Wonder Woman, my ass."

He smiled. "I figured you could rein it in."

"Oh, I can rein it in, but it's still stupid." I pulled in a calm breath. *Statue. Safety bubble. Fine.* "You're familiar with marigolds, are you?"

He cleared his throat. "I took up gardening. Wanna make something of it?"

"It's just you never mentioned it."

He fiddled nervously with his tie. "Didn't think it needed a news flash . . . It's a legit hobby."

I kept my eyes straight ahead, on the glossy wood door with Vonda Allen's name written on it in gold letters. "I know."

Ben checked his watch, getting antsy. "Guys garden."

"They certainly do."

"A lot of cops, too."

"And why wouldn't they? I do a little bit of it myself."

Ben turned to face me. "You're going to give me shit about this, aren't you?"

I grinned back. "Oh, yeah."

Just then Allen's door swung open, and an angry black man elbowed past us, his eyes wild with an outrage he'd obviously been forced to choke down.

"Psychopathic witch," he spat out as he barreled past. Ben and I turned to watch as he stomped down the hall and disappeared into one of the offices, then slammed the door behind him, rattling the glass. Whoever he was, he certainly looked angry enough to have written a threatening note.

I looked at Ben.

"Maintain the bubble," he muttered. "And breathe."

"Enter!" the voice inside the office bellowed. "Shut the door behind you."

Chandler swung in from behind us and elbowed through. Where'd she come from?

Ben stepped forward, whispered, "Keep an open mind."

"Open mind about . . ."

And that was when I got my first glimpse of Allen's inner sanctum and nearly gagged on astonishment. Everything—chairs, sofas, chaise lounge—was covered in butterscotch leather. Bold art hung in gilded frames from walls papered in artisan fabric the color of tomato bisque, and the carpet was so deep, the heels of my shoes nearly disappeared in the pile. I glanced around, looking for the other twenty people the space could easily accommodate, but Allen was all by her lonesome. There were plants everywhere: lush, green palm-looking things sprouting from terra-cotta urns the size of Humvee tires. I felt like I'd just walked into a desert oasis. This was opulence on steroids.

Allen's desk was a grand slab of tawny marble, but there was little on it, just a phone, an iPhone in a gold case, and one half stack of pink paper. Pink, from all reports, was her signature color. Framed photographs of Allen posing with important people—celebrities, the mayor, sports figures—sat on a credenza along the wall. Included in the array, one of a very well connected, very married senator, Robert Devin, with whom Allen was rumored to have had a relationship prior to his untimely death. I had got that tidbit from one of the gossip rags on display near the register at the CVS near my apartment at the time. In short, Allen was a woman with a lot of pull and a lot of juice, and she wasn't a bit shy about letting everybody know it.

She sat poised in a throne-like chair that swiveled without squeaking, her arms regally placed on the armrests. The woman's picture had been taken easily a million times, and as we stood in front of her now, she looked the same as if she'd primped all day for a *Vogue* photo shoot. She was slender but not overly so for a woman in her early fifties, her eyebrows were expertly arched, and her lipstick was flawless. The professional makeup job enhanced an average attractiveness, but the swish of auburn highlights in her dark hair added a little bit more. Allen literally looked like a million bucks.

She didn't bother to stand up. "Detective Mickerson. Come in. Have a seat."

Her smile revealed a mouthful of high-end dental work, but the smile felt oily, reptilian, as though it was something she tossed out there just because she was expected to, not because she felt it. She wore a lavender linen dress with three-quarter sleeves, and a double strand of flawless pearls hung from her neck. Her nail polish matched the dress, each long, tapered finger manicured within an inch of its life.

"Kaye, I won't need you for this. Touch base with Suzette about the hospital gala, and then print out my updated schedule and send it to my phone. I'll take a cappuccino."

Chandler's face fell, and she held herself there at the door for a moment, the sting of the rude dismissal, the orders, showing on her face. She and Allen exchanged a look I couldn't decipher.

"That's all, Kaye."

Chandler quietly eased out of the room.

Allen leaned forward to read from a piece of paper in front of her. "So, this is the private detective you have for me? Cassandra Raines." She didn't bother coming in for a welcoming handshake. I guessed queens didn't do that sort of thing. "And you're on time. Good. If you'd been late, even a minute, you wouldn't be standing there now." She glanced at her platinum watch—two thousand dollars, easy. Bling squared.

Ben and I took seats in chairs angled in front of Allen's desk. Our chairs were considerably lower than hers, though, and I found myself having to look up to make eye contact. In fact, it appeared as though her desk was actually sitting on a riser or something, which meant she had the added advantage of peering down at visitors from just above eye level.

"Mind if I give you some free advice, Ms. Allen?" Ben asked.

Allen lasered in. "I don't accept it, as a rule, Detective. Neither do I give anything away for free nor respect people who do."

Ben rubbed his chin slowly, and I could hear the scratch of his stubble. "Yeah, well, I'd feel better if I gave it, anyway. The letters? The flowers? We've talked about this before, but I really wish you'd take my advice and not ignore what's going on. Maybe it's completely innocent, but maybe it's not. I think it'd be better if you got out in front of it."

She let a few moments pass without responding, then did finally. "Advice noted."

Something small moved in a corner, and I turned to see a white long-haired cat wearing a diamond-studded collar slink out from under the chaise and head for Allen's legs. Allen caught me watching.

"That's Blue, short for Blue Note. Ignore him. He'll do the same to you." She pressed a button on her desk, and the door opened instantaneously to a lanky young black man in a dress shirt, tie, and slacks. He looked to be around college age, fresh faced, short hair. He came in carrying a round silver tray with a linen napkin and a single cup of cappuccino on it, and it didn't look like this was his first time doing it.

He was used to the tray. Used to the walk from the door to Allen's queenly perch with nary a rattle of fine china or silver. I watched every step of his journey. Whoever the kid was, Allen didn't bother to look at him. She did flick a look at the tray, though.

"Progress, Kendrick. This time you remembered the napkin."

He acknowledged her with a nod, put the tray down, and left as quietly as a ladybug.

Her elbows on her desk now, Allen tented her fingers under her chin and stared at me. "There's only you in your agency." She'd obviously looked me up.

I straightened up a bit. *Showtime.* "That's right."

"Why?"

It seemed an odd question right off the bat. I took a second to answer. "I like it that way."

Her dark eyes did not waver. "I don't see what preference has to do with running a business. You could take on more cases if you had more investigators."

I nodded. "Yes, I definitely could do that."

"So, why don't you?"

"I'd rather keep it simple."

Allen's eyes really were piercing. What was her deal? "What does that mean?"

She was like a four-year-old bombarding you with questions about sex, and I was the parent trying to avoid indelicacies by keeping the answers short and broad, hoping she'd lose interest and settle for a juice box and animal crackers.

"I like working alone," I said.

"Why?"

Our eyes held. My patience was waning. "I just do."

I could feel Ben squirm in the seat next to me.

"You won't tell me why."

"No. Sorry."

Allen didn't blink. "You're not sorry."

I thought about it for a half second. "I was being polite."

"I'd like an answer."

"Why?"

She cocked her head. "Why do I want an answer?"

"Yes."

"Hmmm." Allen pushed the button on her desk twice. I hoped she was buzzing Kendrick to see me out. Frankly, I was more than ready to go. How many times did she push that button in a day? I wondered. And was Kendrick compelled to answer every wordless summons? If so, poor kid.

"You like being in control," she said after a time. "So do I."

The door opened. No Kendrick. It was Chandler who walked in this time, but Allen's eyes never left my face. *Goody for me.*

"Kaye, I also need you to tell the studio I want to see the new set before Friday."

"We really need to get in there sometime today," Chandler said. "That'd give us more of a cushion before mock runthroughs, in case we need to make changes."

Allen turned to Chandler, a sudden chill in the air. "Friday. Make the call."

Chandler, apparently startled by the rebuff, turned and walked out without so much as rippling the air.

"Maybe you heard, but I'm about to launch my own show in a few months. National reach. It's a long time coming." Allen angled her head. "Well? Still waiting for that answer."

"Most people want control over the things that matter to

them," I said. "And they try getting it in a number of ways—working alone maybe, or by propping their desks up on platforms."

Ben cleared his throat; the gruff sound was followed by a clumsy stillness.

"I'm wondering if you're going to be a problem for me," Allen said, condescension dripping from every word. "I'm picking up attitude. I don't like attitude. I want team players. Are you a team player, Ms. Raines?"

"If I like the team."

"And if you don't?"

I shrugged. "Then I take my ball and go home."

Allen looked to Ben. "This could be a problem."

Ben leaned forward, his elbows on his thighs. "Do you want good, or do you want easy?"

The look on Allen's face told me she was a woman not used to having to choose. She considered things for a moment more. "Fine. I'll see how this goes. What I need isn't complicated, as I've told you already. I don't know who's behind all this mess, and honestly, I don't care. I have a magazine to run, a show to ramp up for, events, business. I don't want any of that interrupted. Five thousand for the week. The week started the moment you walked in here."

Ben said, "Yeah, we got it."

I just nodded.

Allen barreled on. "I start my day in the gym at seven. I'm here no later than eight thirty, unless I've got an early meeting scheduled, and I don't this week. There's security in this building, but I'd be a fool to rely on it, so both of you will be here during the day. I'll need you both for my evening events. You can divvy up duties however you see fit. I won't need you overnight. My building's secure—doorman, full security staff. They know what they're doing." Allen sat back in her chair. "Unobtrusive protection is what I'm paying for. Questions?"

Allen looked from Ben to me. Ben stayed quiet, so I stayed quiet. The man had a boat to pay for.

"No problems working for someone else, Ms. Raines?" she asked pointedly.

"I guess we'll find out."

"I'm curious. Why take this at all? A PI who prefers working alone?"

"Detective Mickerson asked, and I had the time."

She let a beat pass. "You two are friends, then?"

I nodded.

"And you apparently value that friendship."

I didn't answer. I didn't think I needed to. I asked a question instead. "Why do you think someone's threatening you?"

I had my theories, of course. I'd known the woman less than ten minutes, and working just on first impressions, I imagined she'd easily get on the wrong side of most anybody quickly. She was intrusive. She was rigid, and she didn't strike me as being the kind of person who cut a lot of slack.

Allen blinked and, for the first time, looked away. "I have no idea."

"Everybody knows at least one person who curses the air they breathe." I studied her, but her painted face, her mask, gave nothing away. If Allen had a feeling, any feeling, it was buried bone deep. "For example, the gentleman leaving as we came in didn't seem too happy with you."

Her eyes widened. "Philip?" She chuckled. "I'm not worried about Philip Hewitt. He's a worker bee, a drone. I enjoy his little fits of pique. They give me a chance to cut him down to size."

"What do you know about him, other than that?" Ben asked.

"I know he thinks he's a much better writer than he is. And that he hates female authority figures, which is why I hired him and why I keep him on. It's fun watching him wrestle with it."

I clocked the cat. "Anyone else you like messing with?"

Allen didn't answer.

"Okay, how about this one?" I said. "Why haven't you called the police?"

Allen took a long, thoughtful sip from her little coffee cup before setting it down and taking a few moments more before she graced me with a reply. "Because they aren't needed. This is a private matter, and I'm keeping it private. No hordes of gossip-greedy reporters waving microphones and cameras in my face. Have either of you ever seen my name linked to scandal?"

Allen waited for an answer. I thought of the married senator she'd latched onto a few years ago. There'd been low gossip and covert whispers, but they'd been careful not to draw attention to the relationship. It had been the worst-kept secret in town, and none of my business. Ben shook his head no. I just sat there. She seemed satisfied.

"That's not by accident. Someone's looking for attention, hoping to get it by aligning themselves with me. I won't give them that satisfaction. In the meantime, until they realize they're not going to get what they want, I have you two. You have your orders."

Our orders? I scanned the butterscotch room. "Obviously, money's no object, so why go for a moonlighting cop and a one-woman PI shop instead of a full-scale security firm? There are a lot of them out there."

"For this, big isn't necessary, is it? Or are you saying even this small job is too much for the two of you to handle?" She looked from Ben to me and back again.

Sitting there watching her, I wondered what kind of life the woman lived. What made her so sure of herself and so inflexible and unfeeling toward those around her? Who loved her or didn't? I couldn't know, of course. I was meeting only the public Allen. She could be completely different out of her Prada than she was in it, but somehow I doubted it. Ben tapped the leg of my chair with his foot, and the subtle jolt instantly stopped my mind from wandering.

"Well?" she was asking.

"Excuse me?"

"I asked if we were on the same page."

I let that sit. This was my chance to bolt, and I would have in a New York minute if Ben and I weren't tight and I hadn't given my word.

I smiled. "Absolutely."

Ben breathed out heavily. Relief? What did he think I'd say?

"Good. I can't imagine you'd have any more questions."

I glanced at Ben, who seemed satisfied to let our meeting come to an end without a challenge, so I just nodded and smiled.

Allen leaned back in her chair, her eyes holding mine again. "I can read people pretty well. Had to, growing up where I did." She picked up a tiny spoon from the tray, pointed it at me. "Let me tell you about yourself."

I groaned inwardly. How could I make Ben pay for this? How would I go about sinking a fishing boat? Would I need power tools, or could I do it with just a handsaw and elbow grease? Acetylene torch? I slid Ben a sideways look, but he wisely avoided eye contact. Power tools. Definitely.

"Cassandra," Allen said, smiling condescendingly. Her familiarity pulled me up short. "Do you mind if I call you Cassie?"

Some smiles are warm, friendly; some are cold, a warning, an opportunity given for somebody to rethink, proceed with caution. I gave Allen the latter. Nobody called me Cassie. It didn't fit me. My own mother had never called me Cassie, and who knew me better than she had? I could practically feel Ben sweating through his blazer. My eyes met Allen's; hers met mine and locked. There was a dark twinkle in her eye. She was messing with me, pushing, digging.

"I do mind, actually. Unless, of course, you'd prefer that we all operate on a first-name basis? You call me *Cass*, I'll call you

Vonda, and he's Ben. We can chuck the professionalism altogether and get real homey. You cool with that?"

She recoiled, and the devilish smile melted away. She couldn't
marginalize me without taking herself down a peg, so what to
do, what to do? How important was it that she be *the* Vonda
Allen? I sat and waited for her to work it out.

"Ms. Raines, then."

I was not surprised. Maybe reading people was fun only
when you thought they couldn't, or wouldn't, read you back?
Allen looked a little unsettled, or as unsettled as I imagined she
got. She was definitely hiding something, I thought, but we all
hid something. I wondered what Allen's something might be.

The room got quiet; the silence was so profound, I could almost hear Blue Note licking his privates under the desk.

"Do you play poker, Ms. Raines?"

I shook my head and ignored the impulse to check my watch
for the time.

"People would have a hard time reading you."

"I'm a pineapple," I said.

I'd confused her. "Yes, well, I'll take Detective Mickerson at
his word. Anything else you feel compelled to ask?"

Ben spoke quickly. "No, I think that'll just about cover it."

"Then I'll be ready to go at six." Allen picked up her phone,
punched numbers.

I interrupted the dismissal. "Do you like marigolds, Ms.
Allen?"

Her finger froze over the number pad, and she fixed me with
flat eyes. "I prefer roses and orchids."

And then she turned away and ignored us. Ben and I eased out
into the hall. As we stood there, our backs to Allen's closed door,
decompressing, I suddenly gave in to a perverse urge and elbowed Ben in the ribs, not hard enough to hurt, just hard
enough to make me feel better. He let out a grunt.

"You'll pay for this one, Mickerson. Big-time. I'll dig deep."

"Knew that when you gave her the poker face. Just do me a favor, huh? Keep it above the belt? I'd like to father children someday."

I glared at him. "No promises."

Chapter 3

Nobody, not even me, tried to kill Allen the entire morning. Ben and I spent the time eyeballing the FedEx guy, the mailman, and a couple of office workers from down the hall who'd come to meet friends for lunch. Allen had a designer salad; Kendrick ordered in burgers for Ben and me. No letters. No marigolds. Just the two of us cooling our heels in rich lady chairs outside Allen's door.

I stood after a time, stretched out the kinks. "I'm taking a walk."

Ben shot me a sly look.

"Bubble," I said before he had a chance to remind me. "Got it."

I strolled down the hall, peeking into the offices, at the unhappy people, but stopped at a small room with a copier in it when I saw Kendrick hastily feeding envelopes through a metered stamp machine.

"Kendrick?"

He jumped, reeled around. I'd obviously caught him doing something he shouldn't have been doing. He eyed the doorway behind me. Checking for Chandler? He tried blocking the machine with his body, but it was too late for that. He wanted to bolt. I could tell.

"I didn't mean to scare you."

He quickly gathered up the envelopes, business size, I noticed, no company logo on them. He slipped them into a manila folder, looking guilty as hell. It had to be personal mail, but what twentysomething these days wrote letters and mailed them? Unless they were addressed to Dear Bitch. I looked closely at Kendrick, sizing him up, but you couldn't peg a sociopath by looking.

"I thought you were . . . Never mind. You didn't scare me." He rambled on, shaken, caught out. "Excuse me. I gotta go." He tried slipping past me, but I gently blocked his exit.

"Got a minute?"

"Me? Why?"

"For a couple questions."

He gripped the folder tighter, flicked a look over my shoulder, where escape lingered just beyond his reach. "If it's about the office, I can't. NDA, or did you forget?"

I stepped back, checked the hall. Ben was still sitting in the chair, like an observant lump. No sign of Allen or Chandler. "No, I remember. But we both know something's going on around here. I'd like to get your take. Five minutes, and whatever you say doesn't get back to either one of them. Deal?"

He eyed the stamp machine, then me, as though this was some kind of trap. He narrowed his eyes. "Not even about the stamps I'm borrowing?"

Borrowing? Could you return used metered postage? "What are you mailing, if you don't mind my asking?"

He looked uneasy. "It's personal, okay? I figure she owes me. I worked fifty hours last week, but I'll get paid for only forty. It's always like that."

Maybe it was the truth; maybe it wasn't. "Can I see?"

Kendrick scowled. "And if I say no, you'll tell them about all of this, right?"

I let his question hang for a second. "It's not my postage machine."

If he wouldn't show me what he had in the folder, I couldn't force him, but that didn't stop me from wondering about it.

Kendrick stood there thinking things over, then nodded. "All right. What do you want to know?"

"What's been going on around here?"

He shrugged. "Not sure, but Ms. Allen's definitely spooked. Chandler too. I know it's got something to do with the flowers Chandler's been throwing out, and I heard she's been getting love notes, too. It's got to be a stalker. Somebody messin' with her." He lowered his voice even more. "There's word going around, too, that maybe she's having a thing with Phil Hewitt and that her riding him is just for show."

"Is there a lot of *word* going around?"

"We're not supposed to talk, but we do. People are people. Maybe she dumped him, or he dumped her. The first could explain the flowers, and the second would explain her bitchier than usual mood lately."

Allen and Hewitt? Huh. I didn't see that coming, but what did I know? The exchange I'd witnessed earlier had certainly looked genuine enough. If it had been a put-on, the two of them had given Oscar-worthy performances. Also, how much could I trust the office scuttlebutt when Allen's threatening letters had been mischaracterized as love notes? The staffers were like players in a bad game of slumber-party telephone. There was no telling what other distorted information was flying around. So much for the NDA, though. Like Kendrick had said, people were people.

"Tell me about the phone calls."

The request surprised him. "They told you?"

I nodded, lying. "Sure. I'm just looking for your perspective."

It appeared to satisfy him. "There were a few of them on her private line, but we didn't know anything about those until we heard her chew Chandler out about them. Ms. Allen figured Chandler should know how the guy got her number in the first place, but Chandler said she didn't. When he called the main number, I was covering the desk for Pam."

I eased in closer to him. "Tell me about that call."

"He wanted to talk to Ms. Allen. I guess she'd blocked him by then. He asked if his flowers got here. Then he wanted to be put right through to her."

"What'd you do?"

"I asked for his name and everything, like we're supposed to, but he wouldn't give it. I asked what the call was in reference to, and he said it was personal. He got a little huffy at that point, saying she and him went back almost thirty years and that she'd know what it was about. I transferred him right to Chandler."

"Allen ever mention it again?"

Kendrick shook his head. "It was Chandler who had to know what time it came in, exactly what the guy said and how he said it. She made me go over it at least five times before she let up. I thought for a second she was going to fire me straight-out. If he calls back, we're not supposed to even talk to him, but to transfer it right to her." He eyed the doorway. "If she catches me talking to you . . ."

"She won't. She's in her office. A couple more. How *did* the caller sound, besides being insistent? Angry? Dangerous?"

He thought for a moment. "He didn't sound like anything. Just normal, I guess I'd say. But he wanted to talk to her bad."

So Chandler was doing her job, standing in as a buffer between Allen and the flower guy, trying to work things out, hold them down. "Allen and Chandler. What's with that?"

Kendrick blew out a breath. "I'd say they make a good team. Only, a few weeks ago they had some kind of falling-out. We heard them shouting."

"You know what it was about?"

"No. But things were real cool around here for days. Then, just like that, whatever it was blew over, and Chandler was Team Allen again."

I thought back to the exchange I'd seen earlier in Allen's office, how rudely Chandler had been dismissed. If that was normal operating practice, I would have hated to see Allen and Chandler during their period of open hostilities. Had they argued about the threats? "Anybody else here on Team Allen?"

Kendrick snickered derisively. "Publicly, sure." He shook his head. "We're all just marking time. Meanwhile, we keep our heads down." I could tell Kendrick longed to be rid of me. He tapped the folder nervously against his thigh, bit down on his lower lip. He knew Chandler wasn't going to stay in her office forever. We'd already been in here too long.

"Last one. Promise. What do you think about Allen?"

The tapping stopped, the lip biting, too. His dark eyes locked on mine. I didn't think he was worried about Chandler or Allen at that moment. I think his mind was somewhere else entirely. "She hits that button like she's calling for her house-boy, and I have to come running. Cappuccino, whatever. For the first six months I worked for her, she called me Tony, the guy before me. I don't think much of her, but until I can make my move, I stay and eat it." He paused a moment. "Only I got full a long time ago."

I rejoined Ben. He sat with his legs outstretched, his hands clasped and resting on his stomach. Chandler's door was open; her office empty. I looked to him for an explanation, and he cocked a thumb behind him. "Royal summons. Couple minutes ago it sounded like they were having a little tiff. It's quiet now, though. And a few people have come by to check me out like I'm about to perform magic tricks, or something. I saw you peeking down here. Subtle. You ran into the kid?"

I nodded. "Chance meeting."

"That's how you're playing it?"

I waved him off. "Kendrick took a call from the flower guy, who said he knew Allen from way back and knew she'd remember."

"Obviously, she doesn't."

"Oh, I think she remembers just fine."

Ben rubbed his chin. "So, it's an ex? Then why doesn't she just tell him to buzz off, or let her lawyers do it for her?"

"Maybe she did, and he won't take the hint, or maybe, like she said, she doesn't want to raise a stink, blow the whole thing up. You heard her. She's scandal averse."

"Wouldn't it be something if all this was some stupid lovers'-knot crap? Flowers, pissy letters, and us two sitting here like a couple of hammers ready to clobber the world's smallest nail."

"Yeah, about that . . . There's also a theory going around the office that Allen and Hewitt are a thing, and that whole push-and-pull thing we witnessed between them is an act."

Ben grimaced, shook his head. "I don't buy it. The guy hates her guts, and for good reason. She treats him like he's got one brain cell working."

"I don't buy it, either. I don't see Vonda Allen climbing off her high horse for Philip Hewitt. She goes after senators and CEOs. What'd be in it for her?"

Ben sat upright, winked. "Besides the obvious?"

"She doesn't have to fish around her own office for that."

Ben slid back down in his seat, closed his eyes again. "If you say so."

"Kendrick had a bunch of personal letters," I said. "I caught him feeding them into the stamp machine."

"You get a look at them?"

"I couldn't very well wrestle them out of his hands, could I?" I slid my hands into my pockets and watched Ben lounge. "He's no fan of Allen's desk buzzer." He made a noise, something between a grunt and a growl, confirmation he'd heard me. "So, we're just going to stand here?"

He twiddled his thumbs, grinned. "I'm sitting and choosing to think optimistically, which you refuse to do. I'm the bodyguard. My body's out here watching out for the body in there." He jabbed a thumb at Allen's door.

I waited, thinking there was a *but* coming. A "But I see your point, Cass," or a "But I think we should dig deeper," but it didn't look like Ben was going to make a move. I gave his foot a light kick. "Ben? One of us should check out Hewitt."

He opened one eye. "What?"

"Hewitt. Are you going to take him, or am I?"

He reached into his pocket, pulled out a quarter, and flipped it into the air. "Call it."

I rapped on Hewitt's glass and entered his office. He looked up, and then sneered at me. "I was wondering how long it'd take one of you to make it down here. Call your boss a psychopathic witch, and suddenly you're the new 'it' man."

"I'm—"

"Yeah, skip it," he said, cutting off my introduction. "Bad news travels fast."

Hewitt looked to be about my age, midthirties. He was of average height, thin, dressed neatly in a shirt and tie, the cuffs rolled up to his forearms. Brown eyes peered out of a brown face. Nothing notable about him. I sat down across from his desk.

"Why bad news?" I asked. "Security is a good thing, isn't it?"

"For Allen, unless you two are following me home tonight, too? No? Didn't think so. Look, I'm going to make this easy for you. I didn't write that viper any hate letters. If I had, I'd have signed them. And there's absolutely no way I would lift one nickel out of my pocket to buy her anything, let alone flowers. We done?"

I perked up. "Who told you they were *hate* letters?"

Hewitt offered up a wicked little grin. "Good news travels fast, too."

"I asked who, not how."

"Don't remember, and even if I did, I wouldn't tell anyone connected to *her*."

"You two aren't close, then?"

The smile he gave me was slow to form, like he took time to think about it first before he went for it, but he said nothing.

"And by *close*, I mean on an intimate, personal level," I added.

He let a moment go by, then burst out laughing so loud, so deep, I thought he might strain himself. I waited for him to reel himself in. On the bright side, the sneer was gone. "Unbelievable. That's your angle? Oh, man. I wouldn't touch Vonda Allen even on a bet. I'm too good for her. Honestly, if it weren't for me, this whole place would have gone belly up already. But does she appreciate it, even acknowledge it?" He snorted. "And that show she's getting ready to launch? My pitch. *My* idea. But do I get a slice of the pie?" He stopped, stared at me. He expected an actual answer.

"No?" I said.

"Right. *We* work for *her*, so *our* ideas are automatically *her* ideas. She gets rich, and we get the privilege of working at the pleasure of the queen."

"Why not quit, then?"

He reached down and came up with a briefcase, which he slammed on the desk. He then pulled a drawer open and started tossing files and paper into the case. "I have my reasons. You want to go after someone, go after the guy who called her, like, a million times. Some jilted half-wit, no doubt. But if you're looking for enemies in general? Lady, you've got your work cut out."

"I would think she'd rub a lot of people the wrong way."

The grin he gave me was dark, sly. "Ask around. You'll see."

Hewitt dipped into the drawers, then tossed pens, pencils, a tape dispenser, scissors, legal pads and, finally, a silver letter opener with the magazine's logo on it right into the case. Like he was packing up for good and leaving town, or something. I had to make sure to mention the letter opener to Ben.

I raised my eyebrows. "Clearing out?"

"For the day, yeah, and taking my fair share." He rolled his shirt cuffs down and buttoned them. "But if the shrew wants to prosecute me for the paper clips, she knows where I live, as if I have to worry. Vonda Allen doesn't go slumming."

He slammed his briefcase shut, picked up the phone, and dialed an extension. "Kendrick, I'm out." He listened for a bit but didn't appear to like what he heard. "Man, you can mark it down however you want to. I'm taking the rest of the day." He slammed the receiver down, then slid me a look. "Wait for it."

I was about to ask what I was waiting for when the phone rang. He smiled and picked up. "What took you so long, Chandler?" He listened. "She'll get the story when I've finished with it." He slammed the phone down again, grabbed up his case. "Nothing goes down around here that she doesn't know about. Remember that." He straightened his tie, glared at me. "If someone caps her before the morning, have Chandler call me. I'll wear my red tie tomorrow."

I watched him storm out and head toward the exit, gone for the day with all Allen's stuff. That would be a no on the love-connection idea. That was no act. I stood, eyed Hewitt's near-empty office. Between Kendrick pilfering stamps and Hewitt pinching practically everything else, how did Allen keep her office operating? Was *Strive* operating in the red or in the black?

I glanced out toward the hall and didn't see anyone, so I checked Hewitt's file cabinets and drawers, one eye on my task, the other peeled for Chandler. Nothing in either place jumped out at me as being suspicious. Of course, it would help if I knew what to look for, which I didn't. I was flying blind, and I didn't like the feeling. *My body's out here watching out for the body in there.* That was what Ben had said. I blamed myself. I knew this job was going to be a dog the minute he proposed it to me. I was too nice. That was what it was. I was a sucker.

Just sit in the chair, Cass. Sit and watch, and that's it. If Ben could do it, I could do it. *That's it. I'll just sit. Cash the check and sit.* I gave Hewitt's office one last look, then headed out.

"He does that at least twice a week. Did he take the tape dispenser again?" I nearly bumped into the woman standing in the hall. She gave me a world-weary half smile.

"And a lot more," I said.

"He'll bring it back." She hovered in the doorway across from Hewitt's, her arms crossed against her ample chest. She was short, well dressed, and had an easy way about her. "He always does. I'm Linda Sewell. You're Detective Raines." She shot a look toward Allen's office. "Does she know you're talking to the serfs?"

"She will if we keep standing here."

Sewell's office was identical to Hewitt's, Lilliputian, merely functional. I saw no signs that she'd done anything to personalize it, except to display a framed five-by-seven photo of a tiny child on a desk piled high with file folders, paper, and notepads. She pointed me to the chair, then sat behind her desk and folded her hands on the desktop.

I sat down across from her, eyeing the piles of paper. "Hewitt didn't have much of anything on his desk."

"They're trying to frustrate him until he up and quits, and me, they're trying to overwork. Same goal, though. That's my punishment for suing *the Great Vonda Allen* . . . and winning." She straightened the piles absently, like she really didn't care whether they were straight or not, but needed something to do with her hands. "That doesn't mean I'm after her. I know that's what you're thinking." She glanced out at the hall. "They think she's got a secret admirer—notes, flowers—like we're in some dippy rom-com. It's darker than that."

I slid my chair a little closer to the desk. "How do you know?"

"No one is that jumpy or paranoid over love notes. She's scared and trying to hide it. Either way, admirer or not, she's not getting a lot of sympathy around here. She's burned too many bridges."

"Why'd you sue her?"

"Still thinking it could be me?"

She watched me for a reaction. I didn't think I offered one. But she was right. Why couldn't it be her? I waited for her to answer my question. Instead, she drew a business card from beneath the corner of her desk blotter and slid it toward me. I picked it up.

"My lawyer's card. I'm not *supposed* to discuss it, but since I'm the one everyone suspects, I figured I'd head things off. If Philip had any smarts, he'd do the same, but he won't listen to anyone with breasts." She pointed at the card. "My lawyer's good. I can call him now, if I need to."

I stared at her, then at the card in my hand, wondering what Sewell was into that she needed a lawyer on speed dial.

"Did I miss something?" I said, a bit bewildered. Usually, I had to pull information out of people, like I was a dentist yanking out a rotten molar, but here was Sewell offering it up, taking the lead, shaking up the game. I needed a moment to readjust.

"I am the number one suspect, right? No one could hate her more than I do."

I read the card. I didn't know the lawyer, but I knew the firm by reputation. It was one of the best in the city, with a roster of notable, well-heeled clients, and their sharks didn't work for chump change. If I ever needed a lawyer, I'd want one from this firm, though I'd have to sell my soul to pay for the billable hours. Had Allen handed me the card, I'd have thought, *Well, sure, of course.* Linda Sewell? Allen's employee, toiling away in a glass zoo cage? It didn't fit.

"I'm sorry. Can we back up? What are we talking about?"

"Vonda Allen's on someone's hit list. Secret's been out for weeks, and everyone's making themselves scarce, working from home, at the printing facility, on the off chance he comes for her and misses. She can afford to hire people like you to watch her back. Me and the others? We're all we've got."

I held the card up, wedged between index and forefinger. "You still haven't said why you sued her."

"Vonda Allen's a user, a drafter. If she can get away with buying you cheap, she will. All of us make well below what we could get anywhere else for the same job we're doing here, and for that she expects us to be at her beck and call twenty-four/seven, with no exclusions for holidays, family time, or even your own mother's funeral."

I eyed the card. "Pittance?"

"I reported her for unfair work practices. She fired me. I went to them, and they jumped at the chance to go up against her . . . high-profile celebrity, high-profile case, their firm's name in all the papers . . . right up their alley. She settled. I was back, full pay, with a little extra. Now in order to fire me, she'll have to prove I'm derelict in my duties." Her eyes scanned over the mountain of work at her elbows. "She's stacking the deck in her favor. You want to ask why I'm still here?"

I sat back in the chair, nodded, deciding to just go with it. If Sewell was going to give me stuff without my having to fight for it, I'd take it. "Okay."

"Because it kills her to see me walk in here every day, knowing that she couldn't beat me, that she can't break my spirit. That's some small satisfaction. Also, because I need the job and the health insurance that comes with it. Another reason it isn't me."

I looked at the child's picture. "Your son?"

She smiled. "Jarrod. He's eight. He's why the insurance is so important, and why the settlement, while it was a victory, got used up fast. He's special needs. I'm a single parent. I have only the one paycheck, and therapy, his school, they're expensive."

"I get it. Any idea why Hewitt doesn't quit?"

She chuckled. "He thinks he's smarter than all of us and that if he just sticks it out long enough, the universe will right itself and he'll come out on top. He isn't so smart. He's a gambler. He likes the casinos, blackjack, mostly, but he isn't lucky. He's probably headed there now."

"Does Allen know?"

"There aren't many secrets around here. Information is currency. The more you have, the safer you are. We know something's happening. We've seen the flowers. We just don't know the details."

I paused, fingering the card. "So if it's not you, who do you think it is?"

"Someone she's crossed. Someone she's taken something from. It's how she does business."

I watched Sewell trying to figure her out; she appeared to be doing the same to me. She glanced down at her son's picture, a wistful look in her eyes. "You asked about my son. Vonda hasn't once asked about him. She wouldn't know the first thing about any of us if you walked down there and asked her. We're staff, resources, about as important as that copier across the hall or the telephones on our desks. Did you find her charming?"

"Not particularly."

"Then you got the real Vonda, the one we see. There's also the fake Vonda, the charming, personable, down-with-the-people Vonda who lights up the room at all the galas and glitzy parties. She's a great pretender, an even greater manipulator. If you let her, she'll manipulate the hell out of you." Sewell stood, smoothed out her skirt. "If she knows who's doing this, then your job just got a lot harder, because she'll never tell you. Instead, she'll do what she always does, throw money at the problem, try to bully it. Let's hope that works."

I stood, too, and tried handing the card back, but she waved me off. I slipped the card into my pocket instead, not that I could do anything with it. No one at that firm was even remotely in my price range.

I said, "I don't think money's the answer."

"Then that's too bad, because that's all she's got."

"So?" Ben asked when I got back.

I plopped down into the chair beside him. "We're not working for Mother Teresa."

"You had to go down the hall for that?"

"I suspected it before. Now I have confirmation."

"Hewitt?"

"Tough talker, but maybe this time he got pushed too far?" I told him about Hewitt and Sewell. "I'd love to see their office Christmas parties, wouldn't you?"

"She's definitely rattled," Ben said.

"About that. It still bothers me that she hired us and not a firm. 'Big isn't necessary,' she said."

Ben nodded. "She wants low key."

I sighed, thinking. "Yeah, I'm thinking there's more to it."

Chapter 4

A while later Ben took his own walk down the hall. He said he was going just to make sure things were quiet up front, but I knew better. He was no better at maintaining the bubble than I was. While he was gone, I flipped through one of Allen's ego-riddled magazines, my legs crossed, my eyes periodically lifting off the page to check the hall, Allen's door, and whatever else needed a quick look-see, my ears peeled for anything that didn't sound right.

Kendrick was at the copier. I could hear the clunky whir of the machine. And then there was Chandler, who, for some inexplicable reason, had nothing better to do and was now sitting at the small intake desk outside her office, watching me read. Whenever I looked up, there she was, and to my great chagrin, it appeared she was prepared to keep at it.

"That's a good issue," she said.

I lowered the magazine just far enough to expose my eyes. *It's okay*, I thought. *Great? Hmm.* "It's entertaining."

"Marlon Hinchey is one of our up-and-coming young performers. He came to us. We didn't have to put feelers out. *Strive* is just that good."

I nodded. For a moment there was a lull in the conversation, mainly because I wasn't committed to entering into one. Chandler had been quite the cold fish earlier on; now she seemed ready to engage in polite conversation. Why? Allen wasn't paying me to gab the day away. One might argue she wasn't paying me to read it away, either, but that was a discussion for another time.

"Not very exciting work. Watching someone."

I lowered the magazine to my lap, a finger between the pages to mark my spot. I wondered if Chandler meant my watching Allen or her watching me. She stood up, walked around the desk, leaned back against it, arms crossed. Her smile threw me. I checked the hall. No Ben. *Shoot.* I sighed, stood.

"The less excitement the better."

Chandler seemed to consider that. "I see your point. Exciting would be bad for Vonda."

I tossed the magazine onto the chair and walked over. "You must have more important things to do than watch me read."

"Just making sure things run smoothly. I can't do that closed up in my office."

I glanced over at her office. It was half the size of Allen's but still large enough to corral at least half a herd of cattle. *Nicely decorated*, I thought, and the desk sat squarely on the floor, like a normal person's desk should. *Score one for Chandler.* "Run smoothly for us or for her?"

She lowered her arms, lifted off the desk. "Everyone." She turned to pace around the tight little rotunda. "You and Detective Mickerson are questioning the staff." She stopped, turned back to face me. "Despite what Vonda said. I understand why, and it's good you're doing it. Find out anything?"

"It's early yet."

"Yes, well, I wouldn't place too much stock in what you're being told. Philip and Linda have axes to grind. They may not like Vonda, they may even resent her, but they respect her authority."

I thought back to Philip Hewitt's dramatic walkout, Linda Sewell's legal representation, and Kendrick's liberal use of the postage machine. None of that looked like respect to me.

"She's tough," I said. "Strong willed."

"Absolutely, and if she were a man, those would be considered positive attributes. But I'm sure you understand that. You likely get that yourself."

"Fair amount. How long have you worked for her?"

Chandler sat down again. "I've worked with Vonda almost fifteen years. We started out at the same PR firm. Then we decided to break out on our own, start the magazine."

"Quite a leap of faith," I said.

Chandler grinned. "It was. There were some lean years, and for a long time it was just Vonda, me, and a couple of young writers doing everything, but we made it." She swept her arms around the room, beaming with pride. "We'll celebrate our eighth anniversary this September. And you've heard about the talk show. It's network, not cable access. National reach. Who knows how far we'll go?"

"Your original writers . . . Are they still on board?"

"Oh, no. Long gone. They didn't have the patience to take the long view. When things got tough, they gave up. It takes time to build a successful business. Young people don't get that." Her face turned to stone. "I know you think someone here is doing this, but you're wrong."

I pressed my lips together. I didn't think I was wrong. I could think of at least two people right down the hall who might be likely candidates. Chandler apparently saw only loyalty and unity, while I had seen, almost from the moment I walked in here, anything but that. Still, she was entitled to her delusion. I gave Chandler another studied look, then padded back to my spot. "I'd imagine your responsibilities don't allow for a lot of personal time." There was no wedding ring on her finger, but that didn't mean much these days, and marriage wasn't the only way to be committed to someone, or even to a couple of someones. "All the late hours?"

"You must know something about that, too. I don't mind them at all. Whatever needs to be done."

I picked up the magazine and sat. "The letters . . . Do you remember how they came in? What kind of envelopes, maybe? A return address?"

It looked like Chandler was racking her brain to remember. "I wish I'd paid closer attention, but things get so busy here. And then, when Vonda told me to throw everything out . . ."

"Except for the letter you showed Detective Mickerson?"

Chandler stared at me. "I was worried for Vonda. Sometimes she doesn't know what's for her own good. You think those things were important?"

The envelopes might have offered a clue to their sender's identity. At least they'd have given us a place to start. They might even have traced back to Allen's own postage machine. I offered a small smile. "Could have been."

Ben made it back from his canvass but had little to show for it. No one else had admitted to holding a grudge against Allen, he reported, but neither had they exhibited a willingness to invite her out for a drink after work or nominate her for Boss of the Year. In short, Allen's compliant employees were sad passengers in an oarless canoe hell-bent for Misery Falls.

"Pamela in reception's got one foot out the door," Ben whispered, tapping his fingers on the armrests of his chair. "She's clocking out for good as of this Friday. Scuttlebutt is Allen pegged her as being thicker than a concrete post, and she took offense."

"And she's sticking around till Friday?"

"It's that or not get paid for the time she's already put in.

She's paying for night school. And I ran into your buddy Kendrick. He's got a sneaky look to him. Reminds me of Loquacious Frye. I told you about him. Helped corner him my second year in uniform. He looked clean-cut, upstanding. Butter wouldn't melt in his mouth. Biggest drug slinger on the West Side. Had twenty dealers working under him." Ben's eyes narrowed, and his gaze slid down the hall, toward the copy room. "Kendrick's got Loquacious written all over him."

I shook my head, getting tired of the whole thing at this point. "Not Loquacious. He's sneaking stamps, not slinging drugs." At least not as far as I knew.

"Stamps? Huh. Well, that's a letdown." He readjusted the gun at his side. "I don't see anyone good for the Dear Bitch letters, then. For one, those notes reek of the personal, and nobody down there would voluntarily get anywhere near Allen, unless a lot of money changed hands. Two, Allen doesn't pay any of them enough to buy flowers that're only going to end up head-first down the crapper without her so much as smelling them first." Ben flicked a nod toward Chandler's door. "Nobody likes that one, either. She pops up everywhere and won't breathe unless Allen signs off on it first."

I leaned back in my chair. "Knows all, sees all?"

He sighed. "And keeps her trap shut." He looked over at me. "What're you doing?"

I folded my hands across my stomach, closed my eyes. "Sitting."

"*Now* you're sitting?"

I grinned. "Yep, my body's out here watching out for the body . . ."

He interrupted me mid-snark. "Can it, wiseass."

At five, Allen's office emptied out faster than a brothel during a vice raid. Everyone hit the door at top speed, desperate, it seemed, finally to breathe air Vonda Allen didn't own. However, Allen, true to her word, stuck it out till six; only then was she ready to be escorted home like the monarch she thought she was.

Her shiny black limo idled out front as the three of us hit the lobby. The driver was dressed as you'd expect in black pants and jacket, neatly pressed, a starched white shirt, and a driver's cap. His name was Elliott, and he was all business. He held the door for Allen, waited until she got comfortable, and then eased in behind the wheel, never looking back.

Ben sat up front with him; I sat in the back with Allen, in the seat across from hers, so that we were face-to-face. She ignored me, of course, though I didn't have that luxury. I kept my eyes on her intermittently while also watching the streets as we went along. That was my job. Luckily, Allen didn't live far, only a few blocks away, in a penthouse condo on North Lake Shore Drive, an area where even the pigeons knew better than to relieve themselves on the sidewalk.

Elliott pulled up into the building's circular drive and dropped us off. Ben took point, Allen was in the middle, and I held the back position as the three of us breezed past the security desk and stood waiting for the private elevator to take us up to the residences. We didn't have to wait long. The polished brass doors whooshed open after a few seconds to reveal a sweet-smelling car outfitted in sheeny cherrywood and a thick Oriental carpet. Ben stepped aside to let Allen walk on, and I stepped in after her.

"You see her up," Ben said. "I'll hit the garage. Get the car. Meet you down there."

I nodded; Allen didn't. The doors closed, and the car rose slowly without a single auditory clue that we were moving at all. No squeaks or groans, no Muzak, no nothing, just the sound of the two of us inhaling and exhaling as we rode up to Allen's apartment.

"Kaye told me you questioned the staff today." She didn't bother looking at me. Her eyes were fixed on the shiny doors. "Contrary to my instructions."

I watched Allen's reflection in the sheen. Though it was slightly distorted, I could see her lips pressed tightly, her lifted chin, the hard eyes. "That's right."

"I forbid—"

I stopped her right there. "Forbid?"

"I call that insubordination."

"I call it doing my job."

We rode up a few more floors in chilly silence before Allen spoke again.

"I assume you have a gun?"

I let a moment go by. "Uh-huh."

"And that you know how to use it?" Her voice was so low, it came out almost as a whisper, as though she were afraid someone else might hear, as though saying even those few words opened a window into her deepest, darkest fears.

I turned to face her, really took her in, though she still would not look at me. For all her perceptiveness, tough talk, and high-mindedness, I could see clearly now that she was uncharacteristically vulnerable but too proud to admit it—even to herself. *Who had done this to her?* I wondered. *What or who was she frightened of?* I faced forward again, watched her in the doors, the stiff set of the shoulders, her defiance, even now, as she fought not to exhibit the slightest hint of emotion.

"I know how to use it. I'm hoping I won't have to."

I could almost feel her struggle with herself over whether to say more. Expectant seconds passed before it became clear to me that she wouldn't. It was yet another missed opportunity.

"Maybe tomorrow you'll tell me why you needed to know that," I said.

There was a sudden intake of breath, and then the doors slid open, and she all but bolted into the cocooned safety of her penthouse suite. Only then did she appear to breathe again.

I stood there, my mouth hanging open. If I thought her office was big enough to host a joint session of Congress, it had nothing on this place. The panoramic view of glitz and abundance was so striking that the glare of it nearly knocked me back a step. And the view. Outside Allen's floor-to-ceiling windows stood the skyscrapers of Chicago in all their steel-girded magnificence, and beyond them, close enough to almost reach out and touch, was the blue-green, undulating sparkle of Lake Michigan, pleasure boats bobbing on the water. Sheesh. All I saw from my front windows were the apartment buildings across the street, and they were nowhere close to being this opulent.

A short, wide Hispanic woman materialized from somewhere and planted herself front and center to await her mistress's desires. Dressed in a severely starched maid's uniform of gray under a crisp white apron, her hands clasped in front of her, she nodded at me, smiled, and waited.

"This is Isabella," Allen said without enthusiasm, handing the woman her briefcase, as she likely did every evening about this time. "Isabella, this is Ms. Raines. She's assisting me for a few days." Turning back to me, she said, "You'll accompany me to the gym tomorrow. Be here at six thirty sharp." Judgmental eyes swept over me. "Bring workout clothes, if you want."

I raised an eyebrow, marveling at Old Girl's recovery rate. As quickly as it had taken her to exit the elevator and relieve herself of her briefcase, she'd managed to get ahold of every hint of vulnerability she'd shown and ram it back behind an iron veil of self-absorbed bitchiness. She then turned on imported heels and clicked away from me without a backward glance.

The elevator doors closed on her exit, and I rode down to the garage in silence, this time watching my own reflection. I looked tired, harassed, like a woman who knew there was trouble waiting around the corner. Something was looming, something dangerous, and I hadn't the first clue what it was. *I assume you have a gun? And that you know how to use it?* I scrubbed my hands across my face just as I hit the lower level and the doors whooshed open.

Chapter 5

I slid into the passenger seat of Ben's old Camaro, clicked the seat belt across my chest, then turned in the seat. "Have you seen this woman's apartment?"

He grinned. "Can you technically call that an apartment?"

"Whatever you call it, it's embarrassing."

"If you had her money, you wouldn't think so."

I jabbed a thumb toward the side window. "There are homeless people sleeping in boxes two blocks from here."

Ben snorted, slid me a look. "She can't see them from way up there."

We pulled out into late rush-hour traffic, the street clogged bumper to bumper with cabs, Ubers, daredevils on Divvy bikes and electric scooters, tourist trolleys, and overly trusting pedestrians weaving in and out of it all, their eyes on their iPhones, their heads up their behinds, everybody on the street jockeying to get just ten seconds up on the next fella. One honk of a car horn led inevitably to a chain of frustrated copycats.

"She wants me to follow her around the gym tomorrow," I said.

"We can change up, if you want. I'll take the club. You do the perimeter."

It was a tempting offer, and I almost went for it. Six thirty in the morning was a bit much, and the idea of watching Allen work up prima-donna sweat didn't sound like it was going to be any fun for me. "Nah, I've got it. Besides, you can't follow her into the locker room."

Ben checked his rearview. "Ha. Who says?"

I slid back in the seat and stretched my legs out as far as the Camaro would allow. I was unprepared for the sudden jolt when Ben jammed on the brakes to avoid a checkered cab that had just cut him off. I bolted forward, toward the dash, but luckily, the belt pulled me back.

"What the hell?" Ben yelled. "Did you see that moron? Times like these, I wish I had my old ticket book. I'd write that clown two tickets right off the bat—one for the cutoff and one for being a friggin' jackass!"

I was used to driving with Ben, so I knew the drill. I checked the seat belt to make sure I was harnessed in tight, and then tuned him out. He'd go on for a bit longer about the cab. He was an impatient driver, a hot dog. Both shortcomings came in handy when rushing to a scene or pursuing a suspect, not so much in rush-hour traffic. I was confident he'd stop short of wrecking his car, though.

"Allen's holding back," I said.

"Everybody holds back shit. And don't mind the fact that we almost got tin canned."

"In the elevator? She wanted to know if I had a gun and knew how to use it. Why, if she didn't think I'd have to shoot somebody?"

"Could be she's just curious." Ben rolled down his window, leaned out. "Where'd you learn to drive, dodo? Hell?" He flipped off the languid-looking cabbie, then rolled his window back up and sped through the yellow light. I gripped the shoulder harness for assurance.

"Did she ask you?"

"Nope, but I look like I could shoot the crap out of something. Nobody expects that from a woman." His big cop foot pressed down on the gas, and the Camaro wove around a green Hyundai with pink, fuzzy dice hanging from the rearview mirror. I squeezed my eyes shut. Cars, testosterone, and traffic did not a good mix make.

"But don't shoot the messenger," Ben said, chuckling. "Get it? Shoot the messenger?"

I shook my head, remembering what it had been like riding with him every day. He was a good cop, and we'd worked well together: we'd known each other's moves, strengths, weaknesses, and then there had been times like this when he brought what he thought was The Funny.

"Shoot the messenger," I muttered sourly. "Got it." I flipped the passenger visor down and looked at myself in the oblong mirror, at the frown on my face, the worry lines creasing my forehead. It hadn't been curiosity I'd seen on Allen's face; it had been fear.

Ben dropped me at my car, which was parked at Allen's office, and then we parted ways. I offered up a prayer for his safe deliverance and then headed south, toward home, picking at the edges of Allen's problem. I had a new car, well, new to me. I'd bought the Black Honda Civic used at a dear price just a month earlier. Not by choice. Someone had tossed a Molotov cocktail into the backseat of my old one—a hazard of the job. I'd driven the Civic off the lot with nine hundred miles on the odometer, resentful of having to sign my life away for it, but more than a little enamored of the new car smell.

My cell phone was in my bag, but a buzz sounded through the car speakers, announcing an incoming call. I glanced at the dashboard readout, one of the new age techno whizbangs I hadn't had in my old, reliable ride, now smoked and gone to auto heaven. It was Eli. I smiled and then tapped the snazzy button on the steering wheel.

"Hello, stranger." His voice rolled nice and easy out of the speakers.

I smiled, checked the rearview, changed lanes. "Hey, what's up?"

"I'm standing outside your place with too much Chinese food, an extra pair of chopsticks, and a whole lot of cop swagger."

I sped up just a bit. "Beef and vegetables?"

"My swagger's not enough?"

I turned onto the Inner Drive, just blocks from home, but didn't say anything. Let him think I was trying to decide.

"If it takes that long, I'll take my egg rolls and go home."

I snickered. "Wait. Why are you standing outside? Mrs. Vincent should be home. She'll buzz you up."

"I don't think she likes me like that yet. I get a vibe."

Mrs. Vincent lived on the first floor of the three-flat building I owned. She was part neighbor, part mother figure, gentle, stern as nails, full to brimming with good old-fashioned mother wit. I squinted, curious. "What kind of vibe?"

"The kind that says she knows we're *spending time*, and she's not all right with it."

I whizzed past the green domes of the museum, ready to make the turn, amused by the big, tough cop's unease at coming up against a kindhearted octogenarian in sensible shoes. "Spending time, *really*? She's old, Eli, not dead. She knows I *spend time*. In fact—"

He interrupted me. "Never mind. Forget it. I'll wait in my car."

I chuckled. Couldn't help it. "Five minutes. Keep the food warm."

We ate sitting crossed-legged at opposite ends of my couch, the food between us, watching nothing in particular on television, the sound muted. I picked vegetables and noodles out of the carton using chopsticks, forgoing proper plates and forks, which were way at the back of my apartment, in the kitchen I rarely used. I'd changed out of my suit into an old pair of jean shorts and a faded Chicago PD T-shirt. Eli, fresh from work, was in slacks, shirt, and loosened tie, his police star still clipped to his belt. This was clearly the easiest part of my day.

"And then she tells me I can bring workout clothes."

"Vonda Allen," he said. "That's some high cotton."

I jabbed a chopstick at him. "She's bent."

"What's Mickerson think?"

"He thinks she's bent, too, but he's okay with babysitting her. Sometimes I don't get him. I mean, I get him, but then . . . I don't get him."

Eli speared a baby corncob and stuffed it into his mouth. "Stalking cases are tough. Lot of levels."

"The fact that she's tight-lipped says a lot. She could involve the department without broadcasting her business, so why hasn't she? And she has lawyers, lots of them, I'd imagine. Why not have them work it out? Or, like Ben suggested, just tell whoever it is to buzz off. There are a lot of options out there."

Eli looked at me, shook his head.

"What?"

"Buzz off?"

"In a polite but firm way, sure . . . It can be done." He looked like he didn't believe me. "I've done it. Trust me. Egg roll?" I offered up the bag, but he declined another.

The final score of some game scrolled along the bottom of the TV screen. He took only a passing glance. "I hope I never get that kind of brush-off."

I smiled, took a bite of broccoli, watched him as I chewed.

"No assurances?" he asked.

I shrugged, grinned playfully. "If it comes to that, I promise to let you down gently."

"Brutal . . . but oddly titillating. Too bad they didn't get anything out of the guy on the phone."

"No name, nada. He copped to the flowers, said he knew her, but that's it." I shook my head. "It could be someone else entirely. I don't know enough yet, and Allen's sure not helping."

"What about this Chandler? You might get something from her, if you frame it as you looking out for her boss, not trying to damage her. Aren't you both on the same side, more or less?"

I frowned, considered it. "Unfortunately, in this case, if you're blocked by one, you're blocked by both."

"Well, you're just at day one. You'll figure it out."

"I would, only I'm just supposed to stand there and swat flowers away."

Eli chuckled, tossed me a fortune cookie. "You think you can just stand there?"

"In the spirit of friendship, I've committed to giving it a try. Hands off. Eyes on the prize. Cass Raines, statue." I struck a pose, held it for a second. "Let's hope I don't screw up and blow the whole thing."

Eli leaned back against the couch. "You're perfect from where I'm sitting."

I bit into the cookie, narrowed my eyes. "Perfect, huh?"

He scooted closer to me. "Perfect lips, two very nice eyes . . . cute nose." A little closer still. "Not to mention a world-class . . ." He stopped talking.

"World-class what?"

Eli was a few years older than I was, a little gray at the temples, thin lines at the corners of his eyes, a killer smile that started there and spread across his dark face to two deep dimples in his cheeks.

"Can't say. It could be considered . . . delicate."

I looked around the room. No one in it but him and me. "To whom?"

Eli took another slide down the couch. "Okay, you're sitting on it."

A slow smile crept across my face. "World class?"

"Hands down."

We met in the middle, shared a kiss.

"Well, sometimes the gods do smile."

"They sure did," he replied.

"Are we done talking?" I nipped at his lower lip. "Because I have an idea."

"Hell yeah, we're done talking."

I moved to his ear. "Good."

"Better than good." His hand trailed down my neck. "Great."

I stood, stretched. "Then if we're done, I'm going to take a shower. Early morning tomorrow. Workout. Swanky club. Vonda Allen. Pip-pip."

"What?"

I headed for the hallway, my shower and bedroom at the end of it, grinning, knowing he'd follow.

"I could use a shower, too," he said.

"Then, I'll try to save you some hot water." I took off running toward the bathroom, my bare feet squeaking on the hardwood floor.

"Oh, no you won't."

Eli easily closed the gap. We eventually shared the shower, and the whole time I didn't think of Allen once.

Chapter 6

There must be a better way to find some peace, Philip Hewitt thought as he wove his way from the backseat of his Uber ride to his front door, four gin and tonics, a screwdriver, and half a bowl of stale Bavarian pretzels sloshing around in his sour stomach.

"Damned bitch." He poked his key at the lock, missed his mark, tried again. The weaving didn't help. "Damn bitch lock."

Quiet block, quiet neighborhood, especially at half past one in the morning on a Tuesday. His neighbors were probably all tucked in bed, not letting the bedbugs bite, Hewitt thought as he finally matched jagged key to jagged lock cylinder. The courtyard of his building was still, empty, or so he thought, as he twisted the small silver key, longing for the comfort of his own bed. But something wasn't right. A feeling. Even with the gin buzz, he sensed something, someone, tuck in behind him, too close for him to feel easy about it. He turned to find the last person he ever expected to see on his humble doorstep. He was so surprised, he began to cackle like a loon.

"Are you serious? I can't get a break." He tried correcting

his weave, tried pulling himself together. "What're you doing here?"

But it was too late in the game for talk. Hewitt was a problem. His eyes grew wide as saucers, then slowly lowered from familiar eyes to the glint of gunmetal. "Are you crazy? Get the hell out of here."

He'd misjudged, but didn't he always?

Hewitt turned his back to the gun, a show of disdain fueled by alcohol, but his heart raced just the same, and his blood ran cold. "You've just made the biggest mistake of your life. I'll own you now."

But the mistake was Hewitt's. This was no prank. Not a fake. This was a plan coming together, a mugging gone horribly wrong—or so it would appear later. Just another senseless tragedy, yet another life cut short by random violence. Remember to take his wallet and cheap watch.

Hewitt turned back, jabbed an angry finger in a feeble attempt to intimidate. "You've picked the wrong guy."

He had always been a stupid man, had never been able to read the room. Good to know some people were consistent right to the end. And make no mistake, this was Hewitt's end.

A playful wave. Really, there was no reason not to say goodbye, was there? Hewitt almost laughed but couldn't; he simply didn't have the time. Too quickly, the hand thrust forward to press gun barrel to drunken forehead. There was a look of shock, one muffled pop, a single twitch. One languid slide to oblivion, and that was all. Hewitt lay wasted on cool cement, in a fast-expanding puddle of gore. Some of the human blowback had splattered across his front door.

Hard eyes assessed the carnage. Done. "Such a ridiculous fool he was."

Highland Health Club was *the* place to breeze through a sedate workout, celebrity watch, or close a million-dollar deal over an endive salad and imported water. Allen skimmed the *Wall Street Journal* from a large elliptical, glancing occasionally at the big-screen televisions mounted to the wall, ignoring me. I watched her from a spot a few feet away, off to the side, where I could see the entire room and Allen, too. The whole place smelled of perfumed sweat, damp towels, and just a whiff of pomposity.

Every machine here was designed to tone, sculpt, and tighten whatever sagged or jiggled, and there were toning classes, nutrition counseling, massage rooms, a sauna, and an assortment of European-inspired body wraps utilizing everything from Swiss mud to emulsified kale. And none of it was bargain basement. The hefty membership fee alone discouraged pretenders.

I'd reluctantly left my bed at five-thirty to get to Allen's place by the time she set. Ben tried starting some light conversation in the limo on the way here, but Allen wasn't interested. It was now a little after seven and the room was already packed with stick-figure people, who rushed from apparatus to apparatus, trailing dry towels along behind them. The televisions were tuned to the morning news reports, and one station was running a story on an overnight robbery-homicide, the details of which I could not hear, since the sound was channeled through headphones that plugged into the machines. Everyone moved with a purpose; everyone stared at me and found me interesting. No one tried to hand Allen any flowers or notes. I'd opted out of working out with her. This was business. I didn't like her well enough to blur the lines.

After a half hour, during which time Allen never broke a discernible sweat, the buzzer on her elliptical machine sounded. When the pedals slowed and stopped, Allen tucked her paper under her arm and headed for her massage. She didn't say a word to me, which was just as well. I wasn't lonely. She was a little miffed I hadn't brought my "workout togs." I'd nearly snorted when she said, "Workout togs." As a rule, *togs* wasn't a word many black folks used a lot, and I wondered what Allen was trying to prove. I was dressed instead in a black blazer, a silk shirt, black slacks, and shoes I could run in, if I had to, without twisting an ankle—"bodyguard togs."

Allen kept up the pointed silence all the way to the massage room, where a smiling blond woman with bright blue eyes and a silver nose ring met us at the door, dressed in a formfitting pink tank and spandex pants.

"This is Jade," Allen said as the woman opened the door and led us inside. Allen padded over to the massage table and sat down to start unlacing her shoes. Jade smiled. I smiled.

I checked the small room, with its neat shelves of fragrant oils and freshly folded towels. There was only the one door, so that was easy. I then checked Jade. Harmless.

I started to leave. "I'm right outside the door."

Allen acted as though she hadn't heard me. Rich people tended to do that—act like they didn't hear or see a person. I was starting to expect it from Allen.

"I'll take a mineral water." She didn't bother looking up. "You'll find it at the juice bar. Try getting it to me while it's still cold, will you?"

Allen calmly slipped off her anklets. I assumed she'd been talking to Jade, but when the young woman didn't move, it dawned on me that it was me Allen was sending out for water. I turned, smiled at the perky masseuse. "Um, Jade? Would you give us a minute, please?"

Jade hesitated, unsure what to do. After all, Allen was paying her. She didn't know me from Adam's house cat.

I held up a finger. "Just one minute." I maintained the smile. "Ms. Allen will be with you toot sweet."

When Jade stepped out and shut the door behind her, I walked over to the table and stood directly in front of Allen so she couldn't help but see me. She looked up, a bored expression on her face. I looked down, not bored, deadly serious. We were mere inches from one another, so I didn't have to raise my voice. Sometimes a whisper could be just as effective as a shout.

"I'm not your maid. I'm not your groupie. I don't go for water, cabs, energy bars, or escorts for the evening. You want water, you'll get up off that ridiculously overpriced table and get it yourself. Anybody bursts in here and tries to strangle you, that's when I do what you're paying me for. Capisce?"

She didn't say anything, but it looked like she had loads of things bubbling up inside of her. She flushed, glowered at me, then looked away briefly before turning back to find me still standing there, serious as a heart attack.

"If not, all you have to do is say so," I said.

A tiny muscle twitched in her neck. She was clenching her teeth too tightly. Maybe she was balancing her desire to fire me with her need for someone to cover the door while she got her backside worked over with jasmine-scented oil and emulsified vegetables. Jade seemed like a nice person, but I didn't think Allen believed she'd take a bullet for her. At this point, I wasn't even sure I would.

"I knew you'd be trouble," she said. If steam could have shot out of her ears, I thought it would have. In contrast, I was perfectly calm, not angry in the least, just insistent that Allen fully grasp the true dynamic of our relationship.

"Five thousand dollars I'm paying, or have you forgotten that?"

I hadn't, but money didn't move me. I'd had it, not had it. Money wasn't integrity or self-respect; it wasn't love or death. You couldn't do a thing with it on your deathbed. I could hear activity outside the door, the busy health club going about its business, while I waited on Allen to straighten up and fly right.

Finally, "I'll get my own water."

I stepped away from her, our deal done. "Enjoy your massage, Ms. Allen."

When I pulled the door open to leave, Jade was standing

right there. She looked at Allen, as if assessing her for body damage, but she didn't say anything. In her hand she held a bottle of chilled mineral water.

I smiled. "Oh, looky, looky. Jade brought you your water. How nice." I stepped aside and let her in, then leaned over and whispered in her ear, "Good luck with that."

Chapter 7

I cooled my heels outside the door, giving people who passed the once-over, making sure no one got too close, occasionally glancing up at the television sets to check the news. I was watching an older man in tennis whites pass me on his way to the courts when I heard a gasp go up and turned to see a breaking-news alert crawl along the bottom of the nearest screen. Cop killed. Suspect in custody. The choppy footage, shot from a news helicopter, showed blue-and-whites, lights flashing, cordoning off a city block in Bridgeport. My throat tightened. I couldn't move from the door, and I couldn't hear the report from where I stood. Cop killed. I thought of all the cops I knew, friends, more than that, family. Eli, but it couldn't be him. Not his district. No ID yet on the dead cop. I felt for my phone, but just then it vibrated in my pocket. I slid it out, glanced at the number. Ben.

"Who is it?" I asked before he could say anything.

"No one we know. New detective. Eighteen months in."

I felt a selfish wave of relief that it wasn't any of my friends, but the relief was short lived. A cop was dead. I felt the loss, mourned it, as though I'd lost a member of my family all the same.

"Cass? She was partnered with Farraday." Just the mention of the man's name nearly took my breath away, and it felt like someone had just kicked me in the stomach. "They hit the door without calling for backup. Her first, him bringing up the rear. She caught a round to the head. Dead before she hit the ground." Ben paused.

He was waiting for me to say something, but I was still on Farraday. I was back on the roof where I had almost died, the taste of blood in my mouth as I lay dying; back to another door Detective James Farraday had barreled through, hoping to make his bones. Almost three years ago now. A pit grew in my stomach, my heart raced, and the years fell away. The rooftop was here, now, again.

Ben continued. "I got the details from Corrigan. We used to work the same district. The news is just breaking, but I wanted you to hear it from me."

Farraday was a menace, a danger to himself and others. I'd said as much to the bosses, but they hadn't listened, because Farraday was connected, the latest in a line of top-brass cops who shielded him from his own incompetence.

She. Eighteen months in.

We'd been after a banger on that roof, and I'd nearly talked him down. That was when Farraday had made his play. He had stumbled in, gun drawn, and it had all gone wrong. Jimmy Pick. That was the banger's name. He hadn't meant a thing to Farraday; neither had I, or Ben. I drew my hand up to my chest now, feeling for the healed-over spot where Pick's bullet had pierced my flesh. Pick was dead. I killed him. I wouldn't have had to had it not been for . . .

"And him?" I croaked it out, my voice sounding far away.

"Not a scratch. He's blaming the screwup on her, but this time I don't think it's going to fly. This is about as bad as it gets."

I watched the people passing by, held the door, the phone sweaty in my hand.

"I can sub you out if you want." He was at the front of the club, watching who came in and who went out.

"No. I've got it. Ben? How old was she?"

He took a moment to answer. "Thirty-two. Second-generation cop. Had a two-year-old at home."

I ended the call, squared my shoulders, my fists clenched tight, shaking. "Oh, my God."

Allen, peering through a pair of half-glasses, stared out the window of her limo as we rode up Michigan Avenue a short time later. The quiet was just fine by me. I didn't feel like talking. Besides, I'd known Allen just two days, and already I'd had my fill of her. Elliott was at the wheel, Ben was beside him in the passenger seat, and I sat across from Allen, both of us trying not to look at each other. To pass the time, I stared at the normal people outside the window and longed for their company.

I thought of my grandfather who had worked at a die-cast factory for more than forty years, day in, day out for union pay, and my grandmother who had worked just as long for the phone company before Ma Bell split up and died. They had been working people, not by any means wealthy. I got to college with good grades, a little set aside, and loans, which had taken me years to pay off. No one I knew, and no one they knew, ever rode in limousines, unless someone had died and they were part of a funeral procession.

The three-flat I now owned was the only thing my grandparents had managed to scrape together, and I maintained it now because it had been theirs and they'd fought so hard to keep it. I'd never sell it. Never.

It was not that I held Allen's wealth against her, not really. It was just that, at a time when the gulf between the haves and the chronically disenfranchised had never been wider, the woman's

callousness and high-handedness struck me as niggardly, gar-
ish, almost indecent. I'd read her bio. She hadn't been to the
manor born. She'd grown up in the Robert Taylor Homes, the
projects, just a few miles west from where we were now. But
Allen had obviously forgotten where she came from, and those
few short miles might as well be a million or more for all the attention she paid. I wondered about the working people who'd
gotten her here. Was this how she honored them? Her cell
phone rang. She answered it.

"What do they want? You didn't ask? Tell them I'm too busy
to . . ." She listened for a bit, her mood darkening with every
second. "Kaye, this is absolutely outrageous. I'm on my way
in. I'll give them exactly five minutes." She ended the call and
tossed the phone into her Hermès bag. "The police want to talk
to me. What do either of you know about that?"

"Excuse me?" I asked.

"I said I didn't want the police involved."

Ben turned around in the front seat. "Yeah, we heard you.
Not us."

She stared at me; I stared back.

"And you?"

I cocked my head toward Ben. "Like he said."

Allen removed her glasses, massaged the bridge of her nose.
We were close to the office now, and the closer we got, the
more worried she looked.

I leaned forward, kept my voice low. "Let us help you."

She pulled away, back to the window and the people in the
street. "I run it, Detective. It doesn't run me."

I sighed, sat back, and let her be.

Chapter 8

Allen barreled into the reception area ahead of us, but there were no cops waiting. She gave poor Pamela the evil eye, heat oozing from every well-moisturized pore. "Well?" She made zero attempt to hide the nastiness in her delivery.

The rattled receptionist shot up from her chair. "They're waiting in your office with Ms. Chandler. Should I . . ."

But Allen was gone, already stomping back toward whatever awaited her, determined, it seemed, to shut it down.

Ben let out the mother of all sighs. "I say we hang out here while whatever's going on back there stops going on." But I was already on the move, following Allen back. "Or, second thought, go back and see what's going on."

We were halfway down the hall when Chandler came rushing out of Allen's office and saw us. "Philip Hewitt's dead. Shot. Early this morning." She swept past us. "I need to get his personnel file."

We watched her rush into her office; then Ben and I exchanged a look that had years of knowing each other in it. When we came to a stop in front of Allen's partially open door,

I peered inside her office to find Allen talking to two plain-clothes detectives. I didn't know the sensibly dressed Asian woman with the police star clipped to her belt, but I sure knew her partner. Detective Marcus Jones, who I hadn't seen or heard from in two years, since the night I walked out on him. I registered the surprise first; then nausea flipped my stomach. I could have gone the rest of my life without seeing Marcus Jones again and not regretted it, but here he was. I could practically feel Ben's mood change.

"Of all the gin joints," he muttered sourly. "This day will just not let up, and it's not even ten o'clock yet."

Though I was thinking the exact same thing, I kept my mouth shut. I just stood there in the doorway with Ben, watching the cops and Allen, wishing I were someplace they weren't.

On the surface, Marcus made for a pretty package. Pushing forty, he looked like he hit the gym on the regular. He'd grown a mustache since I'd last seen him. He had sunglasses clipped to his belt, his star hanging from a chain around his neck, suave, conceit all but oozing out of every pore. I'd found out way too late that he was an incubus.

Marcus Jones was a drafter who latched on to whatever coat-tail promised the greatest advantage. He played the power game, Marcus did, currying favor where he could, hoping in the end the other guy's shine worked for him, too. Smooth and measured, he had taken to the glint of police brass and not to the stink of dirty alleys. But I hadn't known half of that until that last night. I couldn't have imagined that the teat he pre-ferred to suckle from belonged to James Farraday, the cop who'd nearly gotten me killed, the same cop who just hours ago had coaxed his partner first through a door to get her head blown off.

"Farraday's guy," Ben muttered under his breath. "Toss-up who's the bigger prick."

I slid him a look. "Don't. All right?"

Marcus turned to see us standing there, but nothing registered on his face. I could have been anyone anywhere anytime, which said everything. I thought back to the last time we'd shared space. How could I forget it?

"I saw the report," Marcus said. "Mickerson got caught flat-footed, and you were slow to fire. You're lucky Farraday was there to cover."

Neither was true. We'd tried to talk a cornered kid off a roof. Farraday had had other ideas. He'd wanted to be a hero. He'd wanted the notch in his belt.

"There'd have been nothing to cover if he'd stayed out of it," I countered.

Marcus frowned, his arms akimbo. "I'm just going by what I read in the report."

"His report, not Ben's, not mine, obviously. And why is that?" I paced the floor, turned back. "Scratch that. I know why. I just can't believe it. He's rotten, reckless, over his head. He shouldn't be a cop. He doesn't have what it takes. A kid is dead, and he shouldn't be. Wouldn't be if Farraday had let us do what we had to do."

"Look, I don't want to fight about this. Take the win, that's all I'm saying. You can literally write your own ticket now. Promotions come next. Stop sweating that dead banger. Stop stirring things up." The words slipped off his lips like warm chocolate, smooth, sickening, a serpent's lie.

Or else, I thought. He hadn't said the words, but I felt them hanging in the air all the same. There was a bullet scar right below my left clavicle. A couple of centimeters to the right and I'd be gone.

He went on. *"You're okay. Out of the hospital. We got one dead gangbanger, no dead cops. That's cause for celebration, so let's celebrate."*

I watched him uncork the wine, stymied for a moment. We were supposed to be cops, not assassins. That was something Far-

raday didn't get, but I'd thought Marcus did. Oh my God. *It struck me at that moment. I didn't know the man at all.*

"I almost died," I said. *"Are you really okay gambling with the next cop's life?"*

He poured a glass of red, took a sip, smiled. "But you didn't, and I'm not gambling with anything. I'm standing on the blue line, where I've always been, where you should be. You want to be a social worker, go be a social worker. If you're a cop, you get done what needs to get done."

I stared at him, seeing then what I'd missed.

"Hold the line, Cass. It's a lot safer that way."

Safer that way. *His words echoed in my head. Was it a threat? I grabbed my bag, turned for the door. "Good-bye, Marcus." By the time I walked out, I'd let him go.*

An elbow poked me in the side. It was Ben nudging me back to the present.

"This is my security detail," Allen said, waving us off. "This doesn't concern them."

Marcus's partner stepped forward and ID'd herself as Detective Tanaka. "Actually, Ms. Allen, we'll need to talk to everybody." She stared at the great lady, no give in the look. "Is there a particular reason you need bodyguards?"

Ben and I stepped into the room. Allen didn't answer, but the look she gave the cops was cold enough to frost glass. Marcus stared at Ben; Ben glared back. Neither liked the other, and they made no pretense to the contrary. Ben stood with me, though. I had brought him with me into the relationship, and he had come with me when I left it.

"Especially a moonlighting cop and a PI?" Marcus added in a tone dipped in flat-out derision.

Allen looked from him to us, suddenly interested in what wasn't being said. "Do you know each other?"

We were silent, her words having landed like a dud grenade.

"Well?"

"Tanaka's the unknown element," Ben offered glumly. "Otherwise, small world."

We stood around in a loose circle, cops, Allen, Ben and I, uncomfortable, awkward, years of crap thought under the bridge flowing back to loom large in our recollections, none of it pleasant.

Allen frowned, took a seat at her desk. I kept my mouth shut; so did Ben. Thankfully, at that moment, Chandler rushed in with Hewitt's file and handed it to Allen, who didn't even bother opening it. Instead, she pushed it across the desk so Marcus could pick it up himself.

"That's all we have on him. He was competent enough. I know nothing about his personal business. Frankly, I'm not sure what else you think I can offer you." Allen leaned back in her chair, crossed her legs, her eyes appraising. "Muggings happen every day, don't they?"

Tanaka leveled her eyes at Allen. "You don't look too broken up over it."

Allen let a moment go by. "His death is unfortunate. He owed me work. Broken up? I see no reason for that."

Marcus asked, "Did he have any enemies you know of?"

She cocked her head. "I have no idea."

"Doesn't sound like you dealt with the man much at all," Tanaka said, clearly getting frustrated by all the nothing Allen was tossing her way. "You like that with all your staff?"

Allen just stared at her. She was the most important person in the room at the moment, and she knew it. "Detective . . . Tanaka?"

There was a moment of silence.

"Yes?" Tanaka shifted so that she faced Allen full on.

Allen grinned. "Nothing. Just making note of the name."

Tanaka reached into her pocket, pulled out a card case, extricated one of her business cards, and set it on Allen's desk, tapping it with a forefinger for emphasis. "Tanaka."

Boss move. I liked her. I slid Ben a look. He was smiling. He liked her, too.

"When's the last time you saw Hewitt?" Marcus asked.

Allen turned from Tanaka, steepled her fingers under her chin, smiled slightly. "Kaye?"

Chandler had positioned herself beside Allen's desk, ever at the ready. "Yesterday afternoon. He left around one. Four hours short of a full day. There were some items missing from his office. I made a list.".

"What can you tell us about him?" Marcus said. He'd addressed Allen, but she made no attempt to answer. Instead, she waited on Chandler.

"He wasn't an easy person," Chandler said. "He was combative, unruly. There is no emergency contact listed in his file. If he had family, he never said . . . I have no idea who to contact."

Tanaka scribbled in her notepad, glared at Allen. "We'll take care of that."

Marcus looked at me. I held his glance, until he looked away. "But there's been no trouble here?" he asked.

"Of course not," Allen shot back. "Now, if that's all—"

"Not hardly," Tanaka bristled. "A man's been killed."

Allen stared Tanaka down. "He wasn't killed *here*."

"Maybe you'd like to answer these questions down at the district," Marcus said.

Allen laughed full out, as though she'd just heard the funniest joke ever. Then she stood up, calm as anything, placed her hands on the desk, and leaned over like some Wall Street titan about to gobble up a working stiff's retirement fund. Her eyes went dark, like two knots of shiny coal, piercing. "Good one." There was an edge to her voice, a concrete mixer of steel and ore. Allen didn't go anywhere she didn't want to go or do anything she didn't want to do. She said, "As much as I'd like to see you try to pull that off, Detective . . . Jones, is it? I'm going to give you a freebie, a one-off. In the interest of time, mine, not yours. You have fifteen minutes to ask your questions—fifteen, not sixteen, not seventeen—or the next conversation the two of you will have will be with my attorneys. And if it comes to that, I guarantee that conversation will not be pleasant ... for either of you."

The threat hung in the air like pestilence, but Marcus and Tanaka held up. Neither flinched nor blinked nor withered under Allen's stare.

Marcus said, "We'll take you first, alone, and then everybody else. How long it takes depends on the answers we get."

That was when Chandler bolted forward to smooth everything over. "I'm the one who works the closest with the staff. I should stay."

Allen slid in behind her desk again. "Shut the door behind you, Kaye. Detectives? Sit. The clock is ticking."

Rudely dismissed, Ben and I headed out, Chandler behind us. Out in the hall, she pulled the door closed, bolted for her office, and slammed the door behind her.

Ben ran his hands through his short hair. "I bet she's in there bawling her eyes out."

I shook my head, stared at Chandler's door. "It's like the ninth circle of Hell in here."

"I don't know about any circles, but I'm down with the Hell part." Ben sat down in his usual chair. I plopped down beside him in mine. I turned to look at him. "Hewitt dead. You don't think—"

"Who says I don't?"

Chapter 9

Forty minutes later, we were still sitting outside Allen's door, growing restless, not saying much. I pulled up the news reports on Hewitt's death on my phone, to check again for updates, but the little we'd gotten from Marcus and Tanaka was apparently all there was for public consumption. The video clip showed red crime tape strung around Hewitt's front door, uniforms milling around, and again in the news crawl, there was the latest news on the cop killed. She was Detective Marie Russo, married, the mother of a two-year-old daughter. Now she was dead, cold on a slab at the city morgue. I wondered where Farraday was right at this moment, and how he managed to live with himself.

"Could be a 'wrong place, wrong time' kind of deal," Ben said.

I put my phone away, my mood even darker than it had been before. "Sure."

"If it was Flower Guy, you'd think he'd go after somebody she might miss, like Chandler."

I turned to face him. "You think she'd miss Chandler?"

"You might have a point there."

"Kendrick told me they got into it a few weeks ago. He didn't know what about, but it apparently blew over."

Ben snorted. "Maybe not all of it."

"What if this guy's starting slow, playing with her? He puts a good scare into her, makes her jumpy as he gets closer. He takes out Hewitt as kind of a calling card. Makes her worry about his next move."

Ben frowned. "Or a mugging's just a mugging. I'm keeping it there till I know different. One thing's for sure, we won't get a thing from Jones. Why? Because you threw him out like yesterday's cabbage, and he knows I hate his brownnosing guts. Add to that he and Farraday are like two vampires in a pod now, and he knows his guy's hanging on to his job by bloody fingernails. Add to *that*, overall, he's an oily operator who, if he keeps goin' how he's goin', could end up being my boss, and that's the day I either turn in my gun or eat it."

I sighed. "You need to breathe."

"And Tanaka's suspect, you ask me. She's partnered with him, and she looks like she's all in. That's strike one." He jabbed a thumb toward Allen's door. "She's in there now, tap-dancing all over this thing. You know that, right?"

"Just a week of standing around, looking intimidating. That's what you said."

Ben's eyes narrowed. "Uh-oh. I don't like the sound of that."

"For a *boat*. White people's mess is what it is. Out in the middle of a lake all day, with a pole and a cooler full of cheap beer and mushy sandwiches. At the end of it, what do you have? Most of the time nothing. Not one fish. If you do happen to luck up on one, all you've done is sign yourself up for some work, because now you have to gut and scale the bug-eyed sucker. Stupid is what it is. Stupid. I could be at home now. I could be out on my bike. Where am I? Here." My eyes narrowed to reptilian slits. "With her. And *him*."

Ben stared at me. "I'm still on white people's mess."

I buried my face in my hands and took a breath. "I knew he'd get somebody killed. I should have done more, screamed a little harder at the right people."

"Hey, that's not on you."

I scrubbed my hands across my face, and then slumped in the chair. "Feels like it. It feels like it's all on me."

When Allen's door opened finally and Marcus and Tanaka came out, Ben and I stood and were divided up and escorted into offices. I, unfortunately, got Marcus. I wondered as I took a seat whether it had shaken out this way because he'd asked for it, or if it'd just been the luck of the draw. Bad luck.

He sat on the edge of the desk. I sat in a chair inches from him, my arms on the armrests, my legs crossed. I was tired of people looming over me from desks, but there wasn't much I could do about it. He hadn't changed much physically in two years, except for the mustache. There were a few more worry lines at the corners of his eyes, a few more gray hairs. I'd lost the ability to gauge his mood by his expressions. Our connection had been long broken; now we were just two people sitting in a room, talking about a dead man. Keen eyes peered out of his dark face. Most women would consider him handsome. I had. Until I found out what came with it.

"I knew our paths would cross again," he said.

"Like Ben said, small world."

"You two are still thick as thieves, I see. You know, I always wondered if there was more to that." Our eyes locked. I wasn't going to talk about Ben, not with him. "Right. So, Hewitt. Tell me what you know."

"I met him yesterday. We talked briefly."

"About?"

"Job satisfaction. He didn't appear to have any."

Marcus lifted off the desk, walked around it, and sat behind it. "Why'd you care about his job satisfaction? What's going on?"

I hesitated, remembering the nondisclosure I'd signed, weighing Hewitt's death against Allen's obsession with keeping her business to herself and against the likelihood that she'd sue me and take me for every cent I didn't have. "You'll have to ask Ms. Allen."

"Maybe I did."

"And maybe she told you to go fish, which is why you and Tanaka are trying to get Ben and me to fill in the blanks."

He shrugged. "That's how it's done, or have you forgotten?"

"I haven't forgotten anything."

He eased back in the chair and let silence sit for a time.

"What's your take on Hewitt?"

"Angry, stressed. He and Allen seemed to have a difficult working relationship, but as I said, I talked to him only briefly."

"Why's Allen need overqualified body work?"

I shrugged. "You'll have—"

Marcus jumped in to finish. "To ask Ms. Allen, right? His wallet was gone, no watch. There was an iPhone in his pocket. Street thug would have made him turn it over, wouldn't you think?"

I tapped my fingers on the armrest, impatient, eager to be away from Marcus. "Unless he was sloppy or high. Maybe he heard someone coming and didn't have time to go for the phone. Maybe he went for the wallet because there was something in it he wanted besides money. Maybe Hewitt never had a wallet on him in the first place. Lot of things to look at."

Marcus nodded slowly and made a show of straightening his tie. "Or maybe it was about the killing. Too bad Hewitt didn't have you two following along behind him." He waited a moment. "You heard about Farraday, of course. Happy?"

I straightened. "That a cop's dead?"

"That he's likely drummed out, done. You ever think that maybe he wouldn't have charged in so hard if he didn't think he had something to prove? You tarred and feathered him pretty good on your way out the door, got the bosses looking at him suspect."

"Not hard enough, obviously."

He shot me a wan smile. "Cass Raines, cop slayer."

I didn't respond. I didn't want to. I didn't care if I talked about Farraday ever again or thought about how Marcus Jones, even now, was perfectly satisfied to carry his water.

"Nothing?"

I gripped the armrests. "When Philip Hewitt left the office yesterday, he didn't say where he was going. I don't know if he had problems with any of his coworkers. He gave no indication that he was afraid of anyone. On the contrary. He appeared to be a bit of a bantam rooster, cocky, a little full of himself. Ben and I escorted Allen home at the end of business. That completed our duties. We picked her up again at six thirty this morning and headed straight to her club, then here."

"All business, that it?"

"It's what you're here for, isn't it?" I shot back.

He didn't like it. I knew he blamed me for Farraday and he wanted to throw his troubles in my face. I remembered another thing about Marcus just then. He didn't have the ability to let a single thing go—not a slight, not a rude remark, not an argument, not anything—and he always kept score.

"Anything else?" he asked.

I cleared my throat. "Hewitt subscribed to a particularly liberal policy on borrowing office supplies."

His brows lifted. He was confused but didn't follow up. "And this morning, in the wee hours, when Hewitt was getting himself killed, you were . . ."

"Define 'wee hours.'"

He shrugged. "One, two."

"At home in bed, like a normal person."

"Can anybody verify that?"

I didn't answer.

He grinned. "Anyone I know?"

I took a moment. "Tell me the name of Farraday's partner."

"Excuse me?" He didn't know it. I knew he didn't. She hadn't been important enough; her coattails, long enough.

"Maria Russo," I said. "That's her name. She won't be going home to her family tonight or any night. Thanks to your buddy."

His face grew grim, stern. "This doesn't have to get ugly."

"It got ugly about two minutes ago." I pulled the card I'd gotten from Sewell out of my pocket, the one for the high-priced lawyer, and sat it on the desk. Let him think I could afford the representation. He glanced at it, then back at me. Nothing slowed a cop's roll faster than expensive sharks in thousand-dollar suits. In my defense, I never said the lawyers worked for me. I couldn't help him making assumptions. I just laid a business card down, but then I goosed it, and that was all me.

"I can do ugly, though. But when you make your play, it better be good, or Farraday won't be the only cop walking out the door."

He flicked a look at the card, then he looked at me. "So, let's go over this again."

I leaned back. "I met Philip Hewitt for the first time yesterday . . ."

Chapter 10

Allen kicked off early, which meant Ben and I got to kick off early, too. We escorted her home, made sure she was secure, and then left her to it. I was glad for the time, because my new tenant was moving into the building. I'd asked Mrs. Vincent and Barb to oversee the move when I thought I couldn't be there, but now I could, and I got home just as the first moving van pulled up to the back gate.

Barb Covey, the youngest of nine rabble-rousing Irish ruffians, and I had grown up together, gotten in scrapes together, and grown out of it together. She was a nun now, a teacher, and would be starting classes at our old school right after Labor Day. Until then, she was playing it loose, or as loose as a nun played it. There'd been three of us punching back at the world back then before Pop put us all straight. Charles Mingo, whom we'd nicknamed Whip, filled out our little trio.

We three had run the same streets at the same time, doing the same stupid stuff. It was funny how we all ended up on completely different life tracks. I had become a cop, Barb a nun, and Whip had spent the better part of his twenties in the state penitentiary, mostly for taking stuff that didn't belong to him. He was reformed now and worked the griddle in a diner on the West Side, so it was all good.

Barb and I watched the van action in the alley from Mrs. Vincent's back porch. Barb had stuffed her unruly red hair under a Cub's hat and looked as though she'd dressed for a Jimmy Buffett concert—Bermuda shorts with little blue dolphins all over them and a Bon Jovi T-shirt. A simple gold cross, the only hint of her vocation, dangled from a chain around her neck. Sometimes it was hard even for me to believe she was married to God.

"This is exciting," she said. "New people, a fresh start."

I kept my eyes on the van. It looked big enough to carry contraband. "Yippie. Two things I hate."

Mrs. Vincent came out of her back door with two glasses of iced tea, handed one to Barb, one to me, then took a seat in her rocker to watch the action with us. "You two going to watch them bring in every box?"

"Barb is," I said before taking a sip.

Barb gave me serious side eye. "Everybody who knows me knows I'm curious by nature. And not *every* box. Just maybe the first ten or so." She sipped some tea. "Too bad Whip couldn't be here."

I took another sip from my glass. The tea was good, sweet. "I don't think he'd give a hoot about what comes out of that van."

Mrs. Vincent's rocker kept up a slow, steady pace. "You said he works for the city? But he's not a policeman. That's not a lot to go on. Don't know why it's all such a big secret, seeing as he's going to be living under our roof."

I hadn't told anyone much about the new tenant other than what Mrs. Vincent knew. I wasn't being secretive, not really, just cautious. I hoped I'd chosen wisely, but I wouldn't know until he settled in and the honeymoon period was over.

"Kinda big van," Barb said. "Must have a lot of stuff."

"Big enough to fit a piano in," Mrs. Vincent said. "Hope he doesn't have one. I need my sleep, and unless he's that Billy Joel fella, I don't want to hear all that plunking on the keys at all hours of the day and night."

I squinted at the movers as they ambled toward the van doors. "He didn't say anything about a piano. Who moves a piano into a person's building, anyway?"

Barb faced me. "Since when are you anti-piano?"

I shrugged. I was thinking mostly about the weight. Second floor. Old building. Insurance liability. Mrs. Vincent flattened in her bed by a baby grand. A gray Subaru Forester pulled up behind the van, and my new tenant got out, waved at us. We waved back.

"There he is," I muttered. "Hank Gray, fireman."

The rocker stopped. "Good-looking fella. Sturdy. Looks like he can handle himself."

Barb sipped her tea. "Quite imposing."

I looked at them one at a time. "He hauls people out of burning buildings for a living. What's your point?"

Barb avoided looking at me. "No point."

Mrs. Vincent cleared her throat. "I got one. You swung that pendulum mighty far to the right, you ask me. From the Kallishes and little Nate all the way to the big fireman, who's probably got a big fireman's ax in one of those boxes. You won't have to worry over him, that's for sure. Almost as big as a tree, I'd say. I just hope it don't come back to bite you, is all. And that's all I'm saying on the subject."

I stared at her. She met my stare, matched it, and threw one right back at me. I then turned to Barb, who still refused to look at me, which told me she agreed with what had just been thrown down by the old sage in the leisure rocker. I turned back to the van, the Forester, the fireman as big as a tree, wondering now about the ax, knowing Mrs. Vincent had nailed it, nailed me . . . again.

It was true, I didn't have to worry about Hank Gray. He could take care of himself. It was my previous tenants whom I couldn't protect from a drive-by shooting meant to send me a message. It was a failure I had no intention of repeating.

The rocker started back up. "You want cookies with that tea?"

Barb brightened. "Homemade?"

"I only got the one kind." Mrs. Vincent stood. "Oatmeal raisin today."

Barb grinned. "Yum. I love oatmeal raisin. I'll come with you to the kitchen." She elbowed me in the side. "Hold my spot. Yell if you see a piano come out."

I sighed. "Go eat your cookie."

No piano came out, but a lot of guy stuff did—a broken-in lounger, a massive flat-screen TV, stereo equipment, along with the usual necessities—bed, couch, rugs. When Gray was all moved in, Mrs. Vincent went up and gifted him a plate of cookies. I followed up with a "welcome to the building" visit and to check to make sure everything was okay. It was. He wasn't half as big as a tree, but he was imposing—muscled arms, broad chest. He told me he was single and had no kids, but I hadn't asked about his personal situation. It wasn't my business.

"By the way," I said. "We're planning a backyard cookout for Labor Day. Last hurrah before winter snows us under. Join us. Invite a few of your friends, if you want."

"I'll do that. Thanks. Hey, what's your take on overnight guests?"

I blinked at him. "Mine or yours?"

He chuckled. "Thought I'd ask, seeing as this is kind of a special setup, family vibe, and all."

"I'm your landlord, Hank, not your mother. We'd just appreciate your being considerate and respectful of the space. Okay?"

He nodded. "Got it. I'll bring the beer for the cookout."

I turned for the stairs, smiled. "Good beer, right? Don't bring crap beer to my barbecue, Hank."

He laughed. "Wouldn't think of it."

Chapter 11

I would have thought that the tragic death of an employee would have prompted Allen to suspend her busy schedule, but I was wrong. The next day, after a full day of flitting around town, meeting with the producers working on her upcoming show and then hitting the printing facility to check on the run of her latest edition, she was as fresh as a daisy at seven and off to the bookstore for a signing, respect for the dead and any adherence to common decency be damned.

Allen was in a pissy mood, had been since Marcus and Tanaka busted in on her yesterday. Chandler had taken the brunt of her boss's crankiness all day but had hung in there like a champ. It was mostly quiet in the limo for the ride over, and I longed for the day to be over.

"Full house," Ben said as we eased past the Barnes & Noble. I peered out the window and saw the lights blazing inside the bookstore and a crowd moving around.

Chandler craned her neck to see. "Excellent. I knew there would be. Vonda has quite the following."

I stared at Allen. She'd disengaged miles back. Her head was buried in her notes as she prepared for her presentation. Business. Always business. The limo had turned the corner, headed for the alley entrance, before Allen finally looked up at me. "You read, don't you?" Her cool, needling smile told me she wanted to play.

I sighed. It really had been a long day, and I wasn't in the mood to go toe-to-toe with her. "I've been known to."

"What? Specifically."

I brushed a slow hand over my slacks, making her wait for it. "Cereal boxes."

Her smile faded. There came a low snicker from the front seat, followed by a round of fake coughing. Ben.

"Cheerios, *specifically*," I added with a straight face.

Allen tuned me out again, which I appreciated. I was tired of her games.

Chandler tapped lightly on the privacy glass, rolled down partway for easy communication. "Pull up to the door, Elliott. Someone will meet us there."

Chandler was taking it all so seriously. Obviously, this event was as important to her as it was to Allen, and she was making sure everything ran like clockwork. Chandler reminded me of a swan serenely gliding on a glassy lake, graceful, quiet. You only had to look beneath the water's surface to see little webbed feet paddling like mad. This may have been Allen's show, but it was Chandler's production.

"Here we are," Chandler said as we came to a stop. Ben immediately jumped out to check the alley.

Chandler reached for the door handle, but I stuck out my arm to stop her. "Not yet. When he says it's clear." Moments passed before Ben rapped on the window. "Now," I said. "Right side, please. Me first, then Ms. Allen."

Allen didn't look like she cared for the order of things. She was likely used to always going first. She pursed her lips into a severe line and leveled flat eyes at me. I smiled back at her, gave her a wink, and watched her bristle. We were out of the car, inside in seconds and were instantly greeted by a young, bookish store rep with curly hair, large glasses, and a toothy grin.

The young woman bounced a bit on the balls of her feet, excited as a playful puppy looking forward to a noonday piddle. "Ms. Allen. You're here. I'm Meghan Fahey. I'm so honored to meet you." She looked around the tight group. "And everyone. Follow me, please. We're ready for you."

A short ride up to the second floor in a compact elevator, a brisk walk down a narrow hall, and a shuffle into a small VIP courtesy room, and the first test of our evening was over. Fahey flitted around the room, pointing out the amenities—coffee urn, powder room with fully stocked vanity table, color TV with cable access, and platters of cheese and fresh fruit daintily diced for VIP consumption. An ice bucket filled with ice and bottled water, soft drinks, and juices sat on a narrow side table. Allen graciously turned down refreshments when they were offered. The graciousness threw me. I hadn't seen a lot of it in the past three days. I shot Ben a look. I could tell the graciousness had thrown him, too, and he'd known Allen longer than I had.

"So, that's our 'green' room," Fahey chirped, making little invisible quote marks with her fingers when she said the word *green*, since the room was actually a pale yellow. "We have a few minutes, so if you'd like to relax and compose your thoughts, we should be ready to get started in about, oh . . ." She checked her watch. "Fifteen minutes?"

"Everything looks just wonderful," Chandler said. "Thank you, Meghan. I'd like to take a look at the space?"

"Oh sure, no problem. It looks great. More than enough room for the crowd out there, and the books are all in. We should do absolute gangbusters tonight." The two hustled off.

"I'll go with them," Ben said. "Get the lay of the land." He leaned in toward me, whispered, "Yell if you need a referee . . . or riot gear."

I sighed. That left me alone with Allen. Again.

It was as quiet as a mummy's tomb when the door closed. Allen looked around for a chair that met her standards. She found one against the wall, but before she sat in it, she examined it, as if she could see all manner of parasites crawling across the upholstery.

Back at the office, after her full day, she'd showered and changed into a silk suit of vivid melon and added a gold and diamond bracelet and matching earrings to set it off. She didn't look comfortable in the chair; she leaned back cautiously and then maneuvered around so as not to let any part of her bare skin touch it. When she'd found a position that worked for her, she crossed her legs, let the top one swing, and then looked at me as if she'd never seen me before.

I also looked around, but not for a chair. The bathroom looked secure, but I checked it, anyway. No outside access. In and out of the VIP room, there was only the one door we'd just come through, so unless Allen tripped over a lamp cord or scalded herself on the coffee urn, she'd make it another fifteen minutes.

I pointed toward the hall. "I'll be out there. Plenty of chilled water behind you." I reached for the knob.

"Wait," she said.

Dang it. I turned. Allen placed her elbows on the armrests, thought better of it, and pulled them away, then folded her hands in her lap instead.

"I misjudged you. You're not like most people I come across. You have a spine . . . and a smart mouth. I'm curious. Exactly when did you stop taking people's shit?"

I raised an eyebrow. It was an interesting question, but a little unexpected coming from a woman wearing eight-hundred-dollar shoes. "Likely about the same time you started shoveling it."

She smiled, but her eyes didn't sign on to it. "You resent my wealth, find it offensive. You think me abrasive, unfeeling."

I squinted. "That a question?"

"An observation. Here's another. You don't like me."

"The jury's still out. You're a bit much."

"How so?"

"Look, if you want to mind diddle Chandler and the others, that's your business and theirs. Me? I could do with a lot less of it." I turned again to leave.

"Mind diddle. I like that. You think I should have canceled tonight."

"Again. All you."

"But you would have. Out of what? Respect for the dead?"

Yep, but I didn't say it. I watched her instead, wondering what tragedy or act of betrayal had made her, because surely her hatefulness could not have been forged by half a lifetime of happiness. What had she wanted and never gotten? What had she needed and been denied? Whatever the answer, it was unmistakable that it was anger and spite that sustained her now. Beneath all the diamonds and silk, beyond all that excess, Allen was flinty of spirit, an emotional pauper, and if she didn't rankle me so, I might have been able to work up a little pity for her.

"Hewitt was a thorn in my side. It would have been hypocritical. I may be a lot of things, but I'm not that. I don't lie."

"Except by omission. You know who's harassing you, but you won't let us in on it. You're at risk as a result, and so are we."

Allen was slow to speak. "You and Detective Jones? What's your history?"

She was still angling for that edge. She waited, watched. I didn't say anything.

"See? Everyone has secrets."

I said, "It's not a secret. Just none of your business."

She turned her head, ignored me.

When I took up my spot right outside the door, I thought about Allen and how alone she was, and a chill went down my spine. I checked my watch. Ten minutes till showtime. *Oh boy.*

Chapter 12

People loved the public Allen—the smiling, sparkling, polished Allen, who hugged everyone, pulling them into her circle of money sunshine, as if they were long-lost friends, family. The store had positioned a simple podium next to a table draped in black cloth and stacked high with copies of her book, her glamorous face beaming on the cover. Lined up in front were folding chairs, filled with awestruck fans grinning back at her, reassuring her that she was, in fact, a star.

Chandler stood across the way from us, hovering, this after already making sure that Allen's pitcher of water had been filled and that she had enough pens to sign her name. She'd left nothing to chance. At one point, as Allen read aloud, I would have sworn I saw Chandler mouthing the words right along with her.

The audience was made up mostly of women, but there were a few men, husbands or boyfriends, presumably, who were along for the ride and didn't seem too displeased with the prospect. Local news crews were spread out along the periphery, taping Allen as she worked the crowd. She'd make the ten o'clock news easily.

As she read aloud, she detailed her early life of poverty and extolled the grit and perseverance that helped her become the woman she was today. I had to admit it was a compelling rags-to-riches story. How much of it was true, well, who knew?

"It almost makes you want to bawl your eyes out, doesn't it?" Ben whispered.

"You're an easy touch."

My eyes kept sweeping the room; so did Ben's. Nothing out of the ordinary. Suddenly, the room exploded in a thunderclap of applause. I'd missed Allen's big finish. Chandler looked like she was proud enough to burst buttons. Allen took a seat behind the table, uncapped a pen, ready to sign her books, as the people lined up. Ben and I moved in, then split up. He took the right side of the table, and I took the left, both of us keeping an eye peeled for anything hinky.

One of the local TV reporters, a woman I recognized from Channel 5, rushed up with a chubby guy dressed in baggy jeans and a station T-shirt, a bulky camera balancing on his shoulder. The reporter, blond, thin—Annie something or other—thrust a microphone into Allen's face, and the camera flicked on, flooding Allen's face with blinding light.

"What a beginning, Ms. Allen," a plump brunette of about fifty gushed when her time came at the front of the line. She seemed thrilled to see that the camera was rolling and that she'd likely make the evening newscast. "What an inspiring life you've lived."

Allen's face lit up. "Why, thank you. And it's not over yet." She winked playfully at the camera, then glanced at the slip of paper passed along to her by Chandler with the gusher's name written on it. "What a pretty blouse you're wearing . . . Elizabeth." This sent the woman swooning. Annie now had a few usable sound bites, Elizabeth had her autograph, and Allen had experienced the mother of all ego strokes.

Meghan Fahey eased in next to me. "You're so lucky to work with her. She's just the best, isn't she?"

I managed a half-committed smile. "She's one in a million."

The parade of the woefully misguided went on for nearly an hour, as store assistants wove in and out of the line, closing up gaps, keeping everybody moving. Allen signed everything put in front of her—books, photographs, even a few body parts. Everyone seemed happy. No signs of trouble.

The line thinned after a while, but healthy pockets of faithful still moved around the floor, sneaking glimpses of Allen, snapping her photo, and comparing the autographs they'd gotten. Most of the news crews had gotten their footage and had packed up and gone; only Annie and her camera remained behind.

As my eyes came back to center, I spotted a black man who hadn't been there before inching forward at the end of the line. I scanned the room, looking for where he might have come from, then turned back. He was holding a bouquet of yellow flowers and a copy of Allen's book. In a sea of mostly white faces, you couldn't miss him, but it was the flowers that made me hold my breath.

Medium complexion, youngish, midtwenties maybe, average height, average build; wearing a denim jacket, black cargo pants, black runners, and a green T-shirt; a healed scar over his right eyebrow. I committed it all to memory, the scar being the most important. He could ditch the clothes; he couldn't ditch that.

I looked for Ben, but he already had eyes on him. The line moved forward. Another Allen autograph, a little more face time. The man's eyes never left Allen's face, but she hadn't noticed him yet. He was so focused on Allen that he didn't appear to have noticed me or Ben, either, or see that we were tracking his every move.

Four people behind in line, the man readjusted his hold on the flowers, wet his lips. Getting ready. I moved in closer to Allen; Ben moved in beside me.

"No crime in bringing flowers," Ben whispered. "Strange choice, though. Carnations."

My eyes were on the guy, only on the guy. "He's staring at her pretty hard."

"He's just a man with flowers. Until he's not."

The more I looked at him, the more I felt there was something about him. "Why does he look familiar?"

"No kidding? You know him?"

I shook my head, still watching. "No, don't think so, but there's something."

"I'll stick with him," Ben said. "She's yours."

I frowned, then nodded. Allen and I were beginning to be a thing. There were now just two people between the table and the flower guy. Ben stepped out in front of the table. The woman in front of Allen moved away. One person to go. Allen smiled at the woman. She'd bought three books, one for herself, the others for her daughters. She wanted them signed and personally dedicated.

His turn imminent, the young man glanced around and saw me watching him. I didn't smile, didn't blink. I gave no indication that my looking at him was coincidental. He blinked once, looked away, and found Ben watching him, too. He suddenly looked nervous, worried, but he held his spot. He was almost there, much too close to give up now. The woman ahead of him moved away from the table. He stepped forward, laid his book down. Allen palmed it, opened the jacket, then looked up to greet him and gasped.

"Hello," he said. "You can make it out to Eric."

Allen's pen hovered over the title page. She drew in a sharp, startled breath, which she seemed physically unable to expel. Conversations went on around her, but I doubted Allen could hear the talk or see anything except for the face of the man holding the yellow flowers.

"These are for you." He laid the bouquet on the table and took back the book offered him.

Allen never looked at the flowers. Her eyes never left the

man's face. He appeared upset. "You don't like flowers? Go ahead and take them."

I moved forward, scooped up the bouquet he'd laid down, checked it. Just flowers, nothing hidden inside. "Sir, I'll have to ask you to please move back. Ms. Allen appreciates the flowers and thanks you for coming." Ben moved in closer, too, flanked him.

The man glanced hopefully at Allen. Surely, she would intervene. "She appreciates the flowers?"

"Yes, sir," Ben said, suddenly right there. "And she thanks you for coming. Would you mind stepping this way, please?"

"No. I want to talk to her."

I gently took the book from him.

"Hey, that's mine!"

"I'm just putting it here," I said, laying it on the table, "while we talk, calmly. You can have it back." I gestured to an empty corner on the far side of the room, away from the crowd, away from Allen. "She can't talk now, but if you'd step quietly this way."

He shook his head, angry now. He didn't want to speak to us. He made no effort to move. His eyes darted around the room. "Look . . . wait . . . That's *my* book."

We blocked his way, standing like a fence between him and the woman he'd come to see. He tried peering around us for a better look. "She's—"

Ben reached out and took a firm grip of his upper arm. "Sir, you're going to have to move back."

The man yanked his arm free. "Get your hands off me."

The murmurs and bits of conversation that had given the room a party atmosphere died out as suddenly as someone flicking off a light switch. Out of the corner of my eye, I could see cell phones emerging from pockets and tote bags, iPads being raised. The reporter and her cameraman inched forward, the camera filming. This was becoming a circus.

"Look, guy," Ben began as he reached in again. I did, too, gently. We needed to move him back, calm him down. But he peddled away from us fast, got beyond our reach, fixing us with wild eyes.

"Back off." His hand slipped into his jacket pocket, and my hand and Ben's cocked back to our holsters at the same time, the confrontation suddenly taking a sickening turn.

"Do *not* do that!" I yelled.

Ben barked, "Get your hand out of the jacket!"

Our stern commands tumbled over each other as we kept our eyes glued on the pocket.

A pocketknife emerged, the blade at least six inches long. Not a gun. I moved my hand away from my gun, relieved, but not relaxed, my heart pounding. Gun versus knife wasn't a fair fight. All we needed to do was calm him down and move him out, not shoot him.

Ben's hands went up, palms out "Whoa. Steady there. What say we bring this whole thing way down, huh? What's your name, kid?"

"It's Eric, right?" I said. "That's what you said?"

The man's eyes swept from Ben to me, then over the frightened spectators, frozen to their spots. "You started this." He jabbed the knife in our direction, swung it in an arc right to left, holding us off. A gasp went up in the room. "I said get back. Let me talk to her."

I kept my eyes on the knife, mindful of the distance between it and us. "Can't do that."

He didn't like that. He began to thrust and parry, bobbing on the balls of his feet, the knife jabbing forward.

"You have guns," someone from the crowd shouted, "shoot him."

"Shut up!" Ben yelled back.

The man's hand tightened on the hilt of the knife. "You gonna shoot me? Go on then. Shoot me. Go on."

"Dammit." Ben muttered it under his breath, resigned. We exchanged a look. "You good?" he asked.

I checked the crowd, the knife, then nodded to Ben. "Yeah, okay."

"My right."

"Yep."

We rushed forward together, fast off the mark. Ben grabbed the guy's right wrist, locked it, tried to loosen his grip on the pocketknife. On my side, I grabbed his left wrist and forearm, twisted both, while at the same time Ben and I rammed the guy back, away from the table, as if pushing a tackling dummy down a football field. We slammed into a shelf of books, toppling most onto the floor. Shrieks went up in the room.

I pinned the guy's arm back, my forearm pressing in against his neck. "Drop it! Now!"

He fought to get his arm free, but I had it twisted. If he moved it too wildly, it would surely break. Close up now, my face inches from his, I noted the scar parting his right eyebrow, the color of his eyes, the shape of his nose, his hairline. I shot a look at the wrist I was clamped down on and saw a small birthmark right at the joint, on the underside—dark, with jagged edges like an inkblot—another identifier.

I looked right into his face. "I said *drop it!*" I hissed it, my teeth clenched, fighting to keep him pinned, pressing in while at the same time kicking his legs apart to get him off-balance. Out of the corner of my eye, I could see Ben struggling on the other side. Ben was a big guy, a cop. What was taking so long?

"Got it?" I asked.

"Not yet." Ben glared at the guy, still struggling. "Is this really the hill you want to die on? Drop it!"

I pressed in harder, kicked out at his legs again, but I couldn't get enough leverage to send him over, not without removing my arm from his neck or letting his wrist go, and that wasn't happening. Suddenly, Ben cried out, stumbled back, and I turned to see blood blossoming on the front of his white shirt.

"He stuck me!"

The guy's right hand was free, and the knife was coming my way. I released his arm, ducked, and peddled back fast out of striking range. The spectators gasped, screamed, and took off running for the stairs like a herd of frightened buffalo, their retreat so frenzied that I could feel the rumble of the panicked exodus through the soles of my shoes.

I checked Ben, watched the knife, the man holding it. He was hopped up on adrenaline and fear in equal measure. I could see it in his eyes. He was cornered and knew it. I shifted slowly over so that I stood between Ben and him. The guy's frantic eyes dropped to my waist and the gun there; then they met mine. "Don't make me," I said.

He dropped the knife and ran for the stairs. I exhaled, then ran to Ben.

Ben lay on the carpet, his hands clutching his stomach. "What the hell? What're you doing? Leave me. Go after the son of a bitch."

There was blood everywhere—his shirt, his hands, on the carpet beneath him. Pain was etched all over his pallid face. I kneeled down beside him to get a better look. The wound was deep. I turned to the bookstore rep. What the hell was her name?

"Call an ambulance!"

She didn't move. She stood there like a zombie, mouth open, a stricken look on her freckled face.

I stood. "Hey! You. Bookstore girl. Call nine-one-one." She fumbled for her phone, dialed the digits. I looked over at Allen and Chandler. "Both of you sit."

Allen began to gather up her things, her purse, her glasses. "I'm not going to stand here in the open. Kaye, call for the car."

"You'll stay where I can see you. Sit!"

Chandler looked as though I'd stuck her with a cattle prod, Allen, too, but they both sat. I went back to Ben. There was too much blood, far too much, and he didn't look good.

He winced. "You let him waltz right out the door? What's wrong with you?"

"Shut up. Let me see."

"Looks worse than it is." He squeezed his eyes shut. "Get me a Band-Aid, Nurse Nancy."

He was joking. Good sign. I spotted a sweater someone had dropped on their mad dash for the exit, and scrambled over and grabbed it. After balling it up tight, I pressed it to Ben's middle, listening out for the ambulance, trying not to think about the blood. I swallowed hard, waiting helplessly for someone to come.

"You're right. It looks worse than it is." I hoped I sounded convincing. "You do worse giving yourself a shave in the morning." He'd gone gray. I looked into his eyes. Dullness stared back at me. *Shit.*

"You always . . . were . . . a lousy liar."

I applied slightly more pressure to the wound. "I could stitch you up myself. I took basic first aid at the academy. I can birth a baby, apply a tourniquet, perform CPR." Maybe if I razzed him, he'd stay alert enough to razz me back.

"I didn't learn . . . half that crap."

I shot Allen and Chandler an evil look as they sat there seething, as though they were the victims here, not Ben. "Well, I'm smarter than you, or didn't you know that?"

"Yeah . . . I know it. Hands down." His lips were beginning to turn blue, and the sweater was covered in blood.

I turned to the rep. "Call again. Tell them to hurry the hell up." But before she could dial, I heard the sirens. Then, a couple of minutes later, there came a ruckus from the floor below, followed by the sound of heavy feet racing up the steps. Finally.

"They're here." I felt Ben's hands, found them cold. His eyes were closed now. "Ben?"

"Relax. Just resting my eyes."

Now who was the lousy liar? The paramedics rushed in, loaded down with gear, followed close behind by a couple of uniformed cops. I got up, stepped back, and let them work, my bloody hands shaking. I looked over at Allen, sitting there, her arms crossed petulantly at her chest, looking just as unconcerned and as disapproving as always, as though Ben, bleeding on the floor, was inconveniencing her. This was on her, every bit of it. She turned her back to me; Chandler, too. I stormed over to the table, grabbed up the book the guy had left behind.

   Eric.

Chapter 13

I rode in the ambulance with Ben, but he drifted in and out, and I didn't think he knew I was there. We rushed through the automatic doors of the ER six minutes later, Ben on the gurney, the paramedics and I trotting alongside it.

"We've got a bleeding cop here!" I yelled. "Bleeding cop!"

A nurse and doctor in scrubs rushed forward, ready to triage, stethoscopes hanging from their necks, bags under bloodshot eyes. Ben's eyes fluttered open, and I almost cried with relief.

"Jeez, I'm not dead yet." His words were slurred, and his voice was low, but it was something. It was everything.

I watched as the busy pair checked Ben out. The paramedics had replaced the sweater I'd used to apply pressure with real-deal bandages, and they had started an IV, meds, and oxygen in the ambulance. When the doctor pulled the bandages away, the gash on Ben's stomach startled me all over again. I looked over at the doctor, but she didn't appear to be rattled by the sight of it. I took that as a good sign.

She whistled. "Well, looks like somebody's going to surgery on the fast track." She flicked a look at the paramedics. "Wheel him back. We'll get him set up."

Ben scowled. "Surgery . . . ? For this?"

The doctor looked at me; the nurse, too.

I shrugged. "He doesn't like hospitals."

"Hate 'em," Ben said. "Pee in this . . . Drop trou . . . Stick tongue out . . ." He faded out again.

The doctor shook her head, smirked. "Let's go, people. Bleeding cop!"

The gurney shot through the doors, and I tried to follow, but the nurse stopped me at the threshold. "Family?"

I watched helplessly as Ben disappeared inside. "Yes," I barked back.

His brows lifted; he angled his head. He'd obviously been here before.

"Practically. For all intents and purposes."

He gave me a sympathetic smile, tucked his stethoscope into his pocket. "Sorry. You'll have to wait out here, then. But don't worry. He's going right up."

He hustled off toward another crisis and left me standing at the doors, Ben's blood on my hands and shirt.

I turned toward the waiting room just as Marcus and Tanaka walked in, spotted me, and headed over. Instantly, everyone in the ER perked up and tuned in, even an old guy hooked up to an oxygen tank. Everyone could peg *cop* when it breezed through the door like it owned the place.

"What the hell went on tonight?" Marcus asked when he reached me. Tanaka just stood there, as animated as bleached-out driftwood staked into winter sand.

I didn't answer, mainly because he'd just asked a question he already knew the answer to—or why else would he be here?—and secondly, because I was done with him. I eyed them both, weighed my options, then decided just to peace out.

"Excuse me, please." I followed the directional signs to the women's bathroom. I needed a minute, a month, a year even, and a quiet spot without anyone in it but me. I peeked under the stalls, looking for sick-people feet and ankles, pushed open a few stall doors just to confirm I was alone, and then stood at the sink, exhaled, and washed my hands, watching as blood and soap swirled slowly down the drain.

My hands looked clean, but I washed them again, the tap still running, then splashed cold water on my face a couple of times. I avoided looking at myself in the mirror, at my shirt with Ben's blood on it. It was bad enough I could feel the hardened smears brushing against my bare skin when I moved. It felt like it weighed a ton, the blood, like I was wearing a shirt of chain mail or one of bricks.

Why did it feel like I couldn't breathe? Had Ben felt like this when it'd been me bleeding to death? I turned away from the mirror, yanked a rough paper towel from the dispenser on the wall, and patted my face dry, a little steadier, but not by much. That was when Tanaka came in.

"No," I said, trying to ward her off before she had a chance to open her mouth. "Go away."

"You know I can't," she said. "You know how this goes."

"I cannot deal with you right now. You should be out there looking for the guy who did this. I gave his description to the uniforms back at the scene, a full, detailed report, before the ambulance pulled off. You've got a roomful of witnesses, including a news crew with footage of the whole thing. And you've got Allen and Chandler, who know what this is about, but won't say. So right now? I need a minute. I need you—"

"Did the guy tonight mention Hewitt?"

Her question surprised me. What did Philip Hewitt have to do with tonight? "Why would he mention—"

But before I could finish, Marcus burst through the door and encroached on all my personal space. I took a step back.

"We're done dancing around with you," he said. "What the hell is Vonda Allen into, and what's it got to do with this dead guy we're working?" He placed his arms on his hips, his eyes hot, intense. He meant to throw his weight around, show me he called the shots, just like Farraday. I faced Tanaka, ignored him.

"You're talking to the wrong person," I said. "The right person's likely at home now, sipping brandy out of a golden snifter. Go harass her."

"Don't get cute," Marcus snapped. "Don't forget I know you. I know how you operate."

"Hewitt was into a few bookies for a lot of money," Tanaka said, ignoring her partner. The seamless way she did it told me she was used to doing it. "Maybe the guy tonight worked for one of them. Maybe he—"

The door opened, and a black woman, maybe about thirty, rushed in with a little boy, about four, with a runny nose and saggy pants. She startled when she saw us.

"You can't come in here," Marcus barked. "We need the room."

"Yeah, I need it, too," she said none too gently. "He's gotta pee, and this is where he's got to do it, unless *you* want to wash his pants out in that sink." She waited for a challenge but didn't get it, then rushed into a stall, dragging the kid behind her. We stood listening to the sound of tiny pants being pulled down and the two of them bumping against the stall door. Tanaka stared at the tops of her shoes, Marcus stared at me, and I found a spot on the wall just over his shoulder to focus on as we waited on a kid's bladder. I was acutely aware that time was being wasted. I needed to know how Ben was doing. I'd been in this bathroom too long already.

Marcus was growing impatient. "You want to hurry it up in there?"

"Mind your business," the woman yelled back.

We all listened as the mother and kid finished up and the toilet flushed. Finally, the pair emerged and hurried over to the sink for the hand-washing portion of the program, the woman shooting daggers at Marcus. Time couldn't have crawled any slower.

"You need to take all that somewhere else besides in here," the woman said as she tossed the paper towel into the bin and headed for the door, with the boy by the hand. She looked Marcus up and down. "*You're* not even supposed to be in here. *Perv.*"

When the door closed behind them, Marcus banged the trash bin against the door to barricade it shut and then stood in front of that to keep out the next toddler in crisis.

"No one mentioned Hewitt tonight," I said, hoping to move things along. "This felt personal. You might want to start there. We done?"

Tanaka searched my face. "I'm surprised you're not gung ho to work it all out."

"I don't work for Allen anymore. I quit tonight. Ben's my concern right now. But if you two are thinking he was some bookie coming after Allen to resolve Hewitt's gambling debt, you've gotten it wrong. Allen could barely tolerate Hewitt. There's no way she'd agree to bail him out of a jam while he was alive, let alone dead."

"She's got deep pockets," Marcus said. "The bookie wouldn't know she couldn't stand the guy."

I stared at him like he'd lost his mind. "So, the *bookie* bought flowers and a book, stood in line for Allen to sign it . . . and then. . . . 'Oh, by the way, would you write me a check for your employee's gambling losses?' Are you serious? Which one of you came up with this?" It didn't look like either one of them wanted to claim it. I couldn't blame them. I wouldn't have.

"Careful," Marcus warned.

"*You* be careful. This was personal. He was there to see *her*, talk to *her*. He said as much, but you'd know all that if you'd talked to the uniforms before rushing over here to waste my time."

Tanaka stood calmly, eyes steady. "You didn't give chase. Why?"

"He'd dropped the knife. Ben needed help. What would you have done?"

Before she could answer, Marcus did. "I'd have run the guy down, like any *good* cop would."

My eyes held Tanaka's. "Hear that, Tanaka? Like any *good* cop would."

She got the message. Marcus Jones would be no use to her when the chips were down. Like Marie Russo, if the worst came to pass, she'd find that her backup was no backup at all.

"I'm done," I said. "You have the knife. Check for prints. Maybe he's in the system. Grab the news footage. They got everything. You even have the book she signed with his name in it." I stepped around them, slid the bin away from the door. "A *good* cop should be able to wrap this thing up in no time. Now leave me alone. I've got a *friend* to check on."

Marcus turned around. "You're not half as smart as you think you are, Cass."

I smiled, let it go. "The next time you two crowd me in a bathroom, you'd better be ready to put me in cuffs."

"Don't leave town," Tanaka warned.

"I'll leave the country if I feel like it." I glared at Marcus. "And you don't know the first thing about me. Never did."

It was well after midnight when Ben got out of surgery. Everything had gone well, the doctors said, and they thought he'd be just fine with a little recuperation. Eli had come to wait with me, and we were sitting in the surgical waiting room for word on when we could go back and take a look for ourselves. When we finally did, we found Ben snoring in a private room, hooked up to an IV, knocked out and floating on a wave of no-joke drugs, his abdomen covered in layers of bandages.

"It's going to take more than a knife to send him on to glory," Eli whispered.

I watched Ben's chest rise and fall. He was alive, on the mend. I glanced at Eli. "I can go now."

A half hour later, I trudged up the three flights to my apartment, having declined the offer of Eli's company. Like Allen earlier, I wanted to be alone. I stepped inside, tossed my keys into the bowl on the entry table, unclipped my gun, and set it there, too. The place was dead quiet except for the ticking of the clock in my kitchen. I slipped out of my blazer, unbuttoned my shirt, peeled out of it, and then, angry, impotent, shaking, flung both toward my living room, not bothering to care where they landed. Half dressed, unable to move, unable to think about where to move to, I fell back against the door and slid down the length of it, then drew my knees up close, and rocked to soothe myself.

Chapter 14

Linda Sewell bumped her old Corolla into the multilevel garage across the street from the *Strive* office. It was almost 10:00 AM. She was late, with piles of work waiting, but first, she had had to drop Jarrod off at school, meet with his teacher, stop at the ATM, and then dash for gas at the Amoco, for the fifteen dollars' worth, which would get her all the way downtown.

Allen would not be in a good mood, either, she knew, not after the trouble at the bookstore. It was all over the news. Some crazed fan with a knife, still on the loose. No, Vonda Allen would be hell on wheels today. Sewell's car clattered to a stop between diagonal yellow lines on level thirteen.

She grabbed her bag and a stack of files from the passenger seat and then all but hurled herself out of the car, her mind on the work ahead and the grief she had coming. So loud were her thoughts that she didn't hear the footsteps. She had the car locked and her bag slung over her shoulder before she sensed she wasn't alone. She turned, clutched the bag and files to her chest, and fixed surprised eyes on the smiling face. One she knew. Still, there was a prickle at the base of her neck as unease crept up her spine and turned her blood to ice.

"You don't park here." Sewell pulled the bag and the files closer to her. They were her only shield, but not much protection.

The smile widened. There was a slow shake of the head.

"Then what . . . ?" She couldn't finish; fear had swallowed her words. There was no one else around, just cars, dim light, and walls of solid concrete . . . and the smile. Sewell took a tentative step toward escape. "I need to get upstairs."

The head tilted. The smile died. A steady hand slipped into a bulky pocket. Sewell knew then she'd die where she stood. She would have screamed if she'd had the time.

I knocked on the door to Ben's room and stood in the open doorway with a monstrous potted plant, watching as he sneered at the indistinguishable items on his breakfast tray. His color was back. He looked like his old self. He noticed me standing there and lifted what looked like a piece of smoked roadkill.

"Can you believe this crap? They're calling *this* bacon. First, it's turkey, so no way in hell, and second, *it's turkey*." He took in the plant. "What's with the dieffenbachia?"

I eased in, smiling, my spirit instantly lifted after a night of wrestling ghosts and haunting what-ifs. I set the plant down near the window so it could catch some sun. "That's what this is? I just asked for something alive and green." I walked over to the bed, stared at the tray. "That looks . . . sad."

Ben snorted. "You're telling me. I think they're trying to starve me out."

I stood at the bed rail, gave his arm a squeeze. "How do you feel?" We exchanged a look. We'd exchanged millions of them in our time together, but somehow this one felt different. I pulled my hand away, suddenly self-conscious, and slid both into my front pockets. Ben took a sip of orange juice from a little plastic cup.

"Like I got flattened by an eighteen-wheeler, but I'm out of here tomorrow, and not a minute too soon. This place gives me the creeps." He winked at me. "Drugs are damn good, though."

"Almost makes up for the bacon, then."

Ben snorted again. "Hell, it does. They should be ashamed of themselves." He tossed the fake bacon back onto his plate. "So where are we with Allen? Who's Ginsu Guy?"

"Ginsu Guy?"

Ben made a slashing motion with his hand.

"Not funny," I said.

He patted the bandages around his middle. "Tell me about it. So?"

"Marcus and Tanaka think he's connected to one of Hewitt's bookies. That maybe since whoever it is couldn't get the money out of Hewitt, he figured he could get it out of Allen."

"So they think the bookie shot Hewitt? *Before* he got his money?"

"They didn't say. I didn't ask."

"Because if that's what they're thinking, that'd make him one dumb bookie. You bleed the fish. You break his jaw, bust his kneecaps, smash his knuckles. You don't blow his head off. Dead men don't pay, and anybody with half a brain working knows that. As for Allen, I don't think she'd pay to ransom her own mother."

I shrugged. "There are dumb bookies."

Ben pushed his tray away. "A dumb bookie is a broke bookie. And since you're here and not with Allen, I assume you told her where to stick it."

"Sorry about the boat."

He waved a dismissive hand. "Who'd I think I was, anyway? Onassis?"

"We offered our help. She turned it down," I said. "Let Tanaka and Marcus figure out her problem. I've got other work, and you have some healing to do."

"Sure as hell can't babysit her in my condition," Ben offered with a sour smirk. "So that knocks us both out." He stared at me. "You let him get away so you could futz around with me, though. That's twice you've saved my life."

"I made the right call both times. And since when are we counting?"

Many seconds passed. "I said I'd let you know when I was ready to talk. I've had a lot of time to think lately, seeing as they took my pants and I've had jack to do but lie here like a dead carp." Ben picked at the flimsy hospital gown. "It's just one indignity after another in here. Anyway, I'm almost ready, is what I'm saying."

"You want to give me a hint?"

He smiled. "You'll know when you know."

A small nurse walked in, smiling, carrying a tray of needles and medicine vials. "Time for meds." She turned to me. "And you need your rest." That was my signal. I moved to leave.

"Get some sleep," I said. "I'll see you tomorrow." I stepped out into the hall, gave him a last look. "Eat that bacon."

"Stop calling it bacon. Hey, tomorrow bring me an Italian beef from Carmine's, dipped, with extra peppers."

"Bye." I headed for the elevator, a grin on my face, but Ben was still talking.

"Tell them to double the giardiniera!"

I jogged up the stairs to my office, stopped cold when I saw my father, Ted Raines, standing outside my door, looking lost. Of course, he'd be here. Why not? I'd had one hell of a night, I'd just quit my job, and Ben was in the hospital. Why, this was the perfect time to have to also deal with a prodigal father. *Yep, Cass Raines, you are one lucky woman.*

Until two months ago, I hadn't seen Ted Raines since the day he dropped me on my grandparents' front stoop. I was twelve, and my mother had been buried two days before. It had been a jerk move. I neared my door, fishing in my bag for my keys.

"Hey, there you are," he said. "I was just about to slip a note under the door."

I looked him over. When he'd stepped into my yard months ago, he'd been dressed like a stiff-necked banker in a stuffy suit. This time he was wearing a navy blazer and khakis, and the collar of his white polo shirt was unbuttoned.

I slid the key in the lock, led him in. "More notes." I slung my bag onto my nap couch and moved to stand behind my desk, where my hands gripped the back of my swivel chair. Since we last met, he'd taken to writing me letters on the regular. I'd received maybe a dozen at last count, though I hadn't yet read a single one. "And another surprise visit."

"I said I'd be back. You didn't believe me."

"You're right. I didn't. Either time."

When he'd left me at twelve, he'd promised to come back and get me. He hadn't. Now here we were.

He looked around the small office. "I said in my last letter I'd be coming. Guess you missed it. It's all right, too, if you didn't read the letter, or any of the others. I'll follow your lead on this." His eyes landed on the wooden coatrack by the door, a worn black crook-handle umbrella hanging from it. "Hey, I used to have one of those racks back in the day. Even had an umbrella like that."

"It was Pop's," I said. "The umbrella, not the rack."

I could tell he didn't want to talk about Pop. He'd admitted to some resentment of him after his death, blaming Pop for having stepped in to be the father he had refused to be. I'd been so angry at his return after half a lifetime that I even thought it possible that he had killed Pop just to take him from me.

"I brought Sylvia and Whitford this time."

"Your family."

"Yours too . . . if you want." He fiddled with his jacket cuffs. "Sylvia said maybe the letters weren't the right thing to do, but I needed to say things I couldn't with us standing like this. I thought maybe we could go to dinner someplace nice, all of us. Get to being comfortable with one another. I'll understand if you don't want to."

"How old is Whitford?"

He grinned, proud. "Twelve going on twenty. He's anxious to meet you. So's Sylvia."

It was times like these that I missed Pop's quiet counsel, though at times I still heard his voice in my head, my grandparents', too, guiding me. They'd have pushed forgiveness. I'd have pushed back. They'd have won in the end. The sound of my name drew me back.

"Sorry?"

"I said I'll leave now if you've got work you need to get back to. Will you think about dinner? Whatever night you say, anywhere you say. It could even be lunch . . . or coffee. No, tea, right? I remember from last time."

"Where are you staying?"

"The Fairmont. There's a restaurant there, if that's easier."

I'd swear I could feel Pop's gentle hand on my shoulder. So real was the feeling that I nearly wept. "Dinner's fine. Today's bad. Can I let you know when?"

He beamed. "You sure can. Absolutely. Anytime. Anytime at all."

"I think we should talk first, just you and me. Breakfast tomorrow?"

He looked as if I'd stunned him. "Yes," he answered in a rush, as though I might change my mind and rescind the invitation. "Yes."

"Nine? You know where I live."

"I can bring juice, doughnuts, fruit? Anything, really."

"Just come for breakfast."

He smiled, gave me a thumbs-up, which I returned, though not as enthusiastically.

"Breakfast at my daughter's." He walked to the door, opened it. "Can't wait."

Then he was gone, and I stood there, behind the desk, not sure what I'd just done. I couldn't feel Pop's hand anymore, but I knew he'd be back the next time I got stretched beyond the point where I felt comfortable. I sat in my chair, exhaled deep, then slid a look at Pop's umbrella. Forgiveness was a big thing, a hard thing. I'd taken the first real step but wasn't at all sure about the second. I was crawling into the unknown with a heart scarred by grief and loss and half a lifetime of hurt. *God help me.*

I spent the next couple of hours getting paperwork in order, sorting files, busy work. Allen's five-thousand-dollar check in my bank account took the urgency out of my having to rustle up new client right away, so I was taking it leisurely, stopping on occasion to glance out the window, my feet propped up on the desk, thankful that Ben was on the mend. When my stomach grumbled, I called down to Deek's for a chicken salad sandwich, but there was no telling when I'd get it. Jung Byson, Deek's delivery guy, was as slow moving as pond water. I put music on, put my head back, and closed my eyes to wait. I had a lot to think about—fathers, knives, Italian beef with extra giardiniera.

I sat up at the knock at my door, then watched as a young white man in an ill-fitting three-piece suit and a tie eased in, carrying a grungy-looking briefcase. It took me a moment to realize it was Jung. It took another moment to believe it. He'd slicked his spiky blond hair back, and he was wearing horn-rimmed glasses. Instead of his usual flip-flops or combat boots, there were shiny wing tips on his feet. I stared at the briefcase, trying to put it together. *Dippy Jung. Briefcase. Suit. Nope.* Didn't compute.

I got up, circled him. "What am I looking at?" I reached over and pinched the suit fabric between curious thumb and index finger. He was real. I wasn't hallucinating. "Jung? Jung *Byson*?"

He grinned, bowed. "At your service."

I took a whiff. He smelled nicer than he'd ever smelled before. "Huh."

A student on the lifetime plan at the U of C up the street, Jung, as far as I knew, had no plans to graduate anytime soon. Instead, he half worked at part-time jobs and kept it loose, his description of his life choice, not mine. He'd surprised the heck out of me back in June, when he had told me he came from money, but it explained his capricious attitude. A poor Jung would have had to hustle.

"How do you like it?" He twirled around, showing himself off.

I eyed the briefcase. "You get a new job?"

"Nope. Still in the delivery game."

I leaned in. "Then what's in the case?"

He unsnapped the latches, drew out a white deli bag with Deek's logo on it, handed it over. "Your chicken salad. Muna threw in an apple and a chocolate chip cookie. On the house."

I craned to see what else was inside, but the case was empty. I went back to my chair, sat the bag on my desk. "So, what gives?"

He eased down into my client chair, crossed his long legs, and leaned back, the case at his feet. He wasn't wearing any socks. Yep, now, that was the Jung I knew. I smiled. The world made sense again.

"I'm conducting a social experiment, not related to my coursework. I wanted to see how it feels to be just another cog in the wheel of the workaday, to feel firsthand the confinement, the regimentation, the total lack of bliss in your average nine-to-five situation. Deek was nice enough to double up on my hours."

I scoffed, dug my sandwich and cookie out of the bag. "Nice enough, huh? Deek. The Deek down the street? The Deek who once tossed an old lady out because she asked for extra cream for her coffee? *That* Deek? A'ight. How's that going?"

He loosened the tie around his neck. "It's been two days, and honestly, I'm not feeling it."

I took a bite of my sandwich, chewed, swallowed. "Two whole days, huh?"

He shrugged. "Maybe tomorrow the enjoyment will kick in. Did you notice the time?"

I checked my watch. Just seventeen minutes had passed from the time I placed my order to the time I got my briefcase delivery. Not trusting my eyes, I tapped the watch face to make sure the thing was still running. It was. *Well, I'll be damned.*

He shot me a satisfied look. "I am now—at least temporarily—a slave to the j-o-b." A beeping started, and Jung reached for his watch. "And that's time." He stood, reached for his case. "As much as I'd like to sit and ponder the universe, commerce must have its due. Ciao." He opened the door to leave and nearly barreled into Kaye Chandler as she approached. "Whoops. My bad." Jung slid past her. "Can't stay. Gotta make the almighty dolla."

Chandler watched him race away and then stood in the doorway, looking uncertain as to whether she wanted to come in or not. I braced myself, hoping Allen wasn't waiting in the hallway for a formal introduction, too regal to come in unannounced. Honestly, I'd had enough of her, both of them, really, but Chandler was, I supposed, the lesser of the two evils.

She walked in, and then stood there staring at me, my desk, my sandwich. There were badly concealed bags under her eyes, makeup caked into the creases, as though she hadn't sleep well, if at all. "I know I should have called, but after . . . Well . . . I didn't think you'd agree to see me. How is Detective Mickerson?"

"He's better. Thanks for asking."

She nodded, smiled slightly. "I'm glad." She walked over to

my client chair but didn't sit. "That man . . . Do you think he really meant to hurt Vonda? That he's the one who's been calling?"

I gestured for Chandler to sit. "I can't answer either question."

She eased down into the chair. "She's hired a security firm. Titan. Do you know them?"

I glanced at my sandwich, my bonus cookie. "By reputation. They're expensive but competent, as far as I've heard."

"But they're not investigating, only escorting. They'll never find out who's harassing her or if Philip's death has anything to do with that."

My brows lifted. "No, but that's CPD's job now." I paused, stared at her. "Sorry. I'm confused. Why are you here? I didn't think I was at the top of your or Allen's hit parade, especially after last night."

Chandler's eyes focused on the window behind me, with its view of the apartment building across the street. She didn't say anything for a bit. Meanwhile, the sandwich kept calling my name. The cookie, too. The heck with it. I reached for the cookie, unwrapped it from the cellophane, and took a bite. Chandler was still ogling the building, off in a world of her own. I'd have rushed her if I had anything pressing, but since I didn't, I was okay with watching her space out in front of me. It wasn't costing me a dime.

She tuned back in to find me working on the chocolate chip. "Another letter showed up. Much worse than the others. It mentions the bookstore. He was angry he hadn't been able to speak to her. When I think how close he came . . . how many people could have been hurt . . ."

I held out a hand. "May I see the letter?"

"I shredded it. She insisted."

I pulled my hand back. "Did you tell Tanaka and Jones at least?" The guilty look on her face told me that she hadn't. "The two of you are not helping matters."

"What if I wanted to hire you myself?"

"To do what?"

"To get everything to stop."

I frowned. Nuh-uh. No way I was signing up for Allen duty again. I'd tried helping her, and Ben had, too, and she'd clammed up like a frightened witness testifying against the Mob, that is, when she wasn't trying to bat me around like a ball of yarn. Not to mention Ben nearly dying. Nope. I was good and out.

"The police are your best bet."

"Detective Mickerson was very lucky." There was a fuzzy look in her eyes, which made me think for a second that she might be on something. "He could have been killed, or you could have."

I put my cookie down, eased back in my chair, folded my hands in my lap. "You want a piece of advice?" I waited for her nod. "You have a connection with her. Use it. Get her to stop all this secrecy."

"And if there are more letters?"

"Call the police."

"She'd see it as disloyalty."

"But she'd be alive to see it."

She spaced out again, then stood up to leave. Maybe the stress of this whole thing was finally getting to her. "I spoke to him. He called to speak to Vonda, and Kendrick transferred him to me. I thought it was just a crank call. We get them all the time, people claiming to know her, wanting to get her on the phone. It's my job to screen them."

"How many crank callers ask if their flowers got delivered?"

Chandler tensed. "He was calling from an unknown number. He wouldn't give his name. I told him not to call again. There wasn't much more I could do. I considered the matter taken care of."

I took a bite of sandwich, then reached down into the trash can, retrieved one of the first copies of *Strive*, and opened it to the masthead. I ran a finger down the list of names—Allen; Chandler; two staff writers, Reesa Loudon and Dontell Adkins. "Could either Loudon or Adkins be holding a grudge?"

She shook her head.

"What about blackmail? Any sign that someone's putting the heat on her for whatever it is she's holding back?"

"Not everyone is comfortable revealing themselves. Can you really be so sure she *is* holding back?"

"Yes."

She pushed the chair she'd sat in back to where it'd been. "Well, I'm not. She's a private person, and she wants to keep it that way. That may be all this is. All of this could blow away tomorrow, and it'd have nothing to do with her, not really. But you're right about one thing. I should talk to her. She won't like it, but it has to be done."

I stood, too. "I think that's the right way to go. Chandler? What'd you two argue about a few weeks ago?"

Her sculpted brows lifted. It looked like the information was news to her. "We didn't argue. We never argue."

"Maybe you were fed up with how she treats you? I haven't seen a lot of respect flowing your way."

The smile she gave me wasn't anywhere close to authentic. It was strained, tight. I believed Kendrick. She had argued with Allen. So why lie about it?

"She's nervous about what's been going on," Chandler said. "I don't blame her. It must be awful knowing there's someone out there targeting you and there's nothing you can do about it. She tries to hide it, but I can see she's afraid. But you're wrong. Vonda does respect me. She couldn't do half the things she does without my being there. Why else would she have named me an executive producer on her new show? It's been a long journey, but we've finally made it. Vonda's on her way." She gave the office a final look. "Thank you for your time. It helps to talk things through. I just wish—"

Her cell phone buzzed. She drew it out of her bag, answered it, and her face lost all its color. "What? When?" Listening to the other end, she grew paler by the second. "Is Vonda okay? Yes, I'm coming." She ended the call, a desolate look on her face. "Linda Sewell's been killed. Shot, like Hewitt." She panicked. "My God, what's going on!"

Chapter 15

They'd found Linda Sewell's body lying next to her car around ten thirty in the morning. She'd parked some distance from the security cameras mounted near the elevator. Her purse was missing; so were her watch and jewelry. It looked like a mugging. I received all of this information on the q.t. from a detective I knew, as she exited the crime scene. Marcus and Tanaka weren't about to share even a crumb of information. I stood behind the cordon, persona non grata, where I'd been for at least an hour. Marcus and Tanaka had barely given me a glance when they'd rushed past me.

What would happen to Sewell's young son? I wondered. I hated this, all of it. The wanton taking of a life, the cavalier way some people decided who got to stay and who went. I hated it for me; I hated it for others. I just plain hated it. It made me angry and sick and anxious, like I was trying to clear a heap of steaming trash one bag at a time, one hand tied behind my back. I'd never get it all; there'd always be more trash; and whatever I did, it would never be enough.

I was still standing by the riot horse when Tanaka and Marcus came back out. These couldn't be random deaths, not two in as many days, not two with a direct connection to Allen. Would there be more? Could Allen be next? At what point would she realize she was in over her head? I glanced over at her office windows, high above the hectic street clogged with rabid onlookers. She was likely up there now, ensconced in her throne room, not shedding a single tear for Sewell, feigning ignorance as bodies, lives, fell at her feet. Chandler would be there, too. She'd rushed from my office as though racing to a fire. Would she decide to finally confront Allen? Get her to come clean? I hoped so. Hewitt, now Sewell. What was happening?

I looked over to see Marcus watching me. He was playing it wrong. I knew it. He knew I knew it. But this wasn't my show, not this time. I had to drop it here. Ben and I were out. When he turned his back to me, I strode back to my car and caught sight of a dark, late-model Buick with tinted windows idling across the street. Likely a crime-scene junkie, drawn to the scene by a police scanner, mesmerized by the drama of someone else's tragic death. It was a thing. Disturbing, ghoulish, but a thing. I stopped and watched as the car pulled away from the curb and slowly drove away.

I went out early the next morning for bagels, eggs, and juice, my breakfast with my father swinging over my head like an executioner's ax. I regretted suggesting the thing now, in retrospect, but I was stuck with it and had to see it through. He rang the bell right at 9:00 AM, and I buzzed him up, then opened the door to him holding a bunch of yellow roses, my mother's favorite. He'd dressed nicely in a suit and tie. He looked like he was on his way to a job interview or church or his own funeral. I took the flowers, and we stood there at the door awkwardly.

"Those are going to need a vase," he finally said.

"Right. Kitchen's this way." He followed me down the long hall.

"I whip up a pretty mean omelet," he said, making conversation. "Matter of fact, I'm known as the omelet king in my house. You up for one?"

"Sure." Passing the pantry, I snagged a clean apron off a hook and handed it back to him. "Things could get messy. The kitchen's not exactly my room."

He chuckled. "Wasn't your mother's, either, if you remember. She had other strengths—intelligence, compassion, a lot of patience, especially with me."

I cocked a head toward the fridge. "Everything's in there. Coffee beans, too."

"I'm going with tea." He winked. "I hear it's good for you."

He was making an effort; he knew I preferred tea to coffee. I placed the kettle on the burner, turned on the heat, and then plucked a paring knife from a drawer and laid it on the table for him.

"Eggs, butter, cheese, green onion, and bacon," he said, turning from the refrigerator, his arms laden down with stuff. "If bacon don't get your motor runnin', nothin' will, right?"

I thought of Ben and his fake hospital bacon and smiled. I looked over to see my father watching me.

"I remember that smile."

That killed it. I gave him some distance, watching appraisingly as he set the food down on the table, perched himself on a barstool, and began to chop and dice, glancing up at me periodically. There were things I remembered, the way he held his head, the way his hands looked, snatches of mannerisms and such buried somewhere in my brain. Nothing flooded back in a great big wave of recollection; it was just the snatches. I set about lining up the bacon in the skillet, monitoring his movements out of the corner of my eye.

"I wanted to talk to you first, before dinner, to . . ." The speed of his chopping increased, and I turned around to see. The knife was working overtime. His face was creased in concentration, and sweat beaded across his forehead. I eased back. "Earl Grey or Irish Breakfast?"

"Oh, doesn't matter to me. No, ma'am. I'll drink anything." *Chop, chop, chop.* He was chopping enough for at least a dozen omelets. "I went to see your mother yesterday." His voice was light, conversational, as if the visit had taken place anywhere else besides the cemetery. "She's in a beautiful spot. I'd forgotten how beautiful. Do you visit?"

I fingered my mother's wedding ring, which I wore on a chain around my neck. I believed it brought me luck. Rubbing the soft gold and the smooth cluster of diamonds always made me feel as if at least some part of her was still with me, was still mine. No, I didn't visit. She wasn't there in that hole in the ground. She was with me; Pop too. So were all the people I'd loved and lost before I was ready to let them go.

I had slept with the ring under my pillow for months after she died, hoping that by some divine miracle or puff of sorcery—I'd have sold my soul for either—when I woke up, the ring would be gone and she would be back. But every morning there was just the ring there and a feeling of desolation, of brokenness I couldn't shake. It was my grandmother who had given me the chain to carry it on, and it was Pop who had blessed them both for me. It had taken years for the small band of gold to signify anything other than sorrow. Only now did it give me peace.

"Cassandra, the bacon's burning."

I jolted, pulled my hand away from the chain, and slid the skillet off the burner.

"I asked if you ever went to visit your mother."

"I don't. No." I hadn't visited Pop, either, or my grandparents. I didn't need to stare at a slab of remembrance to make the loss real. My eyes met his. "I don't trust you. I don't know if I ever will."

The knife stilled. Many moments passed. "You got good reason not to. I hurt you."

"You changed me. I'm a different person than the one you left. I'm not sure I want to make room for you in my life, but I've opened the door . . . for now. That's what I wanted to tell you in private, before dinner with your family. That's what I needed you to hear from me."

He set the knife down and looked squarely at me. "Honesty." He sighed. "I said this was a visit, but that's not the whole truth. I explained in the letters, but . . . we found a place in Rogers Park. A nice house on a quiet street, with a yard and a driveway that I'll have to shovel. Good schools close by. There's still the back-and-forth to go through, but we hope to be in there and settled before Christmas. We talked the whole thing over—Sylvia, Whitford, and me. They understand why I need to be here. They know what I did. This doesn't have to go fast. It doesn't even have to go easy. But, however it goes, I'll be here."

I turned back to the stove, my heart racing, my palms sweating. The cutting started again.

He said, "I'm ready with these vegetables. Where's your omelet pan?"

I handed it to him, but I didn't let go of my end. We stood there for a time, looking into each other's eyes. "I won't let you in easily. I'll protect myself." It was both a warning and a declaration.

"I promise you won't have to."

I let go of the pan. "No more promises."

Chapter 16

Ben's bed was empty when I walked into his hospital room, the smell of Italian beef, extra peppers, wafting out of the greasy bag in my hand. I stood for a moment, confused, having expected to see him sitting up, dressed and ready to go.

"You're here for Detective Mickerson?" I turned to find Ben's nurse, the one I'd seen the day before with the med tray, standing behind me.

"Yeah. Has he already been discharged?"

She placed a hand on my arm, steered me farther into the room. "They had to take him back to surgery about an hour ago. He was bleeding internally, having trouble breathing. Yours was the only number we had, but there was no answer. We didn't know who else to call."

Her voice sounded like it was coming from so far away. I stared at her, half hearing her. I heard *surgery*, *bleeding internally*. I drew my phone out of my pocket, saw the flashing light. I had silenced it during my breakfast with my father and had forgotten to unmute it. I'd missed the call. I swallowed hard. "Is he going to be okay?"

"They're doing everything they can." Keen, sympathetic eyes held mine. "Should we call someone else? A family member?"

I backed away from her, set the high-smelling bag down on the tray table. I couldn't believe what I was hearing. It didn't make sense. "No," I said. "I'll do it."

The nurse nodded and then eased out of the room to give me some privacy. I fell back into a chair, my entire body numb, cold. When I could hold my phone steady, I punched in the numbers for Ben's sister, Carole.

We sat anxiously in the surgical waiting room. His color restored, Ben had looked good when I saw him yesterday. He'd been joking around about bacon and peppers. I glanced over at Carole and at their mother, Ida. Both tense and worn practically to nothing by worry. The Mickersons had also assembled a few cousins and an elderly aunt. We'd all been here for hours already without any word on Ben's condition. Cops, friends of Ben's, had cycled in and out, as had Eli, Barb, and even Whip, who'd left work to make sure I was okay, but I'd sent them all home. There was no sense in all of us being here, and I couldn't leave. It was up to me to take care of Ben's family.

I stood. "Anyone need anything? Coffee? Food?" I turned to Ben's mother, lowered my voice to a soothing whisper. "Mrs. Mickerson?"

The weak, sweet smile she gave me almost broke my heart. It was weird thinking of big, burly Ben as this small, silent woman's baby, but that was what he was to her. I couldn't begin to fully grasp what she was feeling, but I could see the agony on her face. She shook her head, said nothing, but reached over and squeezed my hand gently, a silent thank-you.

Carole stood, as weary, as fearful as I was. "I need to stretch my legs. I'll come with you."

We walked down the hall, rounded the corner, stopped at an alcove of vending machines—bad coffee, snacks, bottles of overpriced water in toxic bottles. Depressing. Carole and I stood blinking at the display, neither of us, apparently, willing to make the first move.

"Off duty and knifed in a bookstore," she finally said, rummaging for change in her oversize bag. "God, I hate the job you two do. Always have. He was fine. He called me yesterday. I chewed him out for not telling us right away he got hurt. Know what he said? 'No big deal.' He said it matter-of-factly. *No big deal.* I called him a selfish prick." Her hand stilled. "That's the last thing I said to him. 'You selfish prick.'" She went back to diving for change, violently, as though she were trying to punch a hole in the bottom of her bag. "What's wrong with me?"

I reached into my bag and pulled out a handful of loose change, kept there in case of emergency. I fed several coins into a slot, but neither of us made a selection. Instead, we stood there staring at the processed poison neither of us really wanted.

"These greedy assholes actually have the nerve to charge one-fifty for sixteen ounces of Pepsi?" Carole rolled her eyes. She looked a lot like Ben—same nose, same eyes—but she was two years younger, slight. "At least when they rob you on the street, you can half respect it."

I punched the button for the pop and watched as the machine thrust it forward off the shelf and it landed with a thud in the tray at the bottom. I handed it to Carole.

She went on. "You two deal with the worst people. Why? What's in it for you? You work yourselves to death, all hours, no time for family, no time for a life. For this? You were shot, for God's sake, and nearly died. Now he's lying in there with his stomach sliced open by some maniac. I don't understand what makes you keep going back for more."

I turned my back to the machine after getting a glimpse of my reflection in the glass, the haunted look on my face. "It's just what we're good at."

"It's tempting fate, and I hate it. How many times do we have to end up here? How many more chances will you or he get before your number comes up? Don't you worry about that?"

I didn't. I couldn't, could I? If I did, I couldn't do what I did for the people I did it for. Those who couldn't stand for themselves, fight for themselves, those who had lived their entire lives under the heel of some fat cat's boot. I hated bullies. I hated unfairness. I couldn't abide needless suffering. Ben understood. I knew he felt the same.

A cold shaft of fear shot up my spine. "Can we talk about something else?" I needed something, and I didn't know what. Damned certain whatever it was couldn't be found in a vending machine, no matter how many coins I slid into the slot. It was an awful feeling.

Dr. Alton entered the waiting room hours later and called out Ben's name. I stood back as his family crowded around for the update, but Mrs. Mickerson pulled me forward to stand with the rest. Ben was out of surgery, in recovery, she said, then off to the ICU. He'd blown a fairly substantial clot, which she thought they were able to fix, but he was now on a respirator, unconscious. I held on to Ben's mother, my hands surprisingly steady, yet the old woman stood far steadier than I felt. We'd have to wait and see, the doctor said. Then she was gone.

I found a quiet spot outside the hospital and stood with my face tilted up to the night sky. It was late, nearly eleven. Everything beyond where I stood felt a million miles away, unreachable. Ben was holding his own, but no one knew how it'd go. We were in an uncertain state, limbo, waiting for the fates and medical science to decide.

Carole eased in beside me. "You just can't sit still, can you?"

I breathed in deep. "Just needed some air."

She gazed up at the sky, breathed in deep. "Same as him. He's always got to be doing something."

I smiled. "Eating mostly."

"True." She turned to face me. "Do you know he has feelings for you? I've always wanted to ask you that. Never had the nerve before."

"What?"

"He'd never admit it, but I know my brother. He doesn't take to a lot of people, certainly not to his first wife. I tried to tell him before the wedding, but he wouldn't listen. Bull-headed. You and he are different, though. I thought you should know, in case he doesn't get to tell you himself."

I shook my head, felt my face flush. "It's not like that."

"Yeah it is. I see you two together. You couldn't be more different, but you're like the same person in a way." She read my face. "You really missed it, didn't you? That's wild. You two have got to be the smartest dumb people I know." She gave my arm an affectionate squeeze. "I'll shut up now. I'm taking Mom home, and then I'll be back."

Shaken, I stood there, not sure what to say. *What* had I missed? *When* had I missed it? I answered Carole absently. "I'll be here."

She moved to stand in front of me. "No you won't. That's what I also wanted to say. We've got this part covered. We—the family, that is—want you looking for the guy who did this."

"That's being handled," I said, my voice rising, adamant. "I'm staying here."

"Why? What can you do besides worry like the rest of us?"

"I can take care of his family. I can be here to do that."

"We don't need it. We want you to do what you're good at." She exhaled, wiped her tired eyes. "He did the same for you, you know. Things weren't looking good. I was here, too, with Father Ray and Mrs. Vincent. They were so nice, so worried about you. We looked up at one point, and Ben was gone. We didn't know where. The nurses found his star on the table next to your bed in the ICU. He'd gone looking for Farraday, we found out later. Thank God he was able to stop himself before he did anything stupid." She smiled weakly. "See? Feelings. Smart dumb, the both of you. You want to take care of the family, then do this for us. Find him. Bring him in. Say yes."

I had no words. I had no idea about Ben going looking for Farraday. He'd never said a thing about it. All I was able to manage was a nod.

Chapter 17

I crawled into bed but didn't sleep. There was too much to think about, none of which I could make sense of. When the sun came up, I was still lying there staring at the ceiling, my head as heavy as lead. My place was at the hospital, but Ben's family didn't need me there. They wanted me out on the street, looking for Ben's attacker. That meant butting heads again with Tanaka and Marcus, which I had no desire to do. Ben had never told me he'd left his badge and gone after Farraday. I had had no idea about his feelings, either. I hoped Carole had read him wrong. I considered Ben a part of my family, the one I'd cobbled together when the real one collapsed beneath me. If he felt differently, wouldn't he have said so? I think he would have. We've never had a problem communicating, but feelings were different, weren't they? Feelings were messy, always delicate. They could mean anything, everything or nothing. I needed to talk to Ben.

Until then I had to get moving. I got up, showered, dressed, and hit the office, tearing into Allen's life for whatever or whomever she was hiding. I pulled up everything I could find on the woman, no matter how small or absurd the item was, keeping an eye out for anything that could be the fuel behind someone's hate. The anonymous caller, the one Kendrick had transferred to Chandler, had said he knew Allen almost thirty years ago. That'd put her at about college age. I couldn't track down everyone she'd known back then, of course; all I could do was cast a wide net, go back as far as seemed prudent, and see if I hit on anything. My odds of success weren't great: there was too much ground to cover.

Break it up, Cass. Pick a starting point. Work your way back.

Allen's magazine. I stacked the issues I had on top of my desk and started in on each one. There was no one in the mastheads named Eric. What about the two young writers who'd bailed after her first year? They'd likely been in the same position Kendrick was in now, underpaid, overworked. Despite what Chandler had said, that had to have led to hard feelings. Maybe one or both were resentful enough to do something about it now? Worth checking.

I found nothing on Loudon in the usual searches. Maybe she had married and wasn't using her maiden name? I had better luck with Adkins, or bad luck, as it turned out. I found a short, cryptic obituary in the paper. He'd died at the age of twenty-two, the victim of a violent hit-and-run. I saved the obit, searched the paper for the news story on the accident, but got only a little more than what I had. No mention of the driver having been found. Adkins was survived by his grandparents. That was all. A life summed up in less than twenty lines of newspaper copy. It was possible Chandler didn't know about the accident, but how likely was it? Would I find that Reesa Loudon had met a bad end, too? And while I was looking at obituaries, I looked for one for Allen's mother but came up empty. Allen's memoir said she'd died when Allen was still in college, that she'd missed out on her success. Maybe she'd died somewhere else? I'd have to come back to that.

I scribbled down names, dates, and particulars on a notepad, not knowing what might be important. Allen had attended Northwestern University for a year before transferring to the Chicago campus of the University of Illinois, from which she eventually graduated. Nothing jumped out from either place. Why the change in schools?

I stuck to it until my eyes began to cross, digging deep until finally I stumbled upon a reference to a write-up on Allen titled "The Magazine Wars" in a women's magazine. It took a while to find the original piece, but I did. It detailed a contentious tug of war between Allen's publication, *Strive*, and a competing magazine called *Veritas*, published by a father-son team, Deton and Henry Peets. The Peetses had accused Allen of stealing their concept, siphoning off readers, and bleeding them dry, and neither had been shy about hurling insults. The father, Deton, had called Allen a Jezebel, a thief in the night. The article was over four years old, and I couldn't find a follow-up article or anything else on the feud.

I printed the story out, stuck it into a file folder, then glanced at my phone, hoping for news from the hospital, but there was nothing from Carole. I stuffed my notes into my bag, grabbed my jacket, and headed out. Dontell Adkins, the mudslinging Peetses, and Allen's university switch were threads I could follow. If I kept busy enough, I might even be able to ignore the sinking feeling in my gut that my world was about to come crashing down on me . . . again.

The UIC campus was a sprawling, fast-moving melting pot of nationalities and academic concentrations, minus a lot of the rah-rah, quad-lounging fervor of its sister campus downstate in Champaign. UIC offered higher education on the down and dirty for those who didn't have a lot of time or money to Jung Byson their way toward a diploma on frat parties, football games, and navel-gazing Proust fests in the back of dusty on-campus bars.

I wanted a look at the alumni lists, hoping to find Allen on them. I parked in the lot across from Hull House and trotted across busy Halsted, dodging heavy traffic, the rumble of the trains running along the CTA Blue Line drowning out the honking horns. I could smell the sausages cooking on Taylor Street from here, and across the bridge in Greektown, lamb roasting on the spit. I'd thought to try my luck in the administration building, where maybe I'd find a staffer I could convince to let me take a look, but I switched gears halfway through the concrete quad and took off for the library instead.

"You're looking for old school papers?" the pudgy boy behind the counter asked. Maybe he was eighteen or nineteen, grungy, beady rat eyes. "How old?"

"Let's start with those between nineteen eighty-seven and ninety."

He blinked. "Seriously? That's, like, a hundred years ago."

I was stressed, scared, pressed for time. "Do you have them or not?"

"Everything's digital now. I'd have to put you in a room and cue up the reader," he said, as though it was an impossible ask, as though the "putting me in a room" part should be enough to get me to reconsider my request.

"Okay," I answered flatly.

We stood there for a time in silence. I didn't know if he didn't think I could handle the reader or if he thought *I* thought I couldn't handle the reader. In either case, it didn't appear that he was planning on putting me next to one anytime soon.

"The papers," I snapped. "It's important."

He pointed over my left shoulder. "The rooms are over there. I'll come around and get you started, I guess."

I had no trouble handling the reader. I scrolled through the digitized papers, looking for Allen's name, a photo, or any mention of her. I started at the year she transferred in, and made my way slowly through to the end of the year, not finding a thing. I did the same for the next year and got the same result. It wasn't until what would have been her junior year that I spotted a grainy black-and-white photo of her taken at a student rally. In it she was standing at a podium, her fist raised defiantly. The caption was a revelation—BLACK STUDENT UNION PRESIDENT BENITA RAMSEY PROTESTS INEQUITIES IN EDUCATION FOR MINORITY STUDENTS.

Benita Ramsey? I zoomed in closer on the face. It was definitely Allen, minus the wealth and the air of pretention. I'd never heard the name before. It wasn't in her bio or her memoir. Why? The photo proved to be just the tip of the iceberg. There were other photos, many of them. Vonda-Benita's junior year apparently was the year she flew out of the gate to make her mark. There were awards and academic honors; she was named student ambassador and student liaison. She campaigned for editor of the paper and got it. She won a prestigious scholarship worth fifty thousand dollars. I stopped at a photo of her looking chummy with a trio of twentysomethings. The caption identified them as staff writers on the paper—Patsy O'Keefe, Angela Dotson, Dennis Seymour. They all looked happy, even Allen. Did she actually at one time have friends?

"I need to see your student and alumni directories." I was back at the counter, but the boy wasn't thrilled to see me again. "I'll take student directories for the same year range, and any alumni listings you have for the years right after."

He didn't ask any questions, just went to get them, glancing back at me like he expected me to jump over the counter and tackle him. I met his look, matched it, and idled at the counter till he came back. I took the short stack of directories back to the small room, then looked for names, addresses, telephone numbers for the three kids in the photograph. When I'd found them in the older directories, I checked the newer ones to see if they were still listed. They were. Score one for me. I jotted down the information and then returned everything to the counter. I then asked for a computer to use and was directed to a room of communal desktops for rent by the half hour.

Ramsey, not Allen. That was likely why I hadn't been able to find an obituary for her mother. I tried again, typing in *Ramsey* and the date range that worked, and found not only a short obituary but also a news story about a shooting death, the victim one Louise Culvert Ramsey, age forty-four. She'd been the manager of a neighborhood dry cleaners when she was shot and killed while walking to her car after her shift. One round to the head. Her valuables taken.

As I walked back through the campus, the enormity of my task suddenly hit me. I had only two legs, two hands, one brain. Allen's mother's death disturbed me. It would have been a devastating loss for Allen to have experienced, losing her mother in such a tragic way. One shot to the head. A random robbery. Did it mean anything that the death of Allen's mother was similar to the deaths of Hewitt and Sewell? If it did, what was the connection? And what, if anything, did any of it have to do with the man who'd shown up at the bookstore?

I stopped, took a seat on a stone bench, and tried calling each of Allen's writer friends but got only voice mail. I left detailed messages for each, then tried Deton and Henry Peets but got the same result at the *Veritas* office. Their automated message said I'd missed them by half an hour, but I could try again when they opened the following morning at ten. It was just past 5:00 PM now.

It was then I noticed the message light blinking on my phone. It was a text from Carole. I held my breath. Ben had a fever they couldn't control, the text read, which hinted at an infection. People whizzed past me; the train rumbled; the traffic sped by. For a moment I wasn't sure which way I needed to go. I should be at the hospital in case . . . but I wasn't needed there. I couldn't get my bearings. I couldn't think straight. Carole and Ben's family were expecting too much. Infection.

I stood, eyed the lot with my car in it, turned to glance down the street toward Greektown across the bridge, fully aware that I was standing at a crossroads. My feet started walking toward the bridge before I even made the decision to go that way. I dialed Tanaka's number. She picked up on the second ring.

"We need to talk," I said. "Can you meet me?"

Chapter 18

I sat at a window table in the Persephone restaurant, watching the other diners pass their time, seemingly content. The waiter, nice enough, had tried pushing the souvlaki, on special today, but I'd shooed him away twice. I had no appetite. My mind was on the hospital, on Ben's fever. I spotted Tanaka the moment she walked in the door, and I straightened up as she walked over to the table.

"Thanks for coming," I said.

She sat across from me. "Your call was the last thing I expected." She eyed her water glass but left it where it sat. We weren't here to pass the time or share a meal. This was business. "You said you had something?"

"Two more deaths tied to Allen. A hit-and-run and another mugging, her own mother. The driver and the shooter were never found. Maybe they're unrelated, but what if they aren't? What if whatever we're dealing with now has deep roots and goes back years?"

"Sounds like you're trying to shoehorn these incidents into a pattern where there isn't one. Anyway, I thought you were out of this?"

"I'm back in."

She watched me but didn't say anything.

"Allen's the link. She has to be. It's worth giving these other cases a closer look." Tanaka stared at me. It didn't look like she was going to give me an inch, but I didn't have time to play it slow. "Were Hewitt and Sewell shot with the same gun?"

Tanaka's brows rose, and she had a curious look on her face. "I thought this meeting would be about you telling me something *I* could use, not me divulging something *you* need."

"Like?"

"Like what Allen's hiding."

So much for Chandler breaking ranks. "Chandler didn't come to you?"

"Was she supposed to?" She waved it off. "Doesn't matter. No peeing babies or Jones to set you off. Tell me."

It didn't take long for me to decide between Ben and Allen. I would always be on Ben's side, and he on mine. "She's been receiving threatening letters, nuisance calls, flowers. He addresses the letters *Dear Bitch.* I know of maybe half a dozen for sure, but there've been more, which they've destroyed. I think this all started a couple months ago. The flowers come delivered to her office, unsigned, apparently untraceable. Creepy. She ordered Chandler to destroy those, too, and they haven't gone to the police, because Allen doesn't want to damage her brand or put her business out on the street. That's why she hired me and Ben. To protect her. She doesn't seem to be too concerned about those around her, Hewitt, Sewell. Allen won't win any awards for altruism."

"You saw these letters?"

"I saw a copy of one of them. Chandler slipped it to Ben. The threat wasn't specific, but the letter was menacing, and it was written in red ink. You might even be able to dismiss it all as some sick prank, but then her employees started dying. And now the hit-and-run and her mother's death. It's curious."

"And you think the bookstore guy looks good for all that?"

I shook my head. "He feels different somehow, outside the pattern, but he's connected to her in some way. We find him, we might get closer to some answers."

"Only he got away." There was a hint of condemnation in her voice. She knew I had let him go and had stayed with Ben. It'd been the right choice then and now, and I stood by it.

"She knows who he is, and she's afraid, not of the letters so much, but of him. I saw the look on her face. It was as if she'd seen a ghost. She's hiding something, something dangerous. I don't think even Chandler knows what it is, not completely, but she may be able to get her to talk a lot easier than you or I could."

"You can't even know for sure the guy who knifed Mickerson's the same one harassing her."

"You're right. He could be somebody totally different, a needy fan. Maybe he didn't come there to do anything to her. He wanted face time. We kept him from getting it. That's when he got agitated and pulled the knife. He scared himself. I could tell he'd gone further than he meant to go with things."

Tanaka leaned back. "You know, you're the only one saying she knows the guy. Just because of a look? She swears she doesn't know a thing."

"She's lying."

Tanaka paused. "Funny. A couple of days ago, you were stonewalling the hell out of us. Now, suddenly, everything's on the table. Pardon me for being just a little suspicious of your motives."

The waiter rolled up again, all smiles, this time with two menus big enough to water-ski on, but he didn't get far.

Tanaka held up a hand, not bothering even to look at him. "Not yet."

Abashed, a little startled by the brush-off, the waiter melted away.

"I want the guy," I said.

"It looked like you'd washed your hands of the whole thing. Now you want the guy?"

Our eyes locked. "Ben's not doing well. He was at first. Then something happened. A clot. He's running a fever now. I don't know what that means. His family wants me to find the man who hurt him. I work alone. I like it that way usually, but I'm only one person. It's slow going, and I don't have the resources you do. He's family. They're family. I can't mess this up, and I'm afraid I might." I pushed past the lump in my throat. "Cooperation is faster. I asked before, but you didn't answer. Were Hewitt and Sewell killed by the same gun?"

Tanaka took a sip of water, set the glass down, then let moments pass. "Striations match. Caliber too. We'll need the gun, of course. Cooperation. What's that mean exactly?"

"I'm operating on the premise that whatever Allen is holding on to is something long buried, so I'm starting in her past and working my way forward. Maybe I'll find this Eric there. Maybe I'll find something that explains him. I could be totally off base. I won't know until I run things down. What I do know is, I can't do it all myself. Time, like I said, might be a factor."

"It's got nothing to do with you trying to show up Jones? Because whatever went on between the two of—"

I cut her off, answered curtly. "Marcus Jones is the last thing on my mind right now."

"I didn't think you were that wild about me, either."

"That was my initial feeling. I'll have to wait and see if it holds."

Tanaka grinned. "Wow. You don't pull any punches, do you? Not even going to try to butter me up?"

"Is that what it's going to take?"

She tapped her fingers on the table, watched me. "So, we open lines of communication, share information. My resources, your pain-in-the-ass-ness?"

"I follow my leads. You follow yours. First one to find something hollers. I don't care who ends this first, only that it ends."

"Two bodies," Tanaka said, "and the possibility that there could be more. That's a lot of dots to connect when you're racing against time."

I looked around the restaurant, at life as it went on while Ben's hung in the balance. "The thing about time is you don't pay it a bit of mind until you have so little of it left." I turned back to Tanaka. "Then you'd trade your soul for even a second more."

She took another sip from her glass. "If I agree, *if*, this *cooperation* better be a two-way street, and you'd better stay in your lane."

"I agree to the first," I said, "but can't guarantee the second if your side drops the ball."

Her lips twisted into a cocky grin. "I've never dropped a ball in my life."

I stood, grabbed my jacket from the back of the chair. "Me either." I flagged the lonesome waiter, who rushed over expectantly. "Try the souvlaki, Tanaka. It's on special today. I'll be in touch."

Chapter 19

They'd dimmed the lights in the ICU waiting room, which was empty except for me. I sat at a table near the window, looking out at the city lights, going over my notes, everything I'd gotten from UIC, everything I knew about Allen, aka Benita Ramsey, from her press and fantastical memoir. The family had gone home to sleep and recharge.

Why not mention her mother's violent death? That would have been a pivotal moment in her life, wouldn't it? My mother's death had certainly been a turning point in mine. I'd grown up and stopped being a child in the few short days between her passing and the morning my father decided he wanted out and left me. Had Allen experienced something similar? Had she walled herself off from the tragedy, or had it propelled her forward, given her drive? Who erased their own mother from their life story? I looked up from my notes when I heard hushed activity from the hall and watched as Whip, Eli, and Barb walked in, laden down with food. It was a weird sight, the red-headed nun, the tall cop, and the barrel-chested ex-con turned model citizen standing in the doorway.

I stood. "What are you all doing here? What's all this?"

Whip held up a bag that smelled heavenly, reminding me that it'd been half a day since I'd eaten anything. "You won't go home, and you won't let us stay with you, so we got to do our thing stealth-like."

I checked my watch. "It's after midnight. You have jobs, stuff. I'm fine, really."

Barb sat down at the table and started unscrewing a thermos. "We all have watches." She unscrewed the cap, sending a puff of soup steam wafting into the air. "Lentil soup. Mrs. Vincent's. Don't bother crabbing about it. We're staying until you eat. We can't do a thing about you getting some sleep, so food will have to do for now."

Eli looked me over, and I knew he was taking a full study, checking to see how much I really had left in the tank. There wasn't much, but I'd never admit it. "How's he doing?"

"The same. No worse. That's good, I think. I'm not that hungry."

Barb poured soup into the little thermos cup. "You're eating."

Whip and Eli pulled chairs up to the table and began unloading everything, ignoring the fact that I was standing there protesting. I finally gave in and sat back down again. Whip reached inside the bag.

"Cheeseburgers," he announced.

I slid my notes aside, making room, my mind still on the pages. "From where?"

Whip's hand stilled. "From *where*? My kitchen is from where. You know I don't waste money on that fast-food junk. Don't make me hurt you."

"Did you cook fries, too?"

He gave me a look of such profound pity before pulling his hand out of the bag. "Now you're just playin'." He'd wrapped the fries in butcher's paper, and the grease was seeping through.

The smell of salt and oil filled the room. When he handed them to me, they were still warm. My mouth began to water.

Maybe I was a little hungry. I smiled, dug in. "Thanks."

Barb handed me the cup of soup. "Drink up."

Eli grinned and pulled a cookie wrapped in plastic wrap from his jacket pocket and handed it to me. "Dessert." I managed a small smile, and then took a sip of soup. I still had so much to get done, and my path was anything but clear, but for now there was this.

Carole and Mrs. Mickerson were back at six the next morning. I gave them an update on Ben's condition. Nothing had changed. Then I filled them in on what I'd learned so far. It wasn't much yet, and none of it got us anywhere close to Ben's attacker, but I wasn't about to stop. We switched off, and I went home to crash for a couple of hours. When I woke up, I showered, dressed, grabbed a yogurt and an apple, and then rushed out of the house, to find Lenny Vine leaning against my car like it belonged to him and not me.

Lenny was a PI like me whom I'd run into a couple of times while doing business. We weren't friends, not even really colleagues, since Vine was a sleazy-looking white guy who'd do anything for money, and I do mean anything. But there was Lenny, dressed in black and gray, a dirty porkpie hat on his bald, square head, leaning on my ride.

"Raines," he said.

"Vine," I said.

"Nice day, ain't it?"

I looked around at the day. It looked all right. "Guess so."

Birds tweeted in the trees, but Lenny and I didn't make a peep.

"Can I help you with something, Lenny?"

He eased up off my car, and I checked it for butt scratches.

He reached into his pocket, pulled out a paper, handed it to me, grinning. "You've been served."

I watched as he swaggered off and poured himself into a ratty-looking Jeep Wrangler with a rusted front bumper. He waved at me as he pulled away. I narrowed my eyes. I hated Lenny Vine. I hated being served, too, especially since I was used to being the server and not the servee. I read the summons. Allen was suing me for violating the terms of her stupid nondisclosure agreement. My eyes narrowed more. I hated Allen, too. I balled the summons up, tossed it on the ground, and walked away. Three steps out, I thought better of it and went back and picked it up, then stuffed the summons ball into my bag. I'd worry about Allen and her seddity nonsense later.

I headed for *Veritas* magazine to talk to Henry and Deton Peets about their legal run-in with Allen, and given the start to my day, it looked like we'd have a lot to commiserate over. I found *Veritas* in a tiny storefront right off Eighty-Seventh and King Drive. In the hood. But light hood, not deep hood. Here, like all over the city, hardworking, decent folks kept it moving, though they were forced by circumstance to fast walk through their lives, eyes wide, heads on the swivel, hands securely over their valuables, dodging random violence and street thuggery. I parked out front, locked my car, and went inside.

"Hello?" I called.

The place was small, dingy. Cheap plastic chairs lined a wall; three clunky desks, empty, dotted the room. The place felt sticky and tight and smelled of mildew and dust. On the wall the word *veritas* had been stenciled in big bold letters painted black, red, and green.

"Hello?" I said again.

"Hold on." The voice came from a back room, and I waited, then watched as an old man emerged and ambled toward me, limping badly, aided by a cane that looked as old as he was. He eyed me cautiously as he made his way, giving me the full sweep. "Help you?"

I recalled the piece I'd read on the Peetses. A father-son team. This had to be Deton. "I hope so. Mr. Deton Peets?"

His dark eyes lasered in, suspicious. He could have been seventy or ninety; it was hard to gauge. His white button-down shirt was open at the collar, and his gray trousers had been neatly pressed.

"You a lawyer?"

I blinked. It was an odd question to ask when just meeting a person. "I'm not. Why?"

"Because I hate lawyers. All of 'em should be sealed in a drum and dropped in the lake."

"That's a bit harsh."

His eyes wouldn't let up. "Not from where I'm standing."

"I'm Cassandra Raines. I'm an investigator. I'd like to talk to you about Vonda Allen."

The suspicious look he'd given me up till then was gone in a finger snap's time, replaced by the meanest, angriest look I'd ever seen on a black man, and that was including Deek, the owner of my neighborhood diner, who could likely give Satan himself a run for his money.

"That witch had the nerve to send you here? After all she's done?" He raised the cane, brandished it like a club. "Turn around. Get out, or I'll throw you out."

I calmly started again, mindful of the cane. "I don't work *for* her. I'm a private investigator asking *about* her, specifically about your dealings with her concerning—"

"Let me stop you right there. I know what's been going on with her. I read the papers same as everybody else. It was only a matter of time before she sent one of her henchmen down here to see if I didn't have something to do with it. Bankrupting us wasn't enough. Now she wants me locked up. Ain't that just like her."

"Ah . . ." This was far more than I'd expected right out of the gate, and I wasn't sure how to reset the conversation. The old man was working himself up. Couldn't be healthy for him "Mr. Peets, maybe we should—"

"She steals from us, cuts us off at the knees, and now *I'm* a killer?" He shook the cane. I backed up. "I don't want you in my place. I'd tell her to go to hell, but she'll get there soon enough."

We said nothing for a time. I used the quiet to try to figure out where I'd wandered off the path. I had no idea what Peets was doing on his end. He banged the cane down on the floor like Gandalf in *The Lord of the Rings*. I checked the distance again between him and me, making sure I was out of old man swinging range.

"You didn't hear me?" he finally said.

"I heard you. Did you hear *me*? Especially the part where I said I *didn't* work for Allen?"

He squared his slanted shoulders. "Don't believe you."

"Why would I lie?"

"Can't say. I got no idea who raised you."

"Here's the deal, Mr. Peets." I eased forward slowly. "*Again*, I'm here about her, not for her. You read the papers? You know what's going on? I'm looking into all that. Whoever's doing what they're doing may be someone she knows. You may know him, too. *That's* why I'm here. That's it. No tricks."

"Why's any of that your business if you're not working for her?"

"Let's just say I have a personal interest."

His thin lips pursed. *"Personal."*

"Yes, sir."

He looked me up and down again. "You talk like a lawyer. Come in here, thinking I'm too old to know what you're trying to do. Swindle me is what. Think I'll just go along. Well, I won't just go along. You can go tell Ms. Vonda Allen her name don't get her nothing down this way."

I eased my wallet out of my bag, showed him my investigator's license. "Do you see the word *lawyer* anywhere on this thing?" Begrudgingly, he slid his eyes to the laminated card showing through the plastic sleeve. He frowned but still didn't look convinced.

I went on. "I'm looking for information on the woman. You've dealt with her. I read about your lawsuit and how it came out. I need you to tell me about that. Two people have been killed already. No one knows why or if they're even connected. That's what I'm after. That's what's happening." I held my arms out, twisted them, lifted up my jacket sleeves. I was really going for it. "Nothing up my sleeves. No rabbits out of a hat. We good now?"

His watery eyes narrowed. "You got some kind of badge or something?"

I waved the license. "This right here, sir, is what I got. I'm not with the police. Did you hear me say I was with the police? Investigator. *Private.* That's what I am. Now, are you going to help me or not?"

Peets leaned on his cane. "Shoulda shown me that first off."

"Would have if I'd known you'd come out here going zero to sixty." I snapped the wallet closed and stuffed it back in my bag. "Well?"

Peets slowly backed up a bit, cocked his head toward the back. "Come into the office, then. Just don't try nothing crazy. I can still take care of myself."

He limped off unevenly, the cane dragging along the musty carpet. I stayed where I was, watching him go, wondering what the hell his problem was. If he was still this angry at Allen four years after the resolution of his lawsuit against her, I couldn't even imagine how contentious the proceedings had been. He was old, he limped, and he wouldn't have been much of a match for Allen head-to-head, but he could certainly write a letter, stamp and mail it.

Peets turned to face me. "You coming or not? I'm old. I don't have all day."

Oh, my God. I glowered at him, then followed.

Chapter 20

Peets's inner office was even more depressing than the space out front—a cheap desk; two cane-back chairs, one behind the desk, one in front of it; and boxes upon boxes of forlorn *Veritas* issues left to rot, as if they couldn't find a home anywhere. Peets caught me looking. He slowly maneuvered around the boxes and sat down behind the desk, wincing as he did so.

"It ain't much, but it coulda been," he said.

I eyed the lumpy chair in front of me, then sat down on it. "You and your son sued her. I know why. But you lost your case, and she got rich. You're still angry about that."

"There you go again, trying to tie me up. I haven't laid eyes on that woman in over four years. I took my last look on the courthouse steps. Henry was there with me."

"Your son."

He nodded. "We watched her prance down those steps, all high and mighty, cool as anything, and then slip into a long black car and drive away. We took the bus home, poor as a couple of church mice then, and now."

"You haven't seen her, but have you reached out in any way? Letters maybe. Flowers?"

His laugh sounded like it rattled something in his chest. "Send that harlot flowers? I wish I would. And there isn't a thing I need to put in a letter that I didn't say in my court papers. She knows where the Peetses stand, yes, ma'am. She knows for sure."

"You couldn't prove she stole your ideas."

"Fancy-talking lawyers and tricky statutes and such. Peets versus Allen, this and that. When it came down to it, it was a 'he said, she said' thing."

"How'd she steal from you to begin with?"

Peets leaned back in his chair, repositioned his leg. "Henry met her at some community meeting. She was big into public relations then, working for some fancy outfit and all. The way he told it, they started talking about what each of them could do for the community, and Henry started in on his idea for *Veritas*. He said she seemed real interested in how it could all go. Thought she might agree to back us. Turns out she was interested, all right, only not for us, for her. She took everything but the name and beat us to market by six whole months. By the time we got out there, she had already pulled in most of the advertisers and the readership we were counting on. We were dead in the water. We couldn't get nobody interested in *Veritas*— sponsors, ads, nothing. The community could maybe keep one magazine going, not two." He looked around the ratty office. "I can't afford to keep people on full-time, even part-time. One ten-page issue four times a year, that's *Veritas* now. Meanwhile, she's living high on the hog, the money just rolling in for her. I hear now they're giving her her own show, which will suit her just fine. High and mighty, yes sir. Always at the center of everything."

"Did she ever say anything to you about your lawsuit?"

"To my face, no. We weren't that important to her. In front of the judge, she told everybody that she and Henry had been together, and because they were, she couldn't very well steal what he was more than happy to give to her. That just about

crushed his spirit then and there. The guilt nearly killed him."
He looked at me. "Here's your information. Vonda Allen is a
heartless woman. She's got no soul. She'd stab you in the back
soon as look at you. I try not to keep hate in my heart, you understand, but you won't find too many people fretting over her circumstances."

"Does the name Benita Ramsey mean anything to you?"

"Should it?"

"Anyone you know connected to her named Eric? He'd be
about midtwenties."

Peets shook his head.

"Your son, Henry. Can I talk to him?"

Peets's face clouded over. "You'll have to take my word for
what I just gave you. My son passed away four years ago." He
pulled a handkerchief from his pocket, wiped it across his nose
and forehead. "Two weeks after we lost our case against her, we
were in a car crash. I got pinned. Henry got worse. He seemed
okay at first, up, talking. Then one thing led to another, surg-
eries, this and that, and then something went wrong. You never,
ever get over losing a child. They never found the driver. He
left us rolled over in a ditch like we were no better than trash."

I muttered a feeble condolence, but I didn't think Peets
heard me. It looked like he was back in that ditch with his son,
and I was in the ICU, waiting for Ben to wake up.

"I keep this place going because it was his dream. I'm too old
for it, and it barely hangs on, but it was Henry's. And every
night I have the same nightmare. The headlights lighting up the
window, the sound of metal twisting all around us. That hateful
woman is always driving the other car. If I didn't go after her
then, Ms. Private Investigator, I got no call to go after her now.
Whoever is, though, I wish them all the luck in the world."

I read Carole's cryptic text while stopped at a light on my
way to see Patsy O'Keefe, Allen's UIC classmate. Carole's note
read simply: **Holding his own, but no real change, bad or good.**

He has to make it. God, Cass, what if he doesn't make it? I thought of Deton Peets. He'd thought his son, Henry, was going to make it, too, but then there'd been one thing after another, just like with Ben. I checked for a text or a voice mail from Tanaka. Nothing. She'd obviously decided to take a pass on my offer. *Fine.* I hit the gas and went.

O'Keefe owned a tiny bookstore named Barnaby's on Church Street in Evanston. I'd called on my way up, so she was expecting me. When I walked in, she was arranging hardcover books on a display table, her back to the door. She turned around when she heard the door open, smiled, and walked toward me, her hand already extended. She looked much as she had in her college paper, only a little fuller, more settled in, her blond hair streaked with gray.

"Ms. Raines? Come in. Come in. Welcome to Barnaby's."

Her hand was cold. I blamed the AC. O'Keefe was wearing jeans and a bulky cardigan with oversize pockets, likely to keep her warm. Maybe she needed the place cold for the books?

"Thanks for agreeing to talk to me."

"Oh, sure. Let's sit." She led me to a small sitting area in the middle of the shop, one with couches, overstuffed chairs, the perfect spot for curling up with a good book. Soft music played, and everything smelled like new books and fresh-ground coffee beans. There was no one browsing the shelves, but it was early afternoon on a weekday.

"Get you something? Coffee?"

I politely declined as I sank into a chair. "Nice place you have here."

Her blue eyes twinkled as she took in the shop. "It's my baby. I love everything about it, except the lack of foot traffic today. How can I help? You said on the phone this has something to do with Benita Ramsey? That's a name I haven't heard in years."

I eyed my phone, which I'd set on the chair beside me. I didn't want to miss a text or a call. "I'm hoping you can tell me a little bit about her, as much as you remember from your time at UIC. Anything would help."

"My memory's good, but that was more than thirty years ago." She chuckled. "She's changed a lot since then. Not just the name, but her entire personality, from what I've seen. I suppose everyone has the right to change their name, reinvent themselves. Heaven knows, I've thought about dumping Patsy often enough."

"Honestly, anything you can recall."

"Well, when I first met her, she didn't look at all like she does now. I guess money makes all the difference. She was a little chubby then, or at least she started off that way. She managed to lose it. I kept asking her, 'What diet are you on?' You always try to find out what's working, but she would always say she wasn't doing anything special, that it was good genes. Don't you just hate those people?" She chuckled. "Benita wasn't much for sharing."

I took out my notebook, pen, poised and ready. "Did she ever tell you why she transferred from Northwestern?"

She pulled a face. "She wasn't much for bonding, either. We were just passing acquaintances, really. Somebody you studied with or got coffee with. I did ask her once about the transfer, curious as to why she had picked UIC after a school like NU, and she gave me some vague answer, which let me know I was venturing into forbidden territory. I didn't push it after that. Benita wasn't the kind of person you could really do that with."

"Was there anyone who might have known her better? A boyfriend? Girlfriend? Someone she might have confided in?"

"I'd have to say no on all counts. She was the same with everyone, as far as I could see—cool, distant. Smart, of course, but not a joiner, not someone you got buddy-buddy with. We worked on the paper for almost three years together, and I don't think in all that time we ever had a conversation that didn't have something to do with what we were working on.

No boyfriends that I knew about, or girlfriends. I never saw her with anyone, really."

I thought back to the photograph. "What about Dennis Seymour?"

O'Keefe nodded in recognition. "I saw Dennis at the last reunion. He edits medical magazines now." She shrugged. "I guess neither one of us turned out to be either Woodward or Bernstein, but we're doing what we love. Benita . . . oops . . . Vonda, never comes to the reunions. But as far as dating? Dennis never mentioned going out with her, and he would have, believe me. Frankly, I don't think he ever worked up the nerve to ask her out."

"Angela Dotson?" She was the other woman in the photo, the one with her arms around Allen and the others.

"She's Angela Dotson-Hughes now, and the only one of us who got close to the Woodward/Bernstein thing. She's a reporter at the *Sun-Times*. She's won a number of journalism awards, too. I read her stuff all the time."

"You three obviously stay in touch."

"Alumni newsletter. I'm a real sucker for all that, and it's good to have the contact information through the directory. It helps with networking."

"Do you have Allen's number?" I was fairly sure I knew the answer to that, but I asked, anyway. "Or would anyone in your group likely have it?"

"Oh, no. She's not listed. She's a celebrity now. I suppose that's why. But if anyone really wanted to call her, all they'd have to do is contact the magazine, right?" O'Keefe watched me. "This is about those shootings, isn't it? And that thing at the signing? You haven't said, but that has to be why you're here. It sounds like some crazy fanatic."

"The police are hard at work on it. Did Allen have any problem with anyone, enemies, that you knew about?"

O'Keefe's brows rose. "Enemies?" She took a moment to think about the question, looking very uncomfortable with it.

"I don't think so. I can't imagine anyone I knew back then having an enemy. We were just kids . . . high on life, our whole lives ahead of us. Will you also be talking to Dennis and Angela?"

"They're my next stop."

"Good. Then maybe one of them will know more than I do."

"One last question. Did Allen ever talk about her mother?"

O'Keefe's expression turned grim. "She didn't have to. She was there whenever Benita gave a speech or got an award. She was really a nice lady, too. Friendly, warm, polar opposite of Benita, to be honest. She did say once that her mother was pushing her to go to medical school, but medicine didn't seem to be where her head was at. Benita always gravitated toward celebrities and society people. She knew about all the high-powered entrepreneurs and business titans. It's like she kept a list or something. It was so sad when her mother was killed, and it happened right before graduation. She never mentioned med school again."

"She had to have talked about her mother's death."

"No. We read about it in the papers. She never said a word or missed a single class, but people cope with things in their own way, don't they?"

I stood, thanked her for her time.

"I would tell you to tell Benita hello if you see her," O'Keefe said, "but I doubt she'd remember me. She had an innate ability to pick out the people who could help her get ahead, and that wasn't me. It wasn't any of us."

Chapter 21

There was a tall, bulky man in a tight suit pacing around the reception area when I got to Dennis Seymour's office. I assumed the man was Seymour; he resembled the young man in the photo, only now with twenty-some-odd years of wear added on to both face and frame. I hadn't called ahead, so I assumed Patsy O'Keefe had done me the favor.

"You're the detective," he said.

"I see Ms. O'Keefe makes good use of her alumni directory."

"Not every day you get on a PI's radar. Patsy's downright fascinated, but she reads a lot of Dashiell Hammett."

"Thankfully, truth, in my case, is not as strange as fiction."

He grinned, his brown eyes peering out at me from behind heavy glasses. His complexion was light, and his cheeks and the bridge of his nose were splashed with freckles. "Mind if we walk and talk? I need a break, and by break, I mean caffeine."

We took the escalator down to the lower level and ended up at a Starbucks doing brisk business. Seymour ordered a large cup of coffee cultivated in Kathmandu, the Hindu Kush region, and I had a bottled water likely poured from the tap three states over. We sat at a small table by the window.

"It's funny," Seymour said. "You kind of forget that Vonda Allen was ever Benita Ramsey. Patsy said you asked about her having enemies. Sounds ominous."

I took a sip of water. It was obvious that O'Keefe had done all the heavy lifting on this one. "Yes. You know of any?"

"I was about to answer no, but then I flashed on something I saw once. I thought at the time I'd walked up on a lover's spat with her and some guy. If it were anybody else, I probably wouldn't have paid much attention at the time, and sure wouldn't still remember it, but with somebody like Benita, who always kept herself so private, it stuck out, you know?"

"Tell me what you remember."

"We were supposed to meet up to work on a story or something. I remember I turned a corner in the liberal arts building, on my way to one of the student lounges, and saw her having it out with this tall black guy. They were keeping their voices low, but you could tell they were angry and some tough words were passing between them. He grabbed her arm at one point, like he was going to yank her, but she pulled back, and then he hauled off and slapped her. Nearly knocked her off her feet, it was so hard. I didn't know whether to step in or stay out of it. I guess I stood there for a while, not knowing what to do. That's when they saw me." Seymour took a sip from his cup. "The guy took off angry, and that was the end of it. I'd say he was an enemy."

"Did you ask her about it?"

Seymour rolled his eyes. "You didn't do stuff like that with Benita. I asked her if she was okay. She said she was. She acted like I'd been spying on her, which pissed me off, so I left her to it. She never mentioned it, and I never brought it up again. That's how Benita was. I never saw the guy again."

"Can you describe him?"

Seymour frowned. "After all this time?"

"Anything might help."

His brows furrowed. "What do you need all this information for anyway, if you don't mind my asking? Patsy said she thought it had to do with those muggings."

I didn't want to divulge too much. "There's been some trouble. I'm trying to figure out where it started."

Seymour watched me over the rim of his cup, savored the mouthful, then swallowed. "That couldn't have been any vaguer."

"Sorry. All I can say. You were going to give me a description."

He sat his cup down. "Don't remember the face, but he was tall. Hoops tall, you know? Our age. A brutha, like I mentioned, but if he played, it wasn't for us. He wore a blue-and-white jacket. Phi Beta Sigma. I know because I was thinking about pledging at the time. My father was Sigma. Told me it'd look good on my college record and for networking after. I took a pass."

"And you saw him just the one time?"

"That's right. But if you want to know more, you're going to have to talk to Benita. There's no way in hell she could have forgotten that slap."

Angela Dotson-Hughes sat feeding the pigeons little bread cubes from a plastic bag from a bench on the Riverwalk, just below the Michigan Avenue Bridge. I'd called her after talking to Seymour, and she had agreed to see me. She'd be wearing an orange baseball cap and a world-weary expression, she'd told me. I had no trouble picking her out. I introduced myself, then sat beside her, and the two of us watched a Wendella tour boat full of giddy vacationers sweep past us on choppy water. The pigeons didn't appear to mind the hubbub.

I smelled French fries and looked down to see a large carton of McDonald's fries sticking out of her jacket pocket. I hadn't eaten since the apple and yogurt that morning, and now I regretted it.

"These fries are calling your name, aren't they?" She hadn't once taken her eyes off the pigeons. "Want some?"

"May I?"

She handed the fries over. "All yours. So, you're the gumshoe."

I popped a fry into my mouth, swallowed. "Yep."

"Doesn't look like it pays much. There's an apple pie in my other pocket, if you need it."

I shook my head. "The fries will do."

We sat there for a time, me eating, her feeding the flying rats. I finished the fries and crumpled the box into a ball. "Thanks."

She gave me a thumbs-up. "So, somebody's after Benita, and you're trying to find out who."

Dotson-Hughes was direct. I liked direct. Direct saved time, and I didn't have a lot of it. The pigeons crowded in, pecking around my feet and hers. She seemed to like it; I, not so much.

"Patsy O'Keefe called Dennis Seymour, and Seymour called you," I said. "Like a daisy chain. It simplifies things. I'm here to ask you the same questions I asked them."

"About enemies and her mother's death. Strange about her people, though. If I were a suspicious person, which I am, I'd say something's definitely up with that. Somebody's trying to do that sick 'I'm inside the house' thing, for sure, put a little scare into her. Me? I'd go right for it, not get cocky. In and out."

I turned to look at her. She chuckled. "Calm down, Nancy Drew. It's not me. But the fact that you're questioning us tells me you're working an angle the cops aren't. Mind sharing?"

"With an award-winning reporter? No."

"A reporter whose fries you just inhaled."

"I should have known they came with strings."

Dotson-Hughes laughed. "That's how the game of life is

played, my dear." She tossed the last cube of bread to the birds and then balled the empty bag up and slid it into her pocket. "Here's your problem, though. You're betting all this current mess has long tentacles that lead back to the old Benita. Only she's about as unknowable as they come, which drops a big, fat nothing bomb smack-dab in the middle of your village."

"You've sure got a way with words. I'd say you chose the right profession."

She drew the apple pie out of her pocket, which got the pigeons' attention. When she began eating it, I'd have sworn the birds gave her the evil eye. "You looking to screw her over?"

I eyed another tour boat as it passed and the blue-green wake it left behind. "Would you care?"

"Can't stand folks—even Benita—getting the short end, so yeah, I'd care."

"There's a cop lying in a hospital right now. A friend. He was hurt when whoever he is came for Allen. That's my immediate concern. I solve that, maybe I solve the other. Everybody wins."

"Loyalty to a friend. I like that." She took another bite of pie. "Fair enough. When Dennis called me, I dug into my notebooks. I keep them close, always have. I pulled out the one I think you'd be most interested in. Just know, Benita never made Miss Congeniality, never even tried for it. She was bound and determined to lift herself up out of whatever hellhole she came out of, though. I respected that."

"Dennis Seymour remembered witnessing what he thought was a lovers' spat—Allen and a boy in a frat jacket."

"He mentioned that when he called, too, and it started a bell ringing." She reached down into the backpack at her feet and pulled out a reporter's notebook, a small, narrow spiral pad whose pages flipped over at the top. It looked old and was bound by a thick green rubber band that had also seen a lot of days. "I write everything down. Big or small. You never know what's going to be important."

"Your notebooks go all the way back to college?" I asked incredulously.

"You scoff, but I got notebooks that go back to grade school. I was born a reporter. I'll always be a reporter. When I stop being a reporter, I'll be dead, and even then, I'll likely rise up and cover my own funeral. That's me doing me." She winked. "Besides, the notes will come in handy when I write my autobiography."

She flipped through pages, licking her thumb before she flipped each one back.

"You know Allen transferred in her sophomore year?" She didn't bother looking up from the page.

"Yes."

"And that her mother got killed outside that old dry cleaners she worked at?"

I leaned over to catch a look at the notebook. "What do you have on that?"

"Random thing," she said. "Never caught the guy. They thought it might have been some zonked-out crackhead from the neighborhood who couldn't even remember his own name, but they never got close on it. Benita just kept on rollin'." Dotson-Hughes flipped to the next page.

"Excuse me." My interruption lifted her head from the page. "Just curious. How many notebooks do you have?"

"Hundreds. I take notes on everybody, everything. Like I said, you never know what's going to be important. In school I could tell Benita was going places. So, in preparation for my 'I knew her when' exposé, I wrote it all down. I'll take notes about this meeting when we're done." She peered over the top of her glasses. "Full disclosure. I'm mentioning the fries."

"Please," I said. "Go back to what you were doing."

She read for a couple of minutes more, turning a page, flipping back, flipping ahead. And then, finally, she stopped and grinned triumphantly.

"I saw the guy. Sophomore year. March. Sporty, medium complexion, tall. He was waiting for Benita outside the library the time I saw him. She didn't look like she was happy about it. I got the impression he'd been out there for a while, waiting. Did I mention it was March? We're not talking balmy breezes. Whatever he had to say, he was bent on saying it, apparently. I didn't hear the conversation, but not for lack of trying. I can smell a story a mile off, and this guy reeked. I just couldn't get close enough. This was a different time from Dennis's sighting, so I guess the guy hit campus at least twice. They argued about sex."

My eyebrows went up. "How do you know it was about sex?"

"As he walked off, leaving her there, he said something. He was angry as hell and sort of growled it, barely holding back the rage. 'You wanted it. I don't owe you a thing.' That's what he said."

"How do you get sex out of that?"

Dotson-Hughes nodded and smiled. "Body language. The ferocity of the delivery. The soul-crushed look on her face when he said it. Trust me. Sex."

"You didn't happen to hear her call him by name, did you?"

"Not unless his mama named him Piece of Shit." She grinned devilishly. "However . . ."

I waited for the however, but Dotson-Hughes let silence hang there longer than I thought she needed to.

"Yes? However?"

She frowned. "PI's aren't patient people, are they? No appreciation for suspense."

I sighed. "Not today. Sorry."

"*However*, I had the good sense to read the name off his

track pants. It was stitched down the leg, right side . . . Grissom. You're welcome."

Dotson-Hughes's revelation was like finding a pinprick of light while trapped in a cavernous tunnel or stumbling upon a pool of cool water after walking blindly for days, ankle deep in blistering sand. My whole body suddenly felt light.

"You never discussed the sighting with Seymour? Compared notes?"

She shrugged. "You'd think we would have, but like I said, Benita was strange. We mostly stayed out of her business, because we knew that's how she wanted it. Seymour never told me what he saw, and I never mentioned my thing until you showed up. The guy wasn't wearing his name on his pants when Dennis saw him. I guess I get the scoop again." She tapped a finger to her temple. "Nothing gets past me. Steel trap, this is."

"Would you happen to know where this Grissom came from?"

Dotson-Hughes looked as if I'd maligned her in some way. "Northwestern. And before you ask how I know that, the school's name was stenciled down the other side of the pants."

I smiled, stood. "Excellent work."

"You'll need to talk to somebody who went to NU about the same time. I got a pal, Mike Kemper. He was a copy editor at the paper before they started the bloodletting. He ended up working nonprofit. Something to do with saving polar bears or marmosets. I'm not into animals. Might be grizzlies, who knows."

Dotson-Hughes reached down and pulled a business card and a pen from her backpack and then scribbled something on the back of the card. "Anyway, he's hooked into their alumni news, and he's got a good memory. Check him out. He may know Grissom or know of him. Anyway, he's a good place to start." She handed me the card with a smile. "I'll tell him you'll be in touch."

"More daisy chain?"

"Don't knock it. It opens doors."

I gripped the card tightly. "You'd make a good investigator."

She chuckled. "Nah. Looks like you miss too many meals."

Chapter 22

Mike Kemper told me over the phone that he was working at Lincoln Park Zoo the entire day, and so if I wanted to meet with him, it'd have to be there, and it'd have to be within the hour. I sped north up the Drive to Fullerton Parkway, then fought the cars full of sugared-up shorties streaming into the zoo's parking lot before naptime. I made good time, despite the bottleneck at the turnoff. Kemper had told me he'd be waiting in front of the gorilla house, and that was where I found a middle-aged white guy in Dockers and a short-sleeved button-down shirt. He held two hot dogs, one in each hand, and had a laptop bag hanging from his shoulder.

"Mike?"

He thrust one of the hot dogs at me. "Detective Raines." I looked at the dog circumspectly. "Angie said you might be hungry. I figured local version, no ketchup."

I took the dog. It was still hot. "You figured right. And Cass is fine." I held the hot dog up. "You know, I can afford to feed myself."

He chuckled. "Angie's a bit of a mother hen. She said feed

you, so I feed you." He eyed a bench nearby, gestured toward it. "Let's sit. I'm coordinating a fund-raising campaign in conjunction with the zoo today, so that's why I'm here, not in my office. This is my lunch break."

For a few moments we just sat and ate.

"So, Grissom? Frat boy. Maybe on the basketball team. We're looking for him at NU around the late eighties, early nineties."

He swallowed, wiped mustard from his mouth with a paper napkin. "Yeah. I'm not a big sports guy, so I don't know who played for us, but . . ." He wrapped his hot dog in napkins and sat it on the bench next to him and then took out his laptop. "I've got the directory here. Just let me boot up . . . and log in."

While I waited, I worked on my own hot dog, watching little kids across the way try to toss peanuts into the animal enclosures with chubby little baby hands. Then I got caught up in counting the number of strollers. The zoo must be a happening place for the toddler set. I was well past a dozen when Kemper drew me back.

"Okay, I'm in, but if this guy didn't sign on to it or didn't graduate . . ." He let his sentence go unfinished.

"I won't hold it against you," I said.

His fingers tapped over the keyboard. "I'll be damned. We got a hit right off the bat. Four, actually, within your year range. Kyle Grissom, Feinberg School of Medicine, graduated nineteen ninety-three. He's with Doctors Without Borders now." He read on. "David Grissom, Weinberg School of Arts & Sciences, graduated in eighty-nine. He teaches at Columbia College." He grimaced. "Wendell Grissom, deceased. Guess he's out. And Stephanie Grissom. Medill, nineteen ninety-eight. New York." He blew a whistle. "Works at the *New York Times*. Big leagues."

Stephanie was out. "Does it say which ones are black?"

Mike fiddled with the search, pulling up class photos. "David Grissom. And, hey, he played ball. Point guard. Freshman, sophomore years." He leaned back, apparently proud of himself. "And he's a Sigma. Looks like we found him."

I finished my dog, balled up the wrapper. "You found him. I just watched." I stood. "Thanks for your help . . . and for lunch."

Kemper went back to his hot dog. "You bet. Hope it works out for you."

I found Grissom in his office, room 455, texting on his iPhone. He looked up when I knocked at the door, but made no effort to welcome me in, so I took it upon myself. I'd done a quick Google search on him after I left Kemper, so I knew a little about him.

Old newspaper write-ups highlighted his once promising basketball career at NU, and his future had looked bright until he blew out his ACL sophomore year. That was when the scouts stopped scouting and any NBA aspirations he might have had withered on the vine. I could find nothing on him between graduation and when he turned up here, but then, I hadn't had time to cover everything. He was in Benita Ramsey's freshman class, though, which gave them every opportunity to meet, get together, and then part acrimoniously.

"Professor Grissom?"

He frowned, went back to the phone. "I don't see students outside of regular office hours. It's in section II of your syllabus. No exceptions. Also clearly stated in section II."

He was dressed nicely, a silver Rolex on his wrist. When I had looked up his address, it had pinged back to a swanky condo on the Gold Coast. High living for a man who graded papers for a living.

I stood in front of his desk, quietly waiting for him to look up again and acknowledge my presence. He didn't for a while. It was a little awkward. Finally, he looked up to glare at me.

"Persistence will not help in this situation."

"I would think persistence helps in any situation, but I'm

not a student. I'm an investigator. I'd like to ask you a few questions about Benita Ramsey, now Vonda Allen." I placed one of my cards on his desk and slid it nearer to him. He picked it up, read it, then put his phone down.

"Benita Ramsey?"

"Now Vonda Allen. Yes."

I looked around the small office, trying to get a sense of the man. His NU diploma was framed and hanging from the wall, as was his college basketball jersey. He'd also framed a few of the newspaper clippings I'd already read trumpeting his athletic exploits—top scores, game winners, and such. But none of the stories on his career-ending injury had made it up. Too painful for him, maybe.

"How'd you get *my* name?"

I glanced at the chair next to me, then sat down on it, though Grissom hadn't invited me to. "Wouldn't you rather know why I'm here first?"

He tossed my card down, sneered at me. "All right. Enlighten me."

"You two have history," I said. "I'd like to ask you about that."

"I knew her. It was a brief thing in college. We moved on. If you're looking for more than that from me, you're wasting your time."

"A brief thing, an easy split, no hard feelings," I said watching him. "What was she like?"

He took a few seconds to answer. "We only hung out a few times. Half a semester, if that. I can't say I remember what she was like. I played ball. There were a lot of girls hanging around."

"Then you got injured," I said. "But Allen left NU before that. Do you know why?"

His smile disappeared. "No clue. We'd split up by then. What's all this about anyway?"

I flicked a look at Grissom's wall of memorabilia. "She's receiving some unwanted attention. Someone she knew back in the day. I thought maybe you might have some idea who that might be."

He chuckled. "Unwanted attention? Somebody put a horse's head in her bed? Slash her limo tires? And you think it's me after all this time?" His chuckle gave way to an all-out belly laugh. I waited for him to finish, not seeing the humor.

"When's the last time you saw her?" I asked.

"Couldn't tell you."

"And your split was amicable, friendly."

"Sure," he said.

I shifted in the chair. "So, if someone remembered seeing you arguing with her at UIC and then slapping her, they'd be lying?"

Grissom tugged on his shirt cuffs, revealing gold mono-grammed cuff links. "Yeah, they'd be lying. I don't hit women."

"And whatever you argued about back then and split over, violently or not, you've let go of and harbor no hard feelings. In fact, you can't even remember the last time you saw her."

He stood. "We're done here. Whatever you're doing, or trying to do, try it somewhere else."

"Nice watch," I said.

He glanced down at his wrist, pulled down his cuff to cover it. "What's your point?"

"No point. Just admiring it."

"Do I have to call security?"

I stood. "No. I'm going. But can I ask where you were two nights ago?"

"No." He grabbed up the receiver from the phone on his desk but didn't dial.

"Again, not even curious why I'm asking?"

He didn't answer.

"A lot of people are afraid of Allen," I said. "She's got money to burn and a vindictive personality. You one of those people?"

He grinned, still not dialing. "Me? Not a chance. I hear she's a real prima donna these days, but that's only because she's been allowed to get away with it. Someone should have cut her down to size years ago."

"You, maybe?"

He put the phone down. "You know how you tame a lion? You do it by controlling the meat."

My eyes held his. "Seems to me a hungry lion would be far more dangerous."

"Not if you declaw and defang it first. Not if you make it fear for its life."

I wanted to make real sure I understood him. "And Allen's the lion."

He smiled. "You can see yourself out."

Chapter 23

I spent the rest of the afternoon in my office, searching. I didn't find any sudden windfalls that would explain Grissom's high living, which left me with a big question mark. I did find Reesa Loudon, though, after checking municipal records, tax liens, all the standard buckets. She lived in Atlanta now, worked for a local news affiliate. I hoped she'd be able to tell me about Dontell Adkins, so I called her, ID'd myself, and explained what I needed. She sounded a bit rattled over the phone, like I was trying to run a scam, but after I had convinced her I was who I said I was, she agreed to talk. She'd quit *Strive*, just as Chandler had said, but the parting hadn't been as amiable as Chandler had led me to believe.

"I just couldn't stand it one more second. They treated us like indentured servants. I quit and left for Atlanta the next day. I lived with my aunt until I could get back on my feet. It took a while since I couldn't count on Allen for a letter of recommendation or as a reference."

"Why not?"

"Allen told me and Dontell from the very beginning that if

we didn't work out to her satisfaction, not to expect anything like that from her. It was her way of punishing us, holding us back. She really is a terrible person."

"Chandler said you and Dontell were young, uncommitted, and unwilling to make sacrifices."

Loudon laughed. "You want to know how Vonda Allen sacrificed? That first year, after telling us there was no money, she bought a big Hermès bag and a Mercedes and flaunted them around, then set off to Paris for ten days, while me and Dontell put the magazine to bed by working all hours. We were committed, committed to not getting taken for suckers."

"Chandler go with her to Paris?"

"Of course. She can't go anywhere without Chandler. Who'd order her lunch or bring her a pen or whatever else she needs? Vonda said it was some conference they needed to go to that'd help them network internationally and grow the business. That was a lie. Dontell and I looked it up, and we couldn't find that conference mentioned anywhere."

"Any idea what's going on with the two of them?"

"No, and I don't care. I'm just glad to be clear of them."

I told her about Dontell and the hit-and-run. She hadn't known. She'd been in Atlanta by that time. She seemed truly upset at the news, and I gave her a moment to process it before I went on.

"Tell me about him."

"He was still there when I quit, but the way he felt, I knew he didn't plan on staying long. He dreamed big. I can't believe he's dead. Vonda did everything she could to keep him from getting any kind of momentum, and it looked like she enjoyed it. But Dontell was fierce. He planned on exposing her."

"Expose her how?"

"Put it all out there. Tell people how she really operated when people weren't looking. She was always so into how people viewed her. I don't think she could deal with everybody knowing what she's really like. And if Chandler had found out that's what he intended to do, she'd have fired him long before he even thought about quitting. Poor Dontell. I'm so sad right now."

She didn't remember ever hearing Allen mention anyone named Eric. She also claimed not to know anything about the threats or who might be making them. Just to be thorough, I asked if she had proof that she was in Atlanta at the time of Hewitt's and Sewell's deaths, and she e-mailed me receipts from an in-town media symposium she had attended, as well as a picture of herself, heavily pregnant with her first child. Not saying that she couldn't have faked the receipts or the pregnancy, but she didn't appear to have much of a motive. She'd left Allen and *Strive* behind long ago and had done well for herself. I bumped her name to the bottom of my list. Not likely or probable.

The names of Dontell's grandparents were mentioned in his obituary, and I was able to find an address for them, but it was getting too late to call on them. It'd have to wait until morning. Still I'd heard nothing from Tanaka.

I locked up the office, beyond tired. I'd been running all day, and it was just now catching up with me. I should've gone home or back to the hospital; instead, I found myself walking over to the lake to stand on the jagged rocks overlooking the water.

The sun would set soon, and the beach was deserted, except for a lone golden retriever frolicking at the shoreline, its owner, a tall woman, her short gray hair windswept, watching from the damp sand. I glanced mournfully toward the beach house down the path, remembering a rainy night not too long ago and the life I couldn't save. He'd called himself GI, and he'd lived rough under a tree just beyond the beach house. It was Pop who had looked out for him, fed him, clothed him. It was GI who had helped me find Pop's killer. I'd almost saved GI, almost.

I felt like I was drowning, flailing. I wanted to talk to Ben about it but couldn't. It came to me then. He was the part of me

I was missing. Had he really shifted from being a partner, a friend, to having feelings? If so, I hadn't seen it. How did I feel? What were my feelings? It was all too much.

My phone beeped. Another text from Carole. **Mom's been crying all day. Doctors haven't had any good news. Please, tell me you're getting somewhere.** My fingers hovered over the keypad. *What do I answer back?* I had nothing. I knew nothing. Hurriedly, I typed my response—**Following leads. Keep you posted.** Then I turned off the phone and put it away, heading off any follow-up. I wanted to be at the hospital, but I was needed out here. I had people counting on me, and I had nothing.

Damn it, Ben. Wake up.

There was a kid sitting on my front stoop when I turned into my yard. He was maybe twelve or thirteen, light, skinny, a head of curly hair. He stood when he saw me. I stopped, eyed the building. It wasn't full dark yet, but the exterior lights were on, set to a timer. Mrs. Vincent's lights and Gray's on the second floor were out. No one was home.

I walked up to him. "Can I help you?"

Big hazel eyes peered out of a baby face. "Are you Cassandra Raines?"

My eyebrows rose. "What's a kid want with me?"

He shoved his arm out to shake my hand formally, like he was out on a job interview and trying to put his best foot forward. "I'm your brother, Whitford. I came to introduce myself."

I shook his hand, taking a long look at the boy. "That so?"

"But you can call me Whit, since we're siblings . . . at least half."

"It's just Cass, by the way."

"I know." He squinted up at me. "You okay? You look weird . . . Oh, I get it. I surprised you. It's okay, though. You don't have to go all ghosty."

I took my hand back. "Ghosty?"

He gave both his cheeks a playful pat. "Pale. Ghosty. Like you might pass out or upchuck. Are you? It'd be okay if you did. I took Red Cross training last summer. I can do CPR, apply a tourniquet, clear an airway, dress a bandage—"

"I'm not going to pass out," I said, interrupting him. "How long have you been waiting here?"

He glanced down at his watch. "Two hours, thirty-seven . . . Eh, hold that. Thirty-*eight* minutes. But I was prepared to wait longer."

"Two hours?" I looked around the block, up and down at the cars passing by, people walking through. Strangers. In the city. And this little kid sitting on my stoop in the wide open, as clueless as a baby bird tottering toward the end of a tree branch. "Did anybody mess with you?"

"Nope."

"Did you ring the bell?" I checked the windows again. Still dark.

"No one answered."

I scanned the parked cars, half expecting to see my father idling at the curb. Then, when I realized he wasn't, I turned back to the kid. "Wait a minute. How'd you get here?"

"Took a couple of buses. I bought a map at a store close to the hotel."

"Buses? By yourself?"

He looked like he didn't get it. "I *am* twelve."

"This is *Chicago*. Do you know how many people go missing from bus stops in this town? Where are your parents? Do they know where you are?"

He didn't look fazed in the least. "I told them I was going to the pool. You're turning red. That's one of the signs of heart attack. I learned—"

I slid my keys out of my pocket. "Oh my God! Get inside. You're going to call your parents and tell them I'm bringing you back." I fiddled with the door, ushered him in, glancing back to give him a disapproving glare. "Buses."

Whitford Raines, vagabond, sat down on my couch and surveyed the apartment, wide-eyed. I sat across from him on an end chair, wondering what to say to him. Whole new territory here.

"Nice place," he pronounced as way of an icebreaker. "Big. Just you live here?"

I nodded.

"You have a dog?"

"No dog."

His feet barely touched the floor as he sat. They dangled just a bit, the toes of his scuffed-up running shoes kissing the carpet. He hadn't had his growth spurt yet, apparently.

"You have a phone?" I asked.

He looked at me as though I'd asked the dumbest question ever. "Yeah."

"Call your parents."

"I will. You got any kids?"

I shook my head.

"You like kids?"

"They're okay."

"Married?"

I shook my head again. I wanted to sleep, though I knew I probably wouldn't. I was done in, my brain fried, and I hadn't made a single bit of progress at all today.

"You don't talk much, do you?" His brows furrowed. I could tell I was beginning to worry him. "*Ever* been married?"

"Do you work for the Census Bureau?"

"Huh?"

"Never mind. Tough day. A lot crammed into it. Sorry. No, I've never been married."

Whit glanced around the living room; his eyes landed on an old CPD sweatshirt of mine strewn over a chair in the dining room. "You're a policeman?"

"Used to be."

He squinted. "What are you now?"

"A private investigator . . . like a policeman, but not a policeman."

"You have a gun?"

I didn't answer that one.

His eyes gleamed. "You'd have to have one, right? Can I see it?"

"No."

He made a face. "That sucks."

I stood, handed him my phone. "Call someone related to you. I'll get you some milk." I padded into the kitchen, more for a much-needed break than anything else. Maybe I had milk in the fridge; maybe I didn't. I'd have to wait and see.

I opened the fridge and pulled out a cold bottle of mineral water and ran it across my forehead before opening it and taking a long drag. A twelve-year-old boy on my front step. Yep. That was what my day had been missing. *Whitford. Weird name.* I grabbed the carton of milk out of the fridge, turned, and jumped back when I found the kid standing there, all *Children of the Corn.*

"Jeez, kid, you scared the crap out of me." I set the water and the milk on the counter, waiting for my respiration to normalize. "Did you make that call?"

He slid onto a barstool. "I'm thinking of what I'm going to say. They might be a little upset."

I chuckled. "I don't know a thing about your particular parental situation, but I can almost guarantee you they're going to be upset. Dial their number. Do it now." I slid the carton of milk toward him. "I'll get you a glass."

"Are you serious? Babies drink milk. I'm twelve."

"So you said." I plucked a clean glass out of the dishwasher.

"My mom let me have half a Starbucks this morning . . . *without* milk."

"Congratulations." I poured him a glass, slid it toward him.

"You're not giving me much."

"Excuse me?"

"I wanted to see who you were."

"So, you've seen me. Who'd you expect? Rihanna?"

He watched me closely. "Not sure what I expected. You're the adult. I thought maybe you would know."

I put the milk carton back in the fridge, finished my water. "Nope. You lost me at 'I'm your brother.'"

"Dad came to see you, but he said it didn't go good."

"Well," I said.

"Huh?"

"Didn't go *well*, not didn't go good."

He stared at me. I stared back. Standoff.

"I'd be mad, too, if he left and didn't come back practically for my whole life." He took a sip of milk, which he appeared to find satisfying, despite his advanced age. "You're still mad at him. That's why you won't really talk to him?"

"It's complicated."

Whit waited, not blinking, which was a little freaky.

"Yes, that's why, and stop stalling. Put the glass down. Call your parents, or I'll cuff you to something and call them myself."

His big eyes danced. Not exactly the reaction I was aiming for. "You have real handcuffs?"

I put the bottle down. "That's it. Get up. Let's go." I sped through the hall, grabbed my bag and keys from the foyer table. "Unreal. *Buses.*"

"But it was fun." Whit trotted behind me, trying to keep up. "A guy I sat next to wanted to sell me his pants. I said, 'Man . . .'"

My stomach lurched. "*Please, please*, for the love of God, stop talking."

I locked up the apartment, nudged Whit toward the stairs. "Move, Magellan."

"Who's that?"

"Google him whenever you get your computer privileges back. Walk."

My father and a woman I assumed was his wife, Sylvia, were

standing nervously in front of the Fairmont when I pulled into the horseshoe-shaped drive. I slowed the car, but the woman had the passenger-side door open before my wheels came to a complete stop. Whit unbuckled his seat belt, and his mother yanked him out of the seat and deposited him on the sidewalk, danger spitting out of her eyes like molten lava. I kept the car running, my foot on the brake.

"Are you kidding me, Whitford?" She held his jacket collar in an impressive vise grip. "What were you thinking?"

Whit opened his mouth to speak but obviously thought better of it and closed it again.

"Stand right there," she barked. "Do not move!"

She couldn't have been more than five feet two, but I would have declined any offer to tangle with her. She looked like she could more than hold her own. My father stood silently off to the side, his hands buried deep in his front pockets. He'd ditched the suit for a pair of slacks and a blue button-down shirt.

Sylvia leaned down, peered inside the car, relief on her face. "Thank you so much for doing this. I don't know how to address you. Do you prefer Cassandra?"

"Cass," I said.

She smiled. "Thank you, Cass, for bringing him back. I went down to the pool, and he was gone. We had practically everyone in the hotel looking for him. We were just about to call the police." She took a breath, a long one, as though she hadn't exhaled in a very long time. Whit had probably shaved a few years off her life. "I don't know what possessed him to do such a thing."

She looked nothing like my mother, I thought as I checked her out. It was funny how I automatically made the comparison. Sylvia was far shorter, rounder, in a motherly sort of way. Her brown eyes crinkled at the corners, and she seemed like a nice person. I wondered what she did for a living, besides mother an independent-minded boy. There was no reason for me not to like her, not that I consciously looked for one.

"I wanted to meet her," Whit said. "I had money for the bus there and back. What's the big—"

Sylvia reeled, her eyes laying down a challenge to Whit to say one more word. He shut his mouth and kept it shut. "Do not finish that sentence. Do not blink. Do not talk. Do not breathe." Whit looked terrified. Sylvia began to turn back to me, then thought of something else. "And you've seen the last of your Xbox for a while . . . and that includes that beeping thing you always carry around with you." She held out her hand, snapped impatient fingers, and waited as Whit dug into his pocket and lifted out some sort of portable game system and placed it reluctantly in his mother's hand. "The cell phone, too."

"What! Awww," Whit whined but handed that over, too.

Sylvia brushed aside a wayward curl that had fallen across her forehead, and then turned back to me and shrugged. "Kids, right?"

I smile sympathetically, having no firsthand knowledge of the species. "Well, I should get going. Nice meeting you."

"Oh, but wouldn't you like to come up? We could have dinner. I could thank you properly."

Thanks, but some other time."

She smiled. "I understand. Anytime then. Standing invitation." She stepped back and closed the car door.

Whit angled around his mother, waving madly. "See ya, sis!"

There was no misinterpreting his mother's glare. "Really? You won't be seeing anyone anytime soon, Whitford Bennett Raines. Get up to that room! Now!"

The two of them disappeared inside, leaving my father alone at the curb with me. For a moment he didn't say anything; neither did I. Finally, he leaned in through the open window, his arms pressing against the doorframe. An impatient taxi driver honked behind me. I'd idled in the turnaround too long.

I made the first move. "They seem nice."

"He's not shy, that's for sure. Thanks for doing this. Sure you don't want to come up?"

"I can't. I'm in the middle of something. I'll call about that dinner."

He tapped the car with his knuckles, then backed away. "Stay safe."

I drove off and took one final look at him through the rearview before I turned the corner.

Chapter 24

At ten the next morning, I drove out to Calumet City, to Dontell Adkins's last address, hoping I'd find his family still there. It was a small community nestled between the expressway and another community just like it, once anchored by a busy shopping mall, now half dead and long out of fashion. There were ten-minute lube joints, car dealerships, tire retailers, and fast-food places hawking greasy sliders, fanciful chalupas, and chicken parts battered and fried and topped off with a biscuit all within five blocks of each other. The kind of community you sped right through on your way to someplace else, like jury duty. The courthouse in Markham was just up the road north.

I rang the bell at a neat, single-family two-level with a wreath of summer flowers on the door, and moments later an elderly black man opened the door and stared at me through a storm door. "Morning."

"Yes, good morning. Mr. Adkins?"

He peered at me as though he was trying to place me. A pair of battered eyeglasses poked out of his shirt pocket, and he slid them on to take a better look. "That's right. I know you?"

He had a thick accent, Southern, which reminded me instantly of my grandfather and Pop, who were both born and raised in Louisiana.

"No, sir. My name's Cassandra Raines. I wonder if I could talk to you about your grandson Dontell?" I held up my license, a business card along with it. "If you have a minute."

His face changed in an instant. It'd been just another morning just seconds ago, but now a veil of grief slid across his face, and it looked like he'd aged decades more just standing there. "We lost our Donny about four years ago."

"Yes, sir. I know. That's what I'd like to talk to you about. I won't take up too much of your time."

He eyed the card, the license, which I still held up. You couldn't be too sure these days of anyone who came to your door unannounced. People could be cruel, evil, and the elderly were among the most vulnerable. I stepped back from the door and waited for him to decide to trust me.

After a time, he took his glasses off, slipped them back in his pocket, and opened the door. "Come on in. A few minutes are about as much as I got. I'll be eighty-seven come April, if I live to see it."

It was cool inside the small house, and dark, the drapes drawn. It felt close, hemmed in, as though the Adkinses had built themselves a tomb for the living inside the four walls. The furniture, old, neat, was encased in plastic covers, just as my grandparents' furniture had been my entire childhood. When nice things were hard to come by, you did whatever you could to keep them nice.

He gestured toward the couch. "Can I get you something? A cool glass of water? Sweet tea?"

I smiled. "No, sir. Thank you, I'm fine." I started to sit, but then an old woman, about the age of Mr. Adkins, walked into the room. I assumed she was Mrs. Adkins, and I popped up to greet her formally.

"Israel, who was that at the . . . ?" She stopped when she saw me and moved to stand by her husband. They made a handsome pair, gray hair, life experience and all, and reminded me instantly of my grandparents, who'd been married fifty-three years when my grandmother suffered a stroke and passed away.

"My wife," Mr. Adkins explained. "I was just about to call for you, Marva. This is an investigator asking after our boy."

Her face changed, too, just like her husband's had—pain, loss, grief, anger, helplessness, all of it carved into the lines around weary eyes. She stepped away from her husband's steadying arm, walked over to me, and looked me straight in the eyes, as though she were facing down Satan himself.

"You find the man who ran over our Dontell?"

Mr. Adkins went to her, placed a gentle, steadying hand on her shoulder, and then passed her my card. She read it, then looked back at me as if to say, "So what?" I rethought the offer of the sweet tea just then, thinking the break for the beverage would take some of the heat out of the old woman's eyes, but at this point, I didn't have the heart to ask for it.

"Why don't we all sit?" Mr. Adkins said. "See what she has to say." He eased down into the two-seater across the coffee table from me, leaving his wife and me standing. It was her house. I couldn't sit until she did. He reached out for her hand. "Marva?"

She finally sat down next to her husband. I sat, too, then took a breath and started. "I read about Dontell's accident in the newspaper. There weren't many details."

"Wasn't an *accident*. They ran our Dontell over in the street like a dog and kept on going. When it's an *accident*, a person, a human being, stops and sees about you. Four years. Now here you come. Do you know who killed Dontell?"

"No, ma'am."

She rose from the two-seater. "Then we got nothing to talk about. I'm done wasting time going over the same information, but ya'll, the police and such, don't do your part."

Mr. Adkins's calm voice broke in. "Marva?" She eased

down again reluctantly, and the look she gave me pierced right through me.

I went on. "I wanted to know if you could give me more details about what happened. Maybe there were witnesses? The paper didn't say."

"Why do you want to know all this now?" Mr. Adkins asked.

"That's right," Mrs. Adkins snapped.

In my head I cycled through what I could say and shouldn't say. "I can't really say too much about why I'm asking."

Mrs. Adkins' eyes fired anew, and I saw her husband's hand squeeze hers tighter.

"I'm sorry. You have no reason to trust me, but I wish you would. If what I'm working on somehow connects with what happened to your grandson, I may be able to get you some answers. At least I'll try to."

I waited while they sat on it for a moment. Then Mr. Adkins spoke for both of them. "Go on, then. Ask your questions."

They relayed much the same information Reesa Loudon had given me about how terrible it was working for Allen. I listened, knowing they were treading over information I already had, but believing it gave them an opportunity to loosen up some before I asked about what I really needed to know about—his death.

"What can you tell me about the day he died?"

"It was a sorrowful day," Mrs. Adkins said. "He left out early, saying he needed to get down to his job and pick up a letter they were supposed to give him recommending him for other work. He said he had to go get it in a hurry, before they changed their mind about giving it to him at all. That's how they were."

"Allen's office."

"Hateful woman." Mrs. Adkins muttered it, as though she were cursing the devil. "He was crossing the street, they say, on his way back. Something a person does a million times without thinking about it. The car came out of nowhere, speeding, and hit him straight on. It never stopped."

Mr. Adkins picked up where his wife left off. "They found the stolen car a couple days later, all beat up."

"People stopped to help," she said. "A nice woman even held his hand while they waited for the ambulance. I thank God for that woman. I just couldn't live if I knew our Dontell died alone and scared. After they took him, she even helped gather up his things that got scattered all over. There's still kindness in this world." She wiped her eyes with the heels of her hands. "He was all we had in the world. I miss that boy every second of every day. I won't have a minute's peace until I see him again."

A letter. Why had Dontell gotten a letter of recommendation? Hadn't Reesa Loudon told me that Allen didn't give them? That it was her way of exacting punishment on employees she wanted to hold back? So, what made Dontell special? I asked about the witnesses.

"I expect it's on the report they gave us," Mr. Adkins said. "We put it with his things."

"Israel can't bring himself to go through the box." Mrs. Adkins turned to her husband. "Me either. But we keep everything in his room. It's all we got left."

"Did you ever hear anything from Allen?"

"Never did," Mrs. Adkins said. "We didn't get so much as a bereavement card. I didn't think it was right, and I just couldn't let it go. I called up there. I asked for her, but they gave me somebody else, who was real cold over the phone. She said she didn't know anything about Dontell being killed, acted surprised to hear about it. That was the end of it. I couldn't do any more."

That had to be Chandler. There had been only three of them working at the time—Allen, Dontell, and Chandler. Reesa had quit by then and had relocated down South. *No condolences?*

"Could I see the police report and his things?"

Neither answered. I was afraid I'd gone too far, asked for too much.

"Where are your people from?" Mrs. Adkins asked.

The question caught me off guard. It was one I wasn't usually asked. "My mother's side comes from Louisiana, Baton Rouge and small towns around there. My father's family . . ." I had to take a moment to recall. "Michigan, I think?"

"You *think*?" she said.

"We aren't close." I could tell by the look on her face that this wasn't going to cut it. "We're working on it. Slow process."

"He's your Daddy, isn't he? What do you mean, you ain't close?"

I could feel sweat trickling down my back, my collar hot. Why was my mouth so dry? "Um."

"Marva, let the woman alone. I knew some folks from Baton Rouge. Babineaux. You know any Babineauxs?"

I shook my head. "I don't, but my grandfather might have."

Mrs. Adkins said, "You ain't close to him, either?"

"I was. He died several years ago. My grandmother, too. I lost my mother when I was a kid." There it was. We'd found our commonality—loss. Mrs. Adkins settled back; her gaze softened. I'd broken through. The three of us sat for a moment without talking. I was thinking about the people I'd lost, and the Adkins were likely doing the same.

She stood up, straightened her apron. "I put his things in his closet. I'll let you look, but I want everything put back just how you found it. Every scrap of paper, you understand?"

I stood, having just been given a gift. "Yes, ma'am."

I called Allen's office and asked for Chandler, and Pamela transferred me to Kendrick. Apparently, Allen was working from home, which meant Chandler was also working there.

"Does she have any events on her schedule for tonight?"

"She's got lunch at noon at the Drake," Kendrick said.

"Perfect. Thanks."

I hung up and drove to Allen's condo, and walked into the lobby to find the lobby desk manned by a thin black man with glasses and a green blazer. We had a polite discussion. I wanted to go up to Allen's, but my name wasn't on the approved list of visitors. He pointed me to the courtesy phone, which sat on a table in an alcove off to the side. If I called up and Allen agreed to see me, he'd let me up. Meanwhile, residents, one-percenters all, glided blithely past me, flaunting their access to the elevators, tacitly rubbing my working-class nose in it.

"Ms. Allen is not receiving visitors at this time," her housekeeper, Isabella, told me in stilted English.

I peeked around the corner at the guy at the desk. He hadn't forgotten about me. I had a sinking feeling that this was as close to Allen as I was going to get without SWAT backup.

"Tell her it's important that I speak with her."

There was a brief hesitation. She was likely consulting somebody. "No visitors. Would you like to leave, por favor, a message for the señora?"

I gritted my teeth. "Tell her it's about Dontell Adkins and David Grissom."

Another pause, more consultation. Nothing I could do about it. I was trapped in the lobby, after all, with floor upon floor of living space separating us. Allen didn't have to talk to me. She didn't even have to talk to the police unless she felt like it. All she really had to do, when you thought about it, was hang up the—

The line went dead. "Hello?"

I bit my lip, peeked around the corner again. Still there. I hung the phone up. There was nothing else I could do.

I passed the lobby desk on my way out. "Next time I'll bring her chocolates," I said to the desk guy.

He winked at me. "You'd do better bringing them for me."

There was more than one way to skin a cat. Allen had lunch plans at the Drake at noon. It was about eleven thirty now. I'd wait. I trotted around the building to the garage entrance, slid in and spotted Allen's limo idling right in front of the private elevator that led to the residences. I approached cautiously and rapped gently on the driver's window.

Elliott slid the window down. "Ms. Raines."

"Elliott. Waiting for your boss?"

He nodded.

"I'm going to stand here until she comes down. Just wanted you to know so there won't be any misunderstanding."

"She'll have a guard with her. Big guy. And Chandler, of course."

"Is the guard armed?"

"Afraid so."

"Twitchy?"

He frowned. "I don't know what that means."

"Never mind. I got it." I glanced over at the elevator door. Nothing yet. "Thanks for letting me know."

I backed away, stood patiently between the car and the elevator. This was a gambit. It might not work. Allen's security might be as impenetrable as their company name suggested. Titan Security. *Get over yourself.* I waited fifteen minutes; then the door opened, and Chandler, Allen, and a white guy as wide as a frigging bull moose stepped off the elevator and made for the car. They all saw me at about the same time. The bull moose switched to high alert, Chandler looked like she'd swallowed her tongue, and Allen looked at me like she wanted to skin me alive. Elliott got out of the car, came around the side, and stood at the passenger door, but Allen stopped to give me the business before she got in.

"You have a nerve. I should have you arrested for harassment." She cocked her head toward the Titan guy. "Norman."

Norman? I looked at him, grinned, but let it go. Naming this guy Norman was like naming a Chihuahua Hercules. It just didn't go together. I kept my hands visible. Chandler stood off to the side, her mouth clamped shut. If anything went down, she was not going to be any help to me whatsoever. I looked over at the guard. He was watching me pretty closely.

"I only need one minute," I said.

Allen sneered at me. "There's nothing we need to talk about, is there? You made yourself quite clear the other night. We're done here."

"I spoke with David Grissom. He teaches now. Looks good for a man his age. Well put together. He had a lot to say about your time together back in college." He hadn't really. I was still trying to figure out that lion and meat thing, but maybe the lie would prompt Allen to cough something up if she thought I already knew most of it. That was my play, anyway. "I see now why you wanted to keep everything quiet."

To borrow Whit's term, Allen went ghosty. Then meanness fought back and took it from there. "Who do you think you are? Do you have any idea who I am? What I can do to you?"

"Cut the crap, Benita. Did it ever occur to you that I'm actually trying to help you? You can burn the letters, shred them, cut them up and eat them, but that's not going to stop what's going on. Two people have been killed. Two people directly connected to you and your magazine."

Her head had jerked back at the mention of her real name, but the shock lasted only a couple of seconds. Meanness roared back again. Her entire body coiled like a heavyweight spring. "I'd be careful if I . . ."

I went on as if she'd said nothing. "I also found Dontell Adkins. Remember him?" I turned to Chandler. "You said you had no idea where he was. Hadn't seen him since the day he quit. He's buried in the cemetery. Run down, interestingly enough, not too far from where you guys started out all those years ago. His grandparents seem to think he'd just come from seeing the two of you. But you knew he was dead, because his grandmother said she called the office and spoke to you personally. Funny, you don't remember that." Chandler looked stricken. I turned back to Allen, checked on Norman. All good there. "I'm going to find out what's going on. That's a promise. However that shakes out for you is just how it shakes out."

"Out of my way. Elliott! The door." Allen brushed past me, signaling Norman to ramp it up with the guarding business.

Elliott opened the limo door and stepped aside to let Allen through. Norman stepped forward. I took the hint and backed way up.

"I'm gone. Don't want to impede Ms. Allen in any way. Besides, I've got an appointment with a couple of cop friends to discuss the latest developments, so I have to run." I had no meeting set but let her go on and worry about it. "We'll talk again soon. Till then, have a nice lunch. You, too, Norman." I turned and left, not bothering to look back to watch the limo pull away.

Chapter 25

John Coltrane blew smooth and easy through my stereo speakers as I sat cross-legged and barefoot on my living-room rug, a glass of red wine within reach on the coffee table, Dontell's box, a footlocker-size plastic tub, gray-green, with matching lid, like oversize Tupperware, sitting in front of me. Mrs. Adkins had been reluctant to let me walk out of her house with it, until I swore an oath to return the box and all its contents to her the very moment I found out what happened to Dontell. Inside, things were stacked neatly—files, books, papers—and on top was a battered laptop, several generations old, and a scuffed cell phone with a cracked screen. I checked them both. They were long dead. It'd been four years since Dontell used them last. No power cords in the box. But I remembered I had a few spare ones in my junk drawer in the other room, left behinds from countless old phones and computers owned over the years. Maybe something would fit.

I dug through the drawer, batting aside old batteries, brittle rubber bands, rusted screws whose rightful place I had long forgotten. I pulled out a handful of old cords just as my bell rang, and I rushed to answer it.

"Who is it?"

"Me." Eli. I buzzed him up and left the door open before going back to what I was doing.

He came in with a pizza box flooding the apartment with the aroma of hot cheese and spicy sausage. The first cord didn't fit Dontell's laptop. I looked up at Eli, smiled, tried a second.

"Hey. Pizza," I said.

He walked over, leaned down to give me a kiss. "I figured you hadn't stopped to eat, so . . . yep, pizza." He sat the pizza box on the coffee table next to me, then eyed my wineglass. "Which'll go good with that. What's all this?"

"Dontell Adkins's personal effects." The second cord didn't fit, either. I tossed it aside, tried another. "He was a kid who worked for Allen. Killed in a hit-and-run. Strangely, the second hit-and-run connected to her. The first involved a father and son who sued her for stealing the whole idea for her magazine." I looked up at him. "Something starting to smell rotten to you?"

He eased down on the couch across from me after putting the pizza on the table between us. "Not necessarily. Hit-and-runs do happen. You thinking she ran them over?"

"I'm just saying it's odd." The third cord fit the laptop. "Hold on." I moved over to the outlet, plugged in the laptop, and opened it. No cracks. The keys worked. I pressed the power button, and it began to boot up. "Ha!"

Eli joined me and peered over my shoulder as the computer slowly came to life.

"Now fingers crossed it's not password protected . . ." But it was. I screeched, shoving the computer away from me in frustration. I had one more cord. If it fit the phone . . .

Eli picked up the computer. "Password might be something simple."

I plugged the last cord into the phone. It fit. "Don't move. Do not breathe." I held my own breath, then plugged in the adapter. The phone lit up. "Please, no password." The home screen popped up, so no password needed. I was in, and it felt as though I'd just won the lottery.

Eli was still fiddling with the laptop. "See if he put the password to this in there."

I scrolled through Dontell's contacts. "Eli, c'mon, nobody puts the password to their computer in another computer. That'd just be . . ." But there it was. Under *lap pass*. "What just happened?" Eli and I looked at each other. "Password. NEWYORKER3. All caps. Try it."

Eli typed it in. It worked. Dontell's laptop was open. "Why password protect the laptop but not the phone?"

I grabbed the laptop, snatched a slice of pizza from the box. "I don't care. I'm just glad he did."

"What do you think you're going to find?"

I took a bite of pizza, sat the slice back in the box, and got to work. "I'll let you know when I find it."

There were video journal entries on the laptop, dozens of them. It looked like Dontell had documented every minute of his time with *Strive*, from his first day there to the day he told Allen to take her job and shove it, which was less than a week before his death. Each entry was date stamped; each one, archived. Dontell and Angela Dotson-Hughes would have gotten along like a house afire. Reesa Loudon was right. It looked like Dontell had planned on writing about his experiences at *Strive*. That wouldn't have played well for Allen or Chandler, not with a new publication starting up, not following their lawsuit with the Peetses. A hit-and-run, the Peetses run off the road into a ditch. Both things an answer to Allen's problem.

Eli slid in beside me, took a sip from my wineglass. "Okay then. Let's see what this guy was about."

The first file was dated October 19, 2017. Dontell, young, intense looking, squinting into the camera mounted in front of him, what looked like a bedroom as his backdrop.

"*I'm on my way! Somebody's actually going to pay me to write! Strive's new, unproven, but I think it could really be something.*" He pumped his fists. "*And I'm in on the ground floor, baby.*"

I closed the file. "God, were we ever that young and unjaded?"

Eli scoffed. "I wasn't. You maybe."

The next few files were more of the same. Dontell was over the moon, until January 3, 2018.

"*We had to work sixteen hours today, but we don't get overtime pay or time back. Is that even legal? What happened to labor laws? I have to look that up. Ms. Allen says we have to make sacrifices, but it's only me and Reesa making them. We were in the office past midnight yesterday. Allen and Chandler left at six for some swanky gala. Why are we the only ones putting in the time?*" Dontell looked haggard, less enthusiastic, and no wonder. He was being worked to near exhaustion.

I skimmed through the next few files, more of the same, before jumping forward to the last two videos he shot.

October 24, 2018. "*I quit today! Allen didn't like it, especially since Reesa quit last week. Can you believe she called me ungrateful? We'll see about that. I got it all locked and loaded, people. I'm a slave set free from the yoke! Dues paid, son. I didn't even wait for them to walk me out. Strolled out easy. Victory!*"

The last file, October 28. The day he died. Dontell shot it while walking into Allen's office, the shaky camera panning to catch the magazine's name on the door, Dontell's voice in the background. "*Last time I step foot in this place. Picking up the letter today. I gave them no option. The pen is mightier than the sword for real. Next stop, revelation. Let's see Vonda Allen handle what I'm about to throw down. Later.*"

I closed the video folder, looked around on the laptop for more, but found nothing else about *Strive* or Allen. I logged off, checked the phone. The numbers in his contacts meant nothing to me. I stopped scrolling at the name Eric Mason. No service on Dontell's phone, so I used mine to dial the number, but it was out of service. I tossed the phone down, stood to pace some.

"What's this kid Adkins got to do with anything?"

"He could be a part of a pattern of deaths. He was in a position to damage Allen and her business, and now he's dead. Sewell, Hewitt, thorns in her side, dead. Eric Mason is a long shot. Eric's a common name. No guarantee he's the guy we confronted the other night. But what if this Eric's the same one in Dontell's phone? What if he somehow holds Allen responsible for what happened to Dontell? That could play."

Eli looked skeptical. "A bit of a reach. Besides, it's been four years. That takes slow burn to a new level, don't you think?" He reached into the pizza box and handed me another slice. "Take a break? Come back at it in the morning?"

"I should swing by the hospital. Check on things." I read his look. "What?"

"It's after eleven."

I'd been at the box for hours without noticing it. "Oh."

I thought of Dontell, so full of promise. A box of things was a poor accounting of a life barely lived. I thought of the Adkinses, too. Sad, old, alone. *Everything* was a word not nearly big enough to describe the enormity of what they'd lost.

I stared at the box of Dontell's things. There was still stuff at the bottom of it that I hadn't gotten to yet. "Another half hour."

Chapter 26

I found Dontell's acceptance letter to Southern Illinois University still folded inside the envelope it had come in, now brown at the edges, as well as the framed graduation photograph of him in his maroon cap and gown, his arms around his proud grandparents, everyone happy.

There was a mangled messenger bag with a broken strap; inside it, a copy of Dontell's résumé, dirtied, creased, as if it'd been trodden upon and manhandled; and a copy of James Baldwin's *Go Tell It on the Mountain*. Underneath sat a sealed plastic bag, the kind hospitals tossed your things in when you were brought in. I turned it slowly over in my hands, almost reverently, aware of its significance, a little sad, even though I'd never met Dontell. This was the tangible sum of his young life? Stuff, bits of paper, so important to the living, worthless to the dead. Eli watched as I shook what was inside onto my lap.

"Not much," he said.

I sighed. "Only what was in his pockets."

I picked up a leather wallet, worn at the seams, its outsides scratched, muddied. There was twenty-five dollars still inside the billfold, and in the slots were a Discover card, an ATM card, and a driver's license, all expired. I inspected his watch. The face was smashed in; the hands were frozen at 11:36 AM on the twenty-eighth. His key ring had four keys on it. One was a car key, one looked like it might go to a bike lock, the other two looked like house keys, presumably to his grandparents' home. The ring sported the BMW logo.

"Did he have a car?" Eli asked.

I shrugged. "I didn't ask. I doubt he could have afforded one on what Allen was paying. Maybe the key is to his grand-father's car?"

There was nothing else in the plastic bag, and nothing else in the box but a pack of Trident, loose change, and a tarnished Swiss Army knife.

Eli checked his watch. "That's thirty."

I looked up at him, lost in thought.

He said, "Call it."

I put everything back in the box the way I'd found it, then closed the lid and stood. Eli did, too. He reached for his jacket.

"Get some rest. I'll call you in the morning."

"Wait."

We looked at each other, saying a lot without saying any-thing.

"Stay?"

He smiled, walked over, took my hand. We headed back, and I hit the light switch in the hall as we passed it, then stopped suddenly.

"Wait. Where's the letter?" I turned to Eli, as if he might know. "The letter of recommendation. Did you see it in the box?"

I flicked the lights back on, rushed back to the living room, Eli on my heels. I flipped the top off the box and rechecked the hospital bag, though I was fairly sure I'd done a thorough job of it my first time through. "He should have had it on him."

I checked the entire box, every inch of it. I didn't find the letter. Dontell had gone to *Strive* specifically to get it. The video showed him strolling into their office to pick it up. He'd called his grandparents right after he left to tell them he'd gotten it. So where was it? I looked at Eli. "It's not here."

"Half his stuff probably blew off to the four winds when that car hit him, and could have ended up halfway down the street. Hectic accident scene. Nobody's going to go picking around in the gutter for every piece of paper."

He was right. Of course, he was right. Our eyes held.

Eli said, "But you don't think so."

The Peetses. Dontell left to die in the street. Hewitt, Sewell, Allen's own mother.

"No way."

I woke to rain beating against my windows but lay there for a time, watching the slanted drops streak down the glass, feeling gloomy, wishing getting wet was the only thing I had to worry about. Eli had left around six thirty, but I hadn't gotten up. I glanced over at the clock on the bedside table. Three hours I'd been lying here, not getting up, wishing I could go back to before the bookstore and the knife, before Allen. Impossible, fantastical thinking. I'd have to deal with what was, like always, like everybody living.

I reached over and grabbed my phone, hoping for good news from Carole, but she hadn't called or left a message. At least that meant no bad news. There was a text waiting from Tanaka, though. I bolted up, read it. Cooperation was a go. She wanted to meet to seal the deal. "Ha! Yes!" That meant speed and access and more hands stirring the pot. "Thank you, Jesus." I sprang out of bed and darted for the shower, suddenly in a much better mood.

Tanaka was waiting for me at Tut's, a dingy, greasy sandwich shop off Roosevelt Road. I found her at a back table, devouring a Gym Shoe sandwich, a South Side rite of passage, or death, whichever way you wanted to look at it. The classic Gym Shoe was corned and roast beef, onions, cheese, gyro meat, all griddled up together and then dropped onto a sub roll. The thing was then topped with shredded lettuce, mayonnaise, tomato, tzatziki sauce, and giardiniera.

The Gym Shoe was usually eaten in a joint like this, where the cashier and the griddle were both behind bulletproof glass, so whatever went on out here, at the tables, was on you. If you were lucky, someone on the griddle side would call 911 if something went down. If you weren't, you died with tzatziki sauce on your chin. Tut's smelled of onions and simmering meat, and the soles of my shoes stuck to the floor as I walked. No menus. You picked your lunch from the board of options on the wall, and since half the letters were missing, you had to take an educated guess. Some Einstein had spelled *cheeseburger* with two z's. No credit cards. Only cash. No shoes, no shirt, no Gym Shoe.

I peeled out of my rain jacket and slung it over the back of my chair, then sat across from Tanaka and watched her kill herself one bite at a time. I laid my phone on the table in case Carole called. We had the place to ourselves, except for the griddle guy and the woman at the register.

"A Gym Shoe? At ten thirty in the morning? Who hurt you as a child?"

"It's my meal break. I'm starving, okay?" There was a slew of balled-up paper napkins littering the table like greasy fake snowballs. Tanaka talked to me between bites. "Besides, it hits all the major food groups, and I only have twenty minutes."

I gaped at her but said nothing. To each his own. "Any new developments?"

She put the sandwich down and wiped schmutz off her hands and wrists. Another snowball hit the table. "We talked to Allen about the letters."

"And?"

She leaned back in her chair, I guessed waiting for the Gym Shoe to Superman its way down to her stomach, bounce, and shoot back up her esophagus. "She says you're a nutcase. You saw a chance to bleed money out of her by threatening to sell this stalker story to the gossip rags. Blackmail, in short."

I almost laughed. "That's ridiculous, but not surprising. I'm hoping you also talked to Chandler, and that she gave you something useful."

"Not a thing. She just stood there. So, no letters, no corroboration, nothing we can do, until there's something we can do."

"This is bananas, you know that, right?"

Tanaka took a moment. "I know. The bookie angle was Jones's deal, just so you know, and it didn't pan out, as we both knew it wouldn't." Tanaka's eyes swept over the room, right to left and back; she watched the door, too. I knew she had it, so I didn't bother. I did turn my chair slightly sideways, though, so I had a side view of the entrance. "But something's going on, because two of her employees are lying in the morgue right now." She began collecting the napkins, brushing them all into a snow hill. "What about you? What'd you come up with?"

I told her about my visits to Deton Peets and David Grissom, also about Dontell's hit-and-run, the videos he shot, and the missing letter. "There's footage of him entering the office, time stamped, and the word of his grandparents that he definitely left with what he came for."

"What's any of that got to do with Sewell and Hewitt?"

I eyed my phone. Nothing. "Pattern."

"So, Vonda Allen ran down Peets and Adkins? One, to shut them up about the magazine lawsuit, and two, to keep the kid from blasting her craziness all over the internet?"

"In both cases, she got rid of potential problems."

"So, Vonda Allen, Chicago celeb, gala queen, is a stone-cold killer?" Tanaka looked skeptical. "A psychopath hiding in plain sight? And what's her old college boyfriend supposed to be able to tell you?"

"I don't know, but there's something there, too. I can feel it. He's too coy, too smug. He's also living too high on the hog for the salary he's likely pulling in. I don't believe he's had no contact with her in all this time. He's hiding something. She's hiding something. I'll take another crack."

Tanaka emptied her cup, stuffed the napkins and the sandwich wrappings into the greasy brown paper bag they came in, and then looked around for a trash can. "This should hold me for another twelve hours."

"Or twelve days."

"You one of those salad and hay people, Raines?"

I shook my head. "Had pizza just last night. But c'mon, a Gym Shoe? Get ahold of yourself."

She grinned. "Do I look worried?"

I shook my head. "Death by Gym Shoe. At least it's original."

Chapter 27

There was a dark car with someone sitting in it parked in front of my office when I got there. It looked like the same one I'd seen pull away from the Sewell crime scene. I leaned over to look inside and saw James Farraday in the driver's seat. He was alone. That was a problem.

He was supposed to be riding a desk until the department could figure out how to cut him loose, but here he was, tailing me. In his twisted mind, he likely thought I was the cause of all his troubles, the one single-handedly responsible for the death of his career. Whatever he was here for, I was sure I wasn't going to like it.

I kept walking, ignoring him, hoping he'd take a moment, catch himself, then have the good sense to drive away. But my heart sank when I heard the car door open and turned to see him get out of the car and walk toward me. I slung my bag cross-body, over my shoulder, so my hands were free.

"We're going to talk." His eyes were red rimmed; his face splotchy. I could smell the alcohol on him. He was drunk. That meant his judgment was impaired, which made him doubly dangerous. "Right here, right now. You and me."

I heard children's voices and turned to see a double line of nursery schoolers approaching, trailing behind a couple of young women, who were leading them in singing nursery rhymes. They were about a block and a half away. Farraday was oblivious and itching for a fight.

"Get back in your car, Farraday. I'll call you a cab."

He snarled at me, full of liquid courage. "You won't be calling anything, believe me."

I didn't want to incite him further, so I didn't respond right away, but I could hear the kids getting closer. "Fine. Let's take this upstairs to my office, then."

"Nuh-uh. I say where, and I say here."

I turned to look. I counted ten little kids. They held each other's hands as they walked along, cheerful, high-pitched baby voices getting louder the closer they got. I took a step back from Farraday. "You're a drunken mess. Get back in your car and get the hell out of here!"

He lunged for me. I ducked and flew through the door to the building, then took the stairs two at a time. As I hoped he would, he chased me in, lumbering up behind me, slowed by his drunkenness, but thankfully off the street and away from the kids passing by.

I double-stepped it all the way to the third floor, my legs burning, then raced down the hall, slid my key in the lock, tumbled into my office, and locked the door behind me. I dug my phone out of my bag and dialed 911 while I pushed my nap couch against the door to slow Farraday down. No shame in any of that. Live to fight another day. I gave 911 all they needed to know, then hung up and waited.

I could hear him coming, but he was half in the bag and still on the stairs. Maybe he'd cool down before he got to me. I stood behind my desk, slid my top drawer open, just in case I needed to reach in and get a thing or two to defend myself. I needed to hold out only until the police got there. I peeked out the window; the kids were just passing the building on their merry way. I breathed a little easier.

After an embarrassingly long time, Farraday's weaving frame filled the glass in my door. He jiggled the knob, found the door locked. He twisted the knob a little harder, then started banging on the glass.

"Think about what you're doing, Jim. Then don't do it."

"Open this door, Raines! Police!"

That was debatable, I thought. I leaned over and checked out the window again, looking for police cars. Nothing yet.

"Seriously, do you really want to go out like this? Have a little dignity."

The next time Farraday banged on the glass, it shattered into a million pieces, and shards of the jagged stuff rained down on the couch. Now I was mad.

"That'll cost you."

Farraday then took his big cop foot to the door, busting the lock, splintering wood, and skidding the cheap couch back enough to squeeze himself through. He stepped in, crunching glass underfoot, his shoulders squared. Another quick peek. Quiet as a tomb out on the street. He stood there, swaying. Jeez, had he really driven himself here?

"You ruined me. *You* ruined *me*. Who the hell are *you*?"

"I'm going to have to ask you to leave, Jim. Just back up, and we forget this entire thing ever happened." Not likely. I was filing charges just as soon as the police showed up. I was done dealing with Jim Farraday and his crazy crap.

"I shoulda done this years ago, when you kept on about that dumb banger. That's on me. I'm ending it now, though."

He unbuttoned his rumpled blazer, flipped it back to reveal the gun in his holster and the detective's star clipped to his belt. I straightened up and focused. I had a gun in my bag, one in the safe beneath my desk, neither an option right at this moment. Besides, I didn't want to escalate this into a shoot-out. I slowly lifted my arms over my head, palms forward, watching his every move.

He pointed to his star and holster. "See these? They say *I* rule *you*. They trump that two-bit PI's license you carry in that rinky-dink private dick wallet of yours. Somebody comes at me, I come back twice as hard." He tapped the badge. "I earned this. *I* did. How do *I* get dinged for Russo getting her head blown off? *You* set it off."

A wave of anger shot through me, setting my gut on fire. He'd killed Russo, just as sure as if he'd put the gun to her head himself. My jaw hurt from clenching my teeth so tightly. I hated Farraday. I'd hate him till the day I died. I just hoped that wasn't today. I heard the sirens then. My eyes locked onto Farraday's, but I didn't say a word. Didn't have to. He could hear, too.

There was the screech of car tires below, then the rumble of cop feet on the stairs. Farraday looked lost, defeated. I would have pitied him were it not for Jimmy Pick and Russo. I stood stock-still behind the desk, my arms still up, ready to drop and roll if I needed to. Farraday stood weaving just inside the door. We exchanged a look.

He shook his head, resignation on his face. "Damn you, Raines."

The cops were at the door now.

I glared at him. I really did hate the man and all the heartache he'd caused. "Damn you back, Farraday."

Four uniformed cops stared down at the broken glass, then pushed their way in as Farraday slowly raised his arms in surrender and I put mine down.

I'd passed on the Gym Shoe at Tut's, but now, after Farraday had got escorted out, his career and what was left of his reputation in shambles, I needed comfort food in the worst possible way. There was a temporary door on my office, and I'd have to pay for replacement glass for the second time in as many months, but it was over, and no one had got hurt.

I walked down to Deek's and ordered a chocolate shake, fries, a double bacon burger, onion rings, and a slice of banana cream pie before I even sat down, then slid into my booth in back and booted up my laptop. I was done with my office for a while. Muna must have suspected something was up with me when I came in, because when she dropped my shake off at the table, I found it topped with real whipped cream and three cherries instead of the customary one.

She loomed over me, big hands on full hips. "Heard you had some trouble down there a while ago. You all right?"

By now, Muna knew everything that'd happened in my office. Word got around fast, which saved me the recap. I took a long drag of the shake, came up for air. "Am now."

Her eyes narrowed. "You ever think about going into cosmetology?"

I looked up, sighed. "Would you trust me with your hair?"

"Good point. Your food's coming up."

She turned and walked away, and I turned back to my computer and a deep dive into David Grissom's bona fides. What I was able to access fairly quickly looked wonky. I'd been right. He expended far more than he took in, and there was nothing to indicate that he'd inherited a windfall from some long-lost auntie. At best, he couldn't make much more than eighty, ninety thousand a year, yet his condo in the building it was in couldn't have gone for much less than a million or a million and a half. And I found a vehicle registration for a 2020 BMW, so what the frick?

Muna walked up with my food on a tray. She eyed the tray, me, the laptop, my chocolate shake. "You gonna tell me why I carted all these carbohydrates out here and you don't weigh but two pounds?"

I looked up at her, the straw still in my mouth. "I'm hungry."

She snorted, put the tray down on the table, then sat across from me, which was a little more attention than I needed or wanted. "Ain't nobody *this* hungry. It's you worrying about Benjamin?" Her eyes bore into mine.

"It's just lunch, Muna."

"Or maybe you got trouble with that long, tall drink of water you going out with?"

I slurped the last of my shake, vacuuming along the bottom of the glass with the end of the straw so that it made that slurpy noise everybody hated but couldn't help making. "You know, sometimes a burger is just a burger."

She looked unconvinced. *Smart woman. I admit it.* Farraday had rattled me. I'd been afraid I might have to shoot him or, worse, he'd shoot me. He had me frazzled, and then there was Ben. She was right about that.

"Because if it's Mr. Long, Tall Drink of Water," Muna said, "I got relationship tips. Guaranteed to set you straight."

I grabbed my burger off the tray, along with my fries, the onion rings, the pie. "Haven't you been married four times?"

"Right, so who knows better than me?"

I ate a fry slowly, staring at her. "I'm good. Thanks anyway."

Her eyes dropped to my one-woman banquet spread. "Then this is about that drunk cop coming after you down at your place."

I knew it. Nothing on this block got past Muna Steele. "Minor disturbance, not even worth mentioning."

"Uh-huh. Says the woman who got conked on the head by a couple of fools not too long ago." She stood up, picked up her tray. "Have it your way, but if you change your mind, you know where to come. But before you mess up with that man, you better call me." She loomed over me, watching me eat. "Anything else you want?" She was being sarcastic. What else could I possibly want or have room for?

"Another shake?"

Her brows lifted. "Another *shake*? Lord have mercy."

She stormed off toward the kitchen.

"Thanks, Muna," I called after her, my mouth full.

I was standing outside Grissom's office door when he rounded the corner and saw me. The look on his face told me he wasn't happy about it.

"How'd you get back up here?"

"Same as last time. Charm and ingenuity. I need to talk to you."

He brushed past me, unlocked the door. I followed him in. He went to his phone, picked up the receiver. "I'm having you thrown out."

"That's a little extreme, isn't it?"

He checked his watch. "I'm not talking to you."

"Why?"

His face flushed. "Leave, or I'll have you arrested."

I stood there quietly, waiting for him to calm the hell down. He barked into the phone for security. I watched. "All right. You brought this on yourself," he said.

We stood on opposite sides of the desk. He checked his watch again, then reached into his bag and got his cell phone out to send a text. Maybe I was making him late for a date. Maybe it was something else. I'd lay bets on the something else. I heard footsteps approaching from the hall. Security, come to toss me.

The guard knocked, stuck his head in. "You called security?"

Grissom looked satisfied with himself. "There she is. Throw her out."

The guard walked in, stood beside me, thick thumbs looped into his belt loops. "You wearing out your welcome, Raines?"

"Didn't think so. I'm just standing here."

Grissom sneered, looked at both of us. "What the hell's going on?"

I knew the guard. I'd worked with him on the job. Detective Terrence Johnston, retired. He was how I had got up here last time and this time, too. I'd been surprised to see him at the desk my first visit. This time, I had brought peanut brittle, the kind I knew he liked.

I pointed at Johnston. "Old friend."

Johnston smiled. "Not *that* old."

Grissom balled his hands into fists and pounded the desk. Johnston and I stood watching, not quite sure what we were looking at, neither of us able to look away. After Grissom stomped around a bit, he stuck his arm out, pointed at the door behind us. "Get out! Both of you." To Johnston, he said, "And I'm reporting you to the administration."

Neither of us moved. I stared at Grissom's left wrist, exposed during the point. On the inside, right above his watch-band, was a round, dark birthmark with jagged edges, like an inkblot. I'd seen a similar one on the man I had fought to restrain in the bookstore. I should have taken Grissom's infantile behavior a little more seriously, but it was difficult to. The birthmark was a link, an opening.

"You threatening me?" Johnston asked, his voice as dry as dust. He was a solid, sturdy fella still, even after a few years of badging people at a desk. He stepped forward, leveled hard eyes on the man in Gucci loafers who was losing his mind. "You're going to want to be careful with that."

I took a step back, still on the birthmark, thinking it through. Birthmarks were sometimes hereditary, right? What were the odds that two men with a similar mark on the same wrist, connected by the same woman, wouldn't have some familial overlap? Allen and David Grissom. A lost year. All the flash, with nothing to account for it. I thought I'd found it, a way in.

"If you're done," I said, "can we talk about your son now?"

Grissom stopped dead. The flush paled. "What the hell are you talking about?"

"You. Benita. All those years ago." I defaulted back to Allen's given name because of Johnston. An unplanned pregnancy. That would explain Allen's transfer, her lost year. Maybe that was what they'd argued about. It might even explain all Grissom's flash. Blackmail? Hush money? I played a hunch. "How much is she paying you to keep your mouth shut?"

Grissom had had a lot to say just a few moments ago, but that was done, apparently. He stood there, his eyes wandering around the room, as though he were looking for a little help from his knickknacks. None was forthcoming. He tried pulling himself together, straightening his cuffs, adjusting his watchband. Then he turned to Johnston. "You can go, but you haven't heard the last of this."

Johnston snorted and gave me a "Can you believe this?" look. I had once seen him pick a three-hundred-pound bruiser high on PCP off the ground and slam him into the side of a building. By the end of the exchange, the bruiser was sitting in the back of an unmarked car, crying for his mommy. My money was on Johnston. "He's got threats."

I winked at him. "I'll catch you on my way out. Save me some brittle?"

"Quit playing, Raines. You know that brittle's half gone already." Johnston glared at Grissom, and then eased out, and closed the door behind him.

Grissom sat. I did, too.

"You're guessing," he said, trying the bluff out for size. "You don't know as much as you think you do."

I pointed to the birthmark. "He has one just like it." Now I knew why he'd looked vaguely familiar when I'd seen him. He favored both Allen and Grissom, but not overwhelmingly so, not so it'd immediately come to me that she could be his mother. "Not conclusive evidence, but if it comes to it, DNA will confirm."

He tapped nervous fingers on his armrests, deep in concentration, maybe trying to find a way out, concoct a lie I might believe. Or maybe he was clicking through, trying to find a way to protect his money and keep Allen squirming on the hook.

"What's his full name, and where can I find him?"

He shook his head, his arms crossed against his chest now, defiant. "Not in my best interest."

My brows lifted. "That's what you're worried about? He assaulted a police officer. He showed up at that bookstore with a knife. He may be responsible for the deaths of two innocent people, maybe more. You need to start talking."

He sat back in his chair, back to cocky. Still, he left me hanging for almost a minute before he spoke again. "So, Benita had a kid. It's out. That was her choice. She had options."

"*Benita* had a kid?"

"It was a mistake. I told her I wasn't on board, that I'd sign whatever I needed to sign. That was the best thing for everybody."

"Then what happened? Why the argument? The slap?"

Grissom grew more and more uncomfortable, squirming a little in his seat. "I told you I don't hit women."

We both knew that was a lie. I waited.

"She started thinking she'd keep it. We had words. She eventually went through with an adoption but wanted to hold it over my head, bleed me. I was headed to the NBA. She knew it. She saw an opportunity and took it."

"But you set her straight."

"That's right."

"Which one of you did he find first?"

He shook his head. "No, that's enough."

"Believe me. It isn't," I said.

We sat in silence for a bit. I wasn't going anywhere. Grissom finally realized it. "He couldn't find Benita Ramsey, for obvious reasons, so I set him straight. Let him go bleed her for a while. Why not? She can take care of herself." He crossed his legs, played with the pleat in his pant leg.

"I'd have made the hall of fame. I was just that good. After what happened, I got distracted, lost focus. She got into my head with all that mess. Final game freshman year, third period, a minute and a half to the buzzer, I come down wrong, snap my Achilles. Tried rehab, but I never got back to a hundred percent. Game over. NBA out. Hall of Fame gone."

"And you blame her?"

"I wish I'd never laid eyes on her. She got what she wanted. Why shouldn't I get what I want? How would all her high-class friends look at her if they knew she was just some white-washed gold digger? I knew she'd pay."

Grissom reached into his desk drawer and drew out an eight-and-a-half-by-eleven-inch box and dropped it in front of him with a thud. "My tell-all. All about the price I paid. All about the real Benita Ramsey, not the Vonda Allen she dreamed up out of nowhere." He grinned. "She'll *keep* paying."

I could see now how Grissom and Benita might have come together all those years ago. They were the same person— greedy, gnarled, blackhearted—both tangled together like two crabs in a barrel, clawing over each other, neither getting anywhere close to out.

I thought of the threatening letters. Had Eric sent them to get back at her? Had Grissom sent them, just trying to have a little fun? "Have you been writing her letters?"

He laughed. "Benita and I communicate only by direct deposit. As long as that keeps going, I've got no reason to even think about her."

"When did he first come to you?"

"Couple of months back, and it was a one-time deal. Haven't seen him since. Doubt I will again. Why hang out with the second string when Vonda Allen's your mother and she's loaded? I got the distinct impression he intended to get in on some of that. I hope he does."

"You gave him her private number, didn't you?"

He smiled. "How else was he going to contact her?"

"Without caring if he might pose a threat to her?"

"Benita's a big girl." Grissom stood, buttoned his blazer. "And that's all you get for free." He glanced down at the box with all Allen's secrets in it. "The rest you can read about."

I got up from the chair, stood there, rooted to the spot. He knew what I wanted. He also had to know that I'd keep coming back until I got it, Johnston or no Johnston.

"You want his name," he said, seeming to enjoy the suspense.

"His *last* name. I know the first. Eric. He had her sign a book to him."

"Then let's blow this whole thing wide open and see what kind of chaos it starts. His name's Eric Rogers, no *d*." He walked over to the door, opened it, and stood waiting for me to get on the other side of it. "He told me he works at a place called Meisner's up on the North Side. It's a flower shop. He's not exactly setting the world on fire, is he?" I walked to the door. "Tell Benita her lawyers know where to find me."

The door closed right on my heels. I should have been elated. I finally had a name, a way to find the man who'd put Ben in the hospital. So why was I beginning to feel sorry for him?

Chapter 28

"Look at you passing the ball," Tanaka said on the other end of the line. I was holding up my end, sharing the lead. Eric Rogers. Meisner's. "We'll take it from here. Good get."

I ended the call, stared out of my car window at the front of Meisner's flower shop. Cooperation didn't mean I was going to just sit on my hands while things went down without me. I had the Mickersons to think about, a job to finish.

I got out of the car and walked in. I didn't think Eric would be here. I mean, he had knifed a cop. If it were me, I'd be halfway to Newfoundland by now, but maybe someone here would know where he lived or where he might go if he had to get there ahead of the law.

It was a tiny shop inside a dying strip mall off Damen Avenue. A giant Costco literally loomed over it from the next block over, a veritable harbinger of doom. Big box? Try death knell. But there was a large empty lot filled with trash, debris, and human castoffs separating the giant from the little shop, a sea of crabgrass and nettles, a tangible line of demarcation between holding on by a thumbnail and raking it in hand over fist.

It was cool inside, large refrigerated cases with colorful flowers in chilled vases helping the air conditioner along. I took one whiff of the cloyingly sweet flowers and thought, *Funeral home*. There were plenty of happy occasions, of course, for which people purchased flowers, but for me, flowers always smelled like death.

There were no customers at Meisner's. Costco sold flowers, too, or maybe it was just because it was getting late in the day. I walked up to the counter and hit the little bell sitting there, calling for service, and a short white woman of about sixty emerged from the back, all smiles. Her eyeglasses hung from a chain around her neck and hit right at a full bosom. I looked behind her, but she appeared to be alone.

"Hello. May I help you?" Her smile was polite; her blue eyes were sharp.

I smiled back. "I hope so. I'm looking for Eric Rogers. Is he around?"

The smiled faded. I wondered why. "I'm Joan Meisner, the owner. Is there a problem?"

"Absolutely not. I'm an old friend of Eric's. Just passing through. His father told me he worked here. I thought I'd stop by and say hello. Catch up before I hit the road."

She relaxed. "Oh, I see. How nice."

"He does work here? I haven't come to the wrong place?"

"He does. He makes our deliveries. Very reliable. We're quite pleased." She reached under the counter, and a buzzer sounded.

I tensed. He'd shown up for work? Seriously? "He's also very good with customers. Efficient, trustworthy."

"Also fast," I said, "sure-footed."

Meisner looked confused, but she didn't have time to dwell on it. Eric walked in from the back, took one look at me, and froze. *I'll be damned*, I thought. There he was. At work. After knifing a cop. Clueless or just plain stupid? I studied him, up close, as his face drained of color and his eyes bore into mine. He stood there, as stiff as a ship's plank, behind his boss. And then something shifted in his eyes.

"Eric, don't even think about it," I said.

Meisner looked from me to Eric and back. "What's happening?"

Eric took off, bounded over the counter and straight-armed me right in the chest as he barreled past me and out the front door, headed for the open field. The hit to my chest took my breath away, and I saw stars. I wasted several seconds, bent over, trying to recover, then took off after him, shooting out the door. I turned for the field, spotted him sprinting through the tall weeds, in the direction of the train station two blocks up.

I ran after him, dirt and city dreck beneath my feet, stumbling over old shoes, bike tires, and discarded clothing, not stopping, but not making any progress, either. Eric was fast. But if I didn't catch up to him before he hit the train, I could hang it up. I dug in.

I'd envisioned this going a different way altogether. I'd planned on calmly talking to Eric while we waited for Tanaka and Marcus to show up. I'd planned on a quiet end to all this. Now I was racing through an obstacle course of garbage, my chest on fire, and coming up short. I jumped over a rusted box spring. No sign of the cops. When Tanaka had said they'd follow up, I had assumed she meant today.

"Stop!" I called out.

Eric turned to see me but kept going. I would have, too. Did I hear him wheezing? Was I actually gaining? Maybe it was the weeds. Maybe he was allergic. He looked back over his shoulder again but didn't slow down.

"I just want to talk!" *Goddammit.* It was hot. I was hot. My boobs hurt. I wanted to stop. I felt something sticky on the bottom of my running shoe and worried about what it might be. I wondered, too, what Joan Meisner was doing. Standing there in all that air-conditioning, smelling the funeral flowers.

"Eric," I called again. "Where do you think you're going?"

The train station would be my bet. He pulled away from me.

My legs burned. Out of the corner of my eye, I saw flashing lights and turned to see an unmarked car speeding toward the edge of the field to cut Eric off at the pass. Guessed Tanaka *had* meant now. I tracked the car as it screeched to a stop in front of Eric, kicking up dirt and debris. Tanaka and Marcus jumped out and approached, guns drawn, barking orders for Eric to put his hands up and get on the ground. I slowed, then stopped, then doubled over, wheezing, holding my chest. It felt like I might actually die right here in this skanky field. By the time I straightened up, Eric was in the back of the police car.

"Cooperation, huh?" Tanaka called out. "Doesn't count if you toss the ball and then run to catch it yourself."

I dismissed her with a wave. It was all I had.

"Need anything? Ice pack? Oxygen?"

"I would have caught up, Tanaka."

She smirked. "Yeah, okay."

It was hours later, and we were watching Eric through a two-way mirror. Marcus was in the next room with him, making a big show of things. He had heard about Farraday's meltdown and had doubled down on his resentment toward me. If Farraday was through, and I hoped he was, that meant Marcus was going to have to haul his own ass into the superintendent's chair, and he didn't have that kind of finesse even on his best day. Still, he was in there strutting around, giving it his best. I had no idea which one of us he thought he was impressing, me or Tanaka, but it didn't really matter. He wasn't scoring any points either way. Eric Rogers was clean. No run-ins with the police until now.

"What'd you want with Vonda Allen?" Marcus asked.

"It's personal."

Marcus circled the table. "Knife in your pocket. What'd you go there to do?"

"Nothing."

"You assaulted a police officer."

"Hey, those two cops put hands on me first. I defended myself."

Marcus flicked a cocky grin at the mirror. The grin was meant for me. He then leaned on the corner of the table, his arms folded. "So, what had you planned on doing with that knife?"

"I told you, nothing. I use it for work, to cut through the wires on the crates. They came at me. Wouldn't let me see her. I had a right."

"*A right?*" Marcus reached across the table and slid an evidence bag with a piece of paper in it in front of Eric. "We checked your place. Tell me about this letter."

Eric stared at the bag, then glowered at Marcus, but didn't open his mouth.

I turned to Tanaka. This was my first time hearing about them finding a letter in the search of Eric's apartment. "They found the letters?"

She shook her head. "*A* letter. Typewritten, addressed to her. Him introducing himself to her, asking for a meet. It doesn't match the one you described seeing—no red ink, no Dear Bitch, and there wasn't a single flower anywhere in his place. Meisner says Eric doesn't know a thing about flowers. He only delivers. Inconsistencies. I hate them."

"Any flowers missing from Meisner's?"

"No. She says Eric bought a bouquet a few weeks ago, then the roses right before Allen's signing. Nothing else. She even gave him an employee discount."

"Hers is not the only flower shop," I said.

"No, but if he used another, we haven't found it yet."

Marcus took a seat at the table. "What about those phone calls to Allen?"

"What about them? How else was I going to get through? She wouldn't even talk to me."

"Where were you three nights ago?"

"Working."

"Where were you Wednesday morning?"

"Working." Eric sat up straight, clearly frustrated, but angry, too. "I'm always working. That's what I do. I work. I had a *right* to be there. I wanted to see for myself who she was. I wanted to know what went on, okay? Why she gave me up. She figured I wanted something from her. Money." His face twisted in disgust. "I didn't want her *money*. She wouldn't even give me the time of day. She's a bitch!"

Tanaka and I looked at each other.

Inside the next room Marcus said, "So, you decided to do something about it? Make a point?"

Eric stared at the letter in the bag. "I never mailed that. I wanted to *talk* to her. I sent flowers *once*. She never even said she liked them. After that bookstore, I was done chasing her. She's not worth it."

Marcus slid photos across the table. I had a good idea what the photos were of and waited to see how Eric would react.

"Linda Sewell and Philip Hewitt. They worked for your mother, if I can use the term. Know anything about them?"

Eric glanced at the crime-scene photos of their bodies and flinched. "Hey, hey, man. I got nothing to do with any of that. I never even saw those people before."

"You sure about that? It'd be a good way to get back at her, wouldn't it?"

"What? No!" Eric began to sweat, his eyes landing on the door, which was locked, penning him in. "She's trying to set me up. All of you are. I told you, I wanted to see her, talk. They came at me. I defended myself. It was self-defense. I didn't even stab that cop. We were struggling, and he was just there. I didn't do it."

Marcus stood. "I'm on your side here, Eric. Trying to help you."

Eric snorted derisively. "Bullshit. Since when does a cop help anybody out? You're not sticking me with this. I didn't kill anybody. It was self-defense. I want a lawyer."

Marcus didn't move.

Eric said the word again, firmer this time, determined. "Lawyer. Lawyer! Lawyer! Lawyer! Lawyer!" He punctuated each word by banging his fists on the table.

Game over. Marcus picked up his evidence and left the room empty handed.

Tanaka moved for the door. "Guess I won't be going home tonight."

I watched Eric, every line on his face, his body language. It didn't look like he had it in him to walk up to complete strangers and blow their heads off. That took a special kind of defect, a special kind of sick. One letter found, but not like the ones Allen had been receiving. No flowers missing from the shop he worked at, except for the ones he had bought himself. And he had no obvious connection to Hewitt or Sewell, and none really to Allen, except for the DNA.

"It'll hinge on his alibi," I muttered, more to myself than to Tanaka.

She stood at the door. "Yeah, that's next."

I turned to her. "I have a feeling it's going to check out. He's good for the bookstore, but I don't think he's good for Hewitt or Sewell, and not for the others. Those feel personal."

Tanaka groaned. She had a tough job ahead of her and knew it.

"Heard about you and Farraday," she said. "Wow, huh?"

I turned to stare at Eric through the glass, trying to get a sense of him. I didn't want to talk about Jim Farraday not one more time.

Tanaka wisely took the hint and headed for the door. "You know, I didn't ask about you not wearing shoes. I wasn't sure I wanted to know. Now I feel I have to."

Eric, still at the table, scrubbed his hands across his face. He was scared.

"I stepped in something in that field. Maybe dead cat," I answered absently.

It had been some kind of viscous goop matted with fur that had slimed the bottom of my shoes. Could have been rat instead of cat. I hadn't wanted to look too closely. I had dumped the shoes in a trash can before I got back in my car. I had spare shoes at my office and shoes at home, but I wasn't at either place. I stood in my sweat socks. I'd have to toss them, too, when I got home.

Tanaka shuddered.

"It could have been anything, really. Raccoon, squirrel, dog," I added.

She backed out of the room, looking a little green.

I smiled. *Score.*

Carole and Mrs. Mickerson were in the ICU waiting room with the rest of the family when I showed up later to tell them the news. Everyone looked like they'd just marched to war and back on half rations; but when they found out Eric was in custody, they revived, clapping, cheering, slapping me on the back; but that wasn't the only thing to celebrate. They'd just gotten news that Ben was improving. It felt like Christmas and the Fourth of July all rolled into one, and the knot of dread that had planted itself in the pit of my stomach for days was suddenly gone. We'd reached the light at the end of the tunnel.

When I ducked in to see him later, I was taken aback by how small he appeared in the bed, not like himself at all. But he was going to be all right. He was coming back. I took the night shift so the family could get some rest and fell asleep in a chair by his bed. It was the easiest sleep I'd had in days.

Chapter 29

All along the winding path, the tree leaves fluttered in the evening breeze, casting eerie shadows along the stone walkway, the thick bushes and bramble hidden by dusk. No fear, just un-filled space, quiet, unseen.

Someone should have called in that broken sewer grate months ago. It teetered underfoot. A slow walk up the path to the stone steps, around the memorial fountain and back, that was the route. The blue light on the emergency phone was reassuring.

A quick rattle of things dropped into big pockets, one heav-ier than the other. Full stop. A moment to listen to the night. Was that movement in the bushes? Nothing in the end.

The gun barrel gleamed blue-silver in the lamplight. When the shot punched through the night, there was a flinch, a des-perate stagger. Pain came next, then blood. It spread fast; the belly burned. The phone. The blue light.

"I've been shot." The whisper could barely be heard, over each labored breath. "Huddleston Park. By the fountain. Hurry!"

Just shy of the grate, the legs gave way and vision blurred. A shaky grope, eyes shut, ears straining for the sound of salvation. Heartbeats sped, then slowed. Then the night took over.

I woke to find him watching me. At first, I thought I might be dreaming, but it was real. Ben was awake. I shot up from the chair, raced to the bed rail. I fumbled with the call button to summon a nurse, and a voice piped in from the nurses' station.

"He's awake." I only half believed it. I placed a hand on his arm to see if he was warm. He was. "Welcome back."

"You believe this shit?" His voice was hoarse, low, and he seemed a little out of it still, but there was that familiar glint in his eye, the one I'd missed and feared I might never see again.

"Which part?"

His eyes traveled around the room, as though he was trying to get his bearings. The nurse rushed in, checked him out, rang for the doctor. The machines beeped steadily. Ben was still hooked up to them, but they'd done their job. He was awake, alert, back.

"Hey," he whispered, so the nurse wouldn't hear. "Where's my sandwich?"

I laughed. I couldn't help it. I stepped away from the bed when the doctor and another nurse came in. They asked Ben questions, checked him out some more. The sun wasn't up yet, but it felt sunny all the same. I dialed Carole's number to give her the news. She cried on the phone. I did, too. It was going to be a good day.

All the Mickersons crowded around Ben's bed to watch him sit up and pick at his soft breakfast. The look on his face told me he didn't like this meal tray any more than he'd like the last one, but there was nothing he could do about it.

"Eat all of it, Benny," his mother ordered. "You've got to get your strength back."

I stood in the background, leaning against the wall, my arms folded across my chest, tickled to death at all the motherly clucking. "That's right, *Benny*. Eat all of it."

He shot me a look, then smiled. "Shut it, smart-ass."

My cell phone rang. Tanaka. I stepped out into the hall. "Yeah?"

"Chandler was shot last night. She's alive. Luckily."

I turned my back to Ben's room so they wouldn't hear, then lowered my voice. "What the hell?"

"She was walking in Huddleston Park. Don't ask me why."

"Rogers?"

"We still have him."

"Then we're back to where we started. I knew he wasn't good for the murders."

"Doesn't look like it. She's in the same hospital as Mickerson, room eleven-oh-six. How fast can you get here?"

"I'm three floors above you. I'm coming down now."

I ended the call, stuck my head into Ben's room. He was in good hands. "I'll be back."

Tanaka stood outside Chandler's room; Marcus was on his cell phone halfway down the hall, his back to us.

"What happened?"

"Walking in the park, like I said, around nine last night. She thinks she heard something in the bushes, and the next thing she knows, she's down."

"Did she get a description?"

Tanaka shook her head. "She says she might have gotten a glimpse as he ran away. Says it could have been the guy from the bookstore."

Our eyes held. "Which is impossible," I said.

"Could be the shock. Things get mixed up. Either that or we took a wrong turn somewhere. Anyway, the bullet's out. It didn't do any major damage, they say."

We watched as Marcus walked toward us. Tanaka sighed, turned her back. I did, too.

"Did you get anything else from Eric?" I asked.

"Not after his public defender showed up. And it looks like

he was telling the truth about his whereabouts for Hewitt and Sewell. He's accounted for." She lowered her voice. "Jones is working overtime to punch holes in it, but he won't. I think we're missing a crucial piece of the puzzle here."

Marcus walked up, looked right through me. "You're not going in there. You've loused this thing up enough, you and Mickerson." He scowled at Tanaka. "And you're going to need to choose which side you're on or get yourself a new partner."

Tanaka returned his stare. "I know what side I'm on, Jones. And I'm way ahead of you. The paperwork's already in."

He made a face, then disappeared inside Chandler's room. Tanaka took a moment and then followed. I stayed in the hall. After I'd paced for some time, Chandler's door suddenly swung open, and Marcus stormed out and headed for the elevator without so much as a glance my way. Tanaka stuck her head out and motioned me in.

"What happened?" I asked.

"Tell you later."

Chandler lay pale in the bed, bandages bulky underneath her hospital gown. She asked for water, and Tanaka poured her a cup of it from a mustard-colored pitcher on her tray table. Chandler sipped just a little, then put the cup down.

"You were right," she said. "If I'd gone to the police at the very start . . . none of this would have . . ." Her voice trailed away, hoarse, groggy.

"You said you might have gotten a look," Tanaka said.

"Maybe I just thought I did."

I moved closer. "Maybe you smelled something—cigarette smoke, aftershave, perfume?"

Chandler thought for a moment. "Nothing. I was walking, and then I felt such a pain in my side. And the blood. I called for help. That's all I remember. He could have killed me." Her eyes searched ours as the reality of her situation began to set in. "Why can't you catch him?"

It couldn't have been Eric. Who else? "Do you always walk that park late at night?"

She nodded. "It helps me sleep. I barely made it to the phone. I don't remember anything else."

Hewitt and Sewell had both been killed by a single shot to the head at point-blank range. Why was Chandler still alive? I looked over at Tanaka. I could tell she was thinking the same thing.

Chandler closed her eyes. "I'm tired. So tired."

Tanaka and I walked out into the hall. Last night this whole thing had been on its way to being wrapped up, maybe. Today it was wide open again.

"You didn't tell her it couldn't have been Rogers?"

"Intentionally. I wanted to hear what she had to say."

"And?"

Tanaka glanced at Chandler's door. "I got nothing."

"What happened with Marcus storming out?"

Tanaka buttoned her jacket on our way toward the elevator. "He went in heavy handed, determined to get something out of her. He wants to solve this thing before you do, like it's a race. He's obsessed with showing you up. We had words. He took offense."

I punched the DOWN button and the UP button. Tanaka was going out; I was going back up to Ben's room. "Who cares who gets there first?"

"Well, one of us better get there first. Bodies are starting to pile up."

Chapter 30

A couple of days went by, and Ben recovered well enough to begin making a pest of himself at the hospital. I brought him his sandwich, extra peppers, and he devoured it like a caveman downing a Flintstones brontosaurus burger. While he slept, I popped into Chandler's room again. I'd done my job: I'd found Eric. But I couldn't stop turning things over in my head—the Peetses, Dontell, the missing letter, the fact that Chandler was alive and the others weren't.

There was an IV going and the blinds were drawn when I stepped lightly into her room. A huge floral arrangement sat on the table near the window, its wild, arched fronds sticking out everywhere. The room smelled like a tropical rain forest. I had a good idea who the flowers were from. Chandler was asleep. I was backing out to leave when she opened her eyes.

"Detective Raines?"

I approached. "I didn't mean to disturb you. How do you feel?"

"Lucky."

I glanced at the frond monster. "Someone went all out."

"Vonda. She's been so nice." She caught the look on my face. "She has her good side."

I doubted it, but okay. "Have you been able to remember anything else?"

"The police keep asking me that, too, but no."

I glanced at Allen's flowers and wondered about the ones she'd received. "The flowers Allen got. Do you remember what kind they were?"

Chandler concentrated, fighting against the medication. "I think so . . . The first was a beautiful lotus. Vonda barely looked at it."

"How about the next one?"

"I can't remember."

"That's okay. Get some rest. We'll talk again."

She faded. Her eyes closed. I let myself out, only to turn and see Allen sweeping off the elevator into a crowd of hospital staff clamoring for her autograph. I could not catch a break.

Norman wasn't with her this time, but there was another Titan Security guy standing close who was almost as big. Allen's fake smile disappeared the moment she saw me. She headed my way, and I stood waiting for her.

"What are you doing here?" She asked.

"Visiting. You don't strike me as the stand-by-the-bedside type."

"Kaye is a valued employee."

"Yes. I saw the flowers. Couldn't find anything bigger?"

She said nothing, but her eyes were communicating loads.

"Maybe when you're done *visiting* Chandler, you'll have time to *visit* your son in police custody. He's going to be hard to sweep under the rug, isn't he?"

The look Allen shot me was as cold as death. She leaned forward, just slightly, and lowered her voice to a chilling whisper. "You're beginning to be a problem for me."

"I know, and I'm beginning to worry about your problem-solving skills."

"I'm going in to see Kaye. Go away."

She brushed past me and entered Chandler's room, her guard going with her. I started to walk away, then got a feeling. Allen didn't like problems. I went back into Chandler's room to make sure she'd still be breathing when Allen left it.

"A lotus? Nice." Ben was eating orange Jell-O out of a plastic cup with a plastic spoon too small for his man hands. He was out of the ICU and in a private room and was sitting up in a chair, in a gown, robe, and those saggy hospital socks with nonskid soles. I sat beside him, watching him eat.

"What's so big about a lotus?"

"I was just thinking about the symbolism."

I looked at him blankly.

"Flowers have meaning. They're symbolic."

Again, a blank stare from me.

"Red roses mean deep, romantic love, right? White roses can mean death. Am I speaking Portuguese?"

We were back to the easy back-and-forth between us. I hadn't brought up what Carole said about him having feelings for me, and if he was aware of her sharing the information, he wasn't letting on. That was good. It meant maybe we could slide right by all of it.

"That's interesting," I said. "So, you're the closet gardener. What's a lotus flower mean?"

He slurped down more Jell-O, swallowed. "It symbolizes estrangement, somebody forgetful of the past."

"So, somebody thinks Allen forgot something that meant a lot to whoever?"

"Or they just like lotus flowers and went with that," Ben said.

"Now, that makes me want to know what the other flowers were. If they mean something, too, that might tell us who sent them. Like maybe Deton Peets. Allen sure forgot about him and his son pretty quickly. Dontell Adkins, too. And you could say Allen was estranged from both Hewitt and Sewell. I don't think she's gotten another delivery since either of them was killed."

"Could be something." Ben finished his Jell-O and three-pointed the empty container into the wastebasket by his bed. He grinned, winked. "Mickerson is back, baby."

I stood to leave. I wanted to touch base with Tanaka.

"Estrangement's not so bad. Could have been a lot worse," Ben said. "It could have been crimson roses."

"What's so bad about crimson roses?" I asked, almost certain I didn't want to know.

"Well, they sure as hell don't mean I love ya," Ben said.

Chapter 31

I walked into Huddleston Park around nine that night, the approximate time that Chandler had taken her fateful stroll. I wanted to see what the park looked like at that hour, get a feel for it. This was Lincoln Park, so condos, bars, and upscale restaurants hemmed the park in on all sides, and there was a lot of open space with playlots, sports fields, and tennis courts set out around the perimeter. I found the pedestrian path and followed it in, a thick canopy of trees mottling the light from the streetlamps. I couldn't see any woman walking alone along this path at night even in this neighborhood, which was known to be safer. Why had Chandler?

I stopped at the head of the path, scanned the empty park, not seeing a soul in it. I turned and looked behind me, toward the bright lights of the street—lots of people out and about on bikes, walking, strolling. Wouldn't someone have heard a gunshot or a scream?

I plucked a small flashlight out of my pocket and walked on, listening, alert, armed. The path forked at a big memorial fountain with water spouting out of the trunks of iron elephants, and a few feet from that, I saw the emergency phone Chandler must have used. I lifted the receiver, got a dial tone, hung up.

They'd cleared away the crime-scene tape, but Tanaka had explained the scene clearly enough to me. Chandler had been found just inches from a broken sewer grate. I trained my flash on the path, swept it right and left till I found the grate. It was rusted, had a gap on one side, where the metal had worn away and fallen off. I toed the grate. It wobbled.

I squatted down and trained the light into the hole but couldn't make out much of anything in the murk, though I could faintly hear water dripping and could smell the stench of stagnation and rot. Overhead the leaves on the trees rustled. So, he came up behind her, shot her, and ran? I stared at the phone again, then at the grate. Maybe a few hundred feet to the left lay a softball field, its lights blazing, but none of that shine made it to this spot.

Why here? I looked around. No cameras. I pulled at the grate to see if I could lift it or slide it, but it was too heavy. I stuck my hand through the opening, flexed my fingers, pulled my hand out clean.

I heard footsteps and shot to my feet, whirled to find Marcus standing on the path yards from me, his hands in the pockets of a dark trench coat, his expression unreadable. I backed up. Neither one of us said anything for a time.

"I knew you'd need to see it," he said finally.

I kept my eyes on him but worried about the rest of the path, the parts I couldn't watch. I worried about who else might be on it and what they planned on doing. I worried that someone might be Farraday, back for more, this time with help. An ambush. I hadn't told anyone where I was going tonight. My mistake. If I went missing from this park and my body ended up in some landfill, no one who loved me would even know where to start looking.

"What are you doing, Marcus?"

"Following up. It's still my case. You and Tanaka seem to have forgotten that." He took a step forward.

"Marcus." It was a warning.

I hadn't meant it to come out so harsh, but he was the last person I wanted to see in a dark park at nine at night. I scanned the bushes, looking for Farraday. Marcus slid his hands out of his pockets, then displayed them so I'd see he had nothing in them. It was no comfort at all. I held my breath, braced.

"I'm a cop, not some street thug after your purse."

I didn't answer. I checked the fountain to see if anyone was hiding behind it. "Is Farraday with you?"

"No reason he would be. I figure he's halfway to the nearest rehab by now. He's dead in the water."

"That leaves you hanging," I said.

"Not as much as you'd think. He wasn't my only connection. I can always make a deal. We never did walk in lockstep."

"Seriously?" I would have laughed if I hadn't been 100 percent worried about walking out of this park alive. "Did you know he was following me? That he'd meant to come after me?"

He didn't answer right away, which made me wonder about his hesitation. "No."

"I don't believe you."

He moved forward again, one step.

I shook my head. "Marcus, I swear to God."

"I'm a cop."

"So you keep saying."

"What happened to our spirit of cooperation?"

"That's Tanaka and me. You? Back it up."

He took a step back, smiled, calm as anything. That was the creepy part. "We found a gun down that hole, a Glock seventeen. Could be the one used on Chandler." He glanced at the grate. "Also found a muddy glove."

I didn't look. I knew where the grate was. I was standing just inches from it.

"Chandler was found right where you're standing," he said. "Why do you think he ditched it?"

"Good question. Why don't you head on out and check on that?"

"Guess I'd better. I wouldn't want to be 'set straight' like Farraday was."

"What's that supposed to mean?"

Another pause. "Your guy paid him a visit, had a little talk about the incident at your office. I heard it got intense. Me? I've got no beef with him, unless he takes exception to this little meet after the fact."

Eli and Farraday? "When was this?"

"Yesterday." The cocky look on his face made my blood boil. "I guess chivalry isn't dead. Funny, though, I didn't think you went in for that sort of thing, but I guess people change."

I glared at him. "Some don't."

He looked around, then back at me. "Have a good night."

He walked off down the path. I didn't follow him. Instead, I waited until he was out of sight, and then darted off across the softball field, staying under the lights, out in the open. I ran all the way back to my car, my legs shaking.

Chapter 32

The air was still as I sat out on my back porch, in my grandfather's wicker rocker, one of my favorite spots. The chair was old, way past its prime, but I remembered being rocked in it when I was a kid and being read to while sitting in my grandfather's lap. I'd repaired the rocker at least twenty times since he'd sat in it last, but it was still good. It felt like a safe place.

I ran my hands along the rests, worn smooth over time, thinking about the park and about landfills and about Eli riding in on a white horse to put a good scare into Farraday. I kept up a slow, steady rock, my eyes closed, wondering about the grate and the gun and the glove and why Marcus had told me about them.

My doorbell rang. I had a good idea who it was. I got up and went inside. I stood, my finger hovering over the intercom button without pressing it, longer than I would have before the park. Then I punched it.

"Yeah?"

"It's me."

I buzzed him up, then walked back to the kitchen. The front

door opened, and he walked back to join me, his tie loosened, his cuffs rolled up.

"I tried calling."

"I was outside, getting some air." I stared at him, wondering what he saw when he looked at me, and how far afield that image was from how I saw myself.

"You okay?"

Maybe it was me who was looking at things from a crooked perspective, causing friction where there didn't have to be any. Maybe I was too independent? Too self-contained? I didn't lean or cling or hang on too long. When you'd lost as much as I had, when almost everyone you counted on had been taken away, you found your feet, you moved under your own steam, distrusting everything else, or you flamed out. I hadn't flamed out yet.

I'd handled my run-in with Farraday. That should have been where it ended. I wasn't angry, not really, just sure of where the line should be, a little worried that Eli had gotten me wrong and wasn't seeing me.

"You went to see Farraday." It was not a question.

He unbuttoned his collar, understanding slowly dawning. "That's it." He leaned back against the counter. "I did."

"Were you going to tell me?"

"Hadn't planned on it. It was between him and me."

I waited for him to say more, but he seemed content to leave it there. "Yeah, I'm going to need more than that."

He pushed himself off the counter, stood close to me. "This doesn't have to get heavy, does it?"

"That depends on what you say next."

"It wasn't about me riding in, okay? He crossed a line. He messed with someone who matters to me. He didn't know that. Now he does."

"Sounds like riding in to me. I had it covered. It was over, done. I know because I finished it. That should have been enough."

He stared at me, intensity in the look. "Look, I told him that if he came at you again, if I or you saw him anywhere close *ever*, I was going to rip his arms off and shove them down his throat. I didn't do it, because you couldn't. I didn't do it to stake a claim. It was him and me coming to an understanding."

The kitchen clock marked the time, the steady brush of the second hand uncharacteristically loud, as we stood watching each other, at a kind of crossroads.

"I didn't ask for your help," I said. "I didn't need it. Man to man doesn't work for me, Eli."

He took a step back, his eyes never leaving mine. "Are we heading in a certain direction?"

"What?" I'd been thinking things through, weighing what I was willing to throw away and what I'd fight to keep.

"You and me. Are we heading in a certain direction?"

I had envisioned this discussion going another way. I was on firm ground, in the right. He'd overstepped. Not maliciously, but he'd done it. And I wasn't okay with it. "I have no idea what you mean."

"You and me," he said. "We get along? Fit nicely together?"

"I thought we did. But that's got nothing to do with . . ."

He stopped me mid-sentence. "Farraday needed a reality check. He got it. First from you, then from me. He needed to know how far I was willing to take things. I let him know straight up."

"I fight my own battles, Eli, always have."

"I know. I've seen you do it. Like I said, I didn't do it because you couldn't." He searched my face, blew out a breath. "But we're still going to talk about this, aren't we?"

I pulled out a kitchen stool, then one for him. I was beat and would have preferred another kind of end to the day, but here we were. This was important, and it wasn't so much about Farraday as it was about me. I wanted Eli to get it before we went another step forward. We sat facing each other, our knees touching, and I told him who I was.

Chapter 33

The next morning, I sat in the kitchen with my laptop, sipping a cup of tea, wondering, not for the first time, about Kaye Chandler and her relationship with Allen. Where'd she come from? She'd mentioned working with Allen at a PR firm before they branched off together to steal the magazine idea from the Peetses. Curious, I had Googled Allen and tapped into the longest bio sheet I'd ever seen. The PR firm, the Halliwell Agency, was mentioned. Had they met there, or somewhere else?

I couldn't find much on Chandler through usual channels. She didn't have an arrest record, she didn't owe the IRS, and she hadn't been foreclosed on or had her car repossessed. By all accounts, she was leading an exemplary life, but all accounts could be deceiving. Nobody skipped through life without picking up a little dirt somewhere. I closed down my laptop, got showered, dressed, and out of the house, bent on finding it. I'd start with Halliwell and work my way back till something started to stink.

The agency was a small firm with, by all accounts, a sterling reputation, started by a husband-and-wife team, Margaret and

Ronald Halliwell, but Ronald was now deceased. I called first and spoke to Margaret personally, explaining what I was looking for. She had heard about the murders and about Chandler's attack and agreed to meet with me, but not in her office, in her home, which was one floor up, in a boutique setup on East Chestnut in the Gold Coast. Separate entrance, she told me, more discreet, away from prying eyes and wagging tongues.

I got there in half an hour, parked, and rang the bell at a red door. The entrance to the agency was around the corner. I eyed the building, wondering if Halliwell owned all of it, knowing that if she did, she'd shelled out millions. The door opened, and a well-dressed black woman in her early sixties, I'd estimate, was standing there. I recognized Margaret Halliwell from the photos I'd found on her agency's website. We exchanged pleasantries; then she saw me in and led me into a swanky living room with east-facing windows overlooking the Ferris wheel at Navy Pier.

"May I get you anything? Coffee?"

"I'm fine. Thanks."

"Sit, please." She offered the sofa, then sat across from me in a wing chair. "I can't imagine what use I can be to you, really, as I explained on the phone. I haven't seen Vonda or Kaye in years."

"I know. I'm interested in their background. Anything about their time with the agency. What you can tell me about their friendship."

"You think they may be involved in what's happened, don't you?"

"That doesn't surprise you?"

She watched me. "It doesn't, no."

Halliwell stood, walked over to a side table where a coffeepot, cups, and saucers were set up. She poured herself a cup and came back and sat down again. "Vonda would drop little things about herself, college, places she'd been, jobs she'd had. Kaye never revealed anything. We hired Vonda first. She was phenomenal, so great with the clients. She'd worked with another firm before us and came highly recommended. A few months after she joined us, we had a position open, and she recommended Kaye, quite highly, as I recall. We hired her, too."

She put down her cup, smoothed her skirt. "They weren't friends in the usual sense, I don't think, but still they were strangely bonded. Vonda was consumed with herself—always just so, always wanting the best. Kaye was the list maker, the priority setter. She had the ideas. Together, they made a good team. Apart, well, Vonda seemed to stall, and Kaye all but melted into the wallpaper."

"So, they knew each other before Chandler was hired."

"Yes, for how long, I have no idea. I do know we were sorry to lose them to Senator Devin."

"Senator Devin? How'd that happen?"

"We didn't know it, but Vonda began seeing him, though he was married at the time. They tried to keep it low key, or at least I think *he* did, but when you're that high profile . . . Anyway, after a few months, she resigned."

"And Chandler?"

"Vonda never told Kaye she was leaving. Kaye seemed genuinely surprised by the news. She became sullen, quiet. It was like a lightbulb had burned out. Then, not long after, she resigned, too. We discovered later that she'd gone to work as Vonda's personal assistant, of all things. We heard rumors that Kaye and Devin weren't getting along, but I could see why they wouldn't. Kaye always stayed very close to Vonda, and no man likes a third wheel.

"The senator had a daughter, but I don't think either Vonda or Kaye got along with her. She was very close to her father. Vonda wouldn't have liked that. She needs to be the center of everyone's attention, and, of course, Kaye doesn't like whatever Vonda doesn't like."

"Sounds . . . unhealthy."

Halliwell smiled. "I agree. The two of them are like a puppeteer and her puppet. One pulls the strings, and the other dances, each dependent on the other."

"So, if Chandler got tired of dancing at the end of Allen's strings . . ."

Her eyes widened. "Kaye? Oh, no. You've got it the wrong way around. It's Kaye holding the strings, not Vonda. Vonda's a star, shrewd in many ways, but it's Kaye who has the vision and the drive. Vonda couldn't make a move without her."

Chandler in charge, not Allen? That couldn't be right. What about the way Allen ordered Chandler around, dismissed her? "You're sure?"

Halliwell nodded. "Very sure."

You wouldn't happen to have Chandler's résumé or old contact information, would you?"

She rose. "Wait. I keep business files here, in the office and off-site. Redundancies. I just may have a copy."

She walked out of the room, and I waited impatiently, checking my watch, glancing out the window at the wheel. I had a feeling something was about to shake loose. I nearly pounced on Halliwell when she came back, a file in her hands.

"Here it is," she said.

"You kept it all this time?"

"I keep all personnel files. We're a small firm. I see no reason to do away with them." She handed the file to me and sat back down.

I tore into it, hoping I'd reached a turning point in this whole mess. She was Kaytina Chandler, shortened to Kaye. High school, community college, whatever. Work experience, not much. Office assistant at a Realtor's, manager at a local department store. I looked up. "What position was she hired to fill?"

"Executive assistant," Halliwell said. "She was the best we ever had. She eventually moved up to handle her own accounts. Managed them wonderfully, working closely with Vonda."

"There are no references here."

"We had Vonda's word she was just the person we needed. She was right."

Hold on. I read the address she'd listed, then smiled. "Her address. It's the old Robert Taylor Homes."

"That's important?"

"That's where Allen grew up." I stood, smiling. I held up the résumé. "You wouldn't happen to have a copier around, would you?" I called Tanaka from the car to fill her in and to find out if she'd learned anything about that gun found in the park.

"You've forgotten how long this takes, right?"

I hadn't, but one could hope. "They came from the same place, knew each other, well enough for Allen to vouch for her at Halliwell's, long enough for them to be the keeper of each other's secrets. I need to talk to Senator Devin's daughter. An address might help."

There was silence on Tanaka's end. In my opinion, it went on far too long. "Fine," she said finally, "but remember, *cooperation.*"

"How could I forget?"

I hung up, started the car, and pulled into traffic. By the time I hit the first light, Tanaka had texted me an address, and I was seriously starting to wonder about Senator Devin's heart attack.

Chapter 34

Sabrina Devin taught nine-year-olds in a public school on the Southeast Side. It was another couple of weeks before the start of the fall term, but it looked like the school was open and running some kind of summer event in the playground. Kids were clustered around a tall white guy directing a lively word game involving letter tiles laid out on a giant game board on the ground. The kids appeared completely enthralled by the game play, laughing, cheering, working the tiles. It was still technically summer, but no one looked like they minded throwing in a little learning early.

I'd found a photo of Sabrina Devin by Googling, so I recognized her standing off to the side, watching the kids play. She was heavily pregnant, at least six or seven months, and she looked hot and uncomfortable in a sleeveless maternity dress, her long, curly hair pulled back into a ponytail. I walked up to her and introduced myself, told her what I needed, watching as her friendly smile disappeared and the walls went up.

"Fun game," I said, hoping to get her back.

She glanced over at the kids. "They love it. They don't even care they're learning."

"Mind if we talk inside?"

Reluctantly, she signaled to another teacher to watch the kids, and then led me inside. We walked up two flights in silence, slowly for Devin's benefit, and into an empty classroom that smelled of fresh paint, chalk, and disinfectant. Devin took a seat at the desk at the head of the room and pulled a lunch bag out of the drawer.

"You don't mind if I eat while we talk?"

I didn't and told her so. There was a full-size chair next to the desk. I sat there, thankful I didn't have to try to squeeze into one of the tiny kid chairs lined up in rows behind me. While she got herself situated food-wise, I looked around at all the clean metal desks with pressed-wood tops and the empty cubbyholes, which in just a few weeks would be crammed with backpacks, sweaters, and superhero lunch boxes.

Devin unwrapped her lunch. "I would offer you some of my sandwich, but it's a little unusual—ham, cheese, sweet pickles, mustard, and chunky peanut butter."

I made a face. Couldn't help it.

Devin chuckled. "That's what I thought. Second trimester. It's weird what I'll eat these days . . . and at what hour. So, what's she done now?"

I wasn't sure if she was referring to Allen or Chandler. "And by *she*, you mean . . . ?"

"Vonda. She obviously crossed someone."

"Any idea who?"

She shrugged. "Haven't seen her since my father died. It could be anyone, really. She's not a very nice person."

"Not close, then?"

"She had an affair with my father while he was still married to my mother, so, no, we weren't close. When the divorce went through, things quieted down, but then he died."

"A heart attack," I said.

"No one saw it coming. He was healthy, or so we thought. You're never ready to lose a parent. At least, I wasn't."

"It's your impression of Allen that I'm trying to get a sense of."

She bit into her sandwich, thought about it. "She's cold, distant, cruel. Self-absorbed . . . polar opposite of my father. I don't know what drew them together, except that I think she really wanted to be a senator's wife. He died before she could pull that off. Up until then, they both seemed to be getting what they wanted. My father got a trophy on his arm. Vonda got a free pass into a very exclusive club—celebrities, politicians, power brokers. They photographed well. They were both very vain."

"And after he died?"

"Vonda got a lot of mileage out of their relationship, which by then was no big secret. She started *Strive* with connections he had helped her cultivate. The rest, I don't know about. There was no reason for me to pay attention to her after that. The last time I laid eyes on her was at my father's funeral. She cried more than I did, but believe me, it wasn't genuine."

"What about Kaye Chandler?"

Devin hesitated, fiddled with her sandwich. "Yes . . . very efficient."

"Devoted," I said, watching her closely, noting the change in her body language, but Devin wouldn't look at me. "You don't want to talk about Chandler. Why?"

"You wanted to know about Vonda."

"I'm quickly learning you can't discuss one without including the other. She seems oddly devoted and hangs on Allen's every word. But I found out just today, surprisingly, that it's Chandler who drives the bus. I'd like to know what you think. Is she stable? Prone to lies? Capable of violence?"

Devin put her sandwich down, wiped her hands on a paper napkin, glanced down at her stomach. "I didn't know her that well. I can't say."

"I think you can say but won't."

She looked up at me. "She is prone to lies, and she's more than capable of violence. I don't think she's completely stable. I'd rather you didn't tell her I said so."

I sat back. "Okay then."

Devin exhaled, placed a gentle hand on her middle. "In a crowded room, you wouldn't even notice her. Chandler. She's like a lamp, a coffee table, and who notices a lamp? But come too close to Vonda, and she'll sure notice you. For a while, when all those deaths began to happen, I thought maybe Chandler . . . but when I read in the paper that she was shot, too . . ."

"What'd you think?"

"It sounds crazy. It *is* crazy. My senior year of college, during school break, I came home with a new puppy, Mimi. At my father's place, Vonda had all but moved in, and of course Chandler was always with her. This time, they were all working on a speech my father was to give to some women's group somewhere. Vonda didn't like dogs. She wasn't allergic to them or anything. She just didn't like them, so I tried to keep Mimi away from her. Somehow, she got to the speech, chewed it to pieces. There was no backup, apparently. To this day, I don't know how she got into the study."

I smiled. She couldn't be serious. "So, Chandler killed your dog?"

"Yes."

I looked for signs that she might be putting me on, but she wasn't joking.

"I found Mimi on her bed, under a blanket. Her neck had been broken. I don't have any proof that she did it, but I know she did. Vonda didn't like the puppy. Vonda was furious with the puppy. Chandler got rid of the puppy. I never stayed at my father's house again."

"Ms. Devin—"

She interrupted me. "I know it sounds crazy, but after, when

I was cleaning up, I found Mimi's food and collar in the kitchen trash bin. The things had been thrown away *before* I found her. Chandler knew I wouldn't be needing any of that stuff anymore, so she just tossed it away, but she left Mimi for me to find. How sick is that?"

Chapter 35

I had my hand on the car door, wondering about Chandler. Margaret Halliwell and Sabrina Devin had painted quite a different picture of the dutiful fixer who stood behind Allen, taking orders, handling the details, while "the boss" worked the room. What if she was actually running the show, the one holding the strings? She was as close to Allen as anyone. She knew everything that went on in the office. She knew the Peetses and Dontell Adkins. Had she known Allen's mother, too? She must have. Allen didn't like problems. Chandler was her problem solver. Was it that simple? I needed to know what Tanaka had turned up on that gun from the park. Maybe it held the key to this whole thing. I sensed someone behind me and turned to find a man and a woman in dark suits standing too close.

"Cassandra Raines?" the man said. He was white, stocky, solidly built. I stared at him, then at the white, stocky, solidly built white woman standing next to him. They both wore sunglasses, *Men in Black*–style.

I slid a glance toward the playground. Empty now. Minutes

ago, it had been swarming with happy kids tossing letter tiles around, and now, when I might need a witness, zilch.

"Absolutely not." Cocky right to the end, that was me. They'd likely allude to my cockiness on my tombstone. HERE LIES WISEASS. SHE SHOULD HAVE SHUT UP, BUT SHE JUST DIDN'T HAVE IT IN HER. RIP.

"That's her car you were about to get into," he said.

I noted the use of the past tense, a little worried about what that might be leading to. "Borrowed it. Mine's in the shop."

The stocky twins smiled.

"Relax," she said. "Ms. Allen would like to see you."

These jokers were Titan Security hacks? I exhaled. I'd been accosted on the street before, and none of those encounters had been pleasant, but knowing this one was some of Allen's diva mess, and not the start of a one-way trip to Dead Town, put my startled mind at ease. Then it pissed me off.

I looked up and down the street, and my eyes landed finally on the black SUV parked two cars down from mine. "Were you two following me?"

Neither answered, which meant yes.

"And for how long?"

"Ms. Allen doesn't have all day," Mr. Stocky said. "Mind coming with us?"

"Very much," I said. "I'm working, and not at Allen's beck and call. If she wants to meet with me, she knows where to find my office, or she can call me herself, and I'll consider coming to her. This little . . . whatever this is . . . doesn't work for me. Now, if the two of you will excuse me?"

"This doesn't have to get ugly." Ms. Stocky said it with a tone. Like she had just stepped out of a Mafia movie and she was Al Pacino, if Al Pacino had sixty extra pounds, a bad perm, and hit five-nine in flats.

I looked up at her, my brows lifted, and I let go of the car door. "What *exactly* doesn't have to get ugly?"

He sighed. "Ms. Allen doesn't like waiting. Let's go."

I didn't move. They didn't, either.

"You deaf?" he muttered.

I glared at him, at his partner, then back at him. "I heard you. My answer's no." I said it as bold as you please, then stood there waiting for them to challenge me on it. "Do I really have to say the words 'buzz off'?"

The woman grinned. "You're getting in the car."

I pursed my lips, pretended to think it over. "Nope. I don't think I am."

"Yeah you are," he said.

I shook my head. "Um, nope, and I'm done talking to—"

That was as far as I got. Swift as anything, they grabbed me up off my feet and shifted me horizontally, one holding me at the chest and arms, the other at my knees and ankles, and hauled me along. For a second, it was almost like flying. I was in the backseat of the SUV before I knew it, and all I had seen during the brief—and it was surprisingly brief—lift and carry was snatches of black polyester blend and hands. Hadn't had time to yelp or cuss, not that it would have made a difference. Under different circumstances, I might have marveled at the speed of the grab. Not today. I was in the backseat of a strange car, bookended by two wannabe tough guys. Trapped. Squeezed. On my way to Allen's, like she'd ordered out for PI pizza and I had fifteen minutes to get there. There was a driver up front, not Elliott, but he acted like he didn't see me.

Mr. Stocky chuckled. "Told you."

"Unlawful restraint," I said. "The minute my feet left the sidewalk. Illinois Criminal Code, Article ten, section ten-three, 'A person commits the offense of unlawful restraint when he or she'—that's you two ninnies—'knowingly without legal authority detains—'"

Mr. Stocky shoved me into Ms. Stocky; Ms. Stocky shoved me back. "Can it," he said. "What are you worried about? It's a meeting. You got the round-trip ticket, so settle the fuck down."

Nobody talked as the SUV pulled away from the curb and drove away. There was no use fighting about it, so I sat back, folded my arms across my chest, and fumed.

"Exactly how long were you following me?" I hadn't noticed a tail, but frankly, I hadn't been looking for one. I had had business to take care of.

"Does it matter?" Ms. Stocky asked.

"I'll need it for the police report."

"Then just put down too damn long for you not to notice," she said. "What kind of private dick are you, anyway?"

I clenched my fists, closed my eyes, praying for calm. Allen had now officially worked my last nerve. She'd tried before and failed, but she'd finally gotten to the last one. I inhaled deep, exhaled deep, then settled in for the ride, which took about forty minutes in pre–rush-hour traffic. When we got to Allen's condo building and turned into the garage, everybody piled out, and I got pushed along toward the private elevator.

"The kidnapping charge kicked in the second we pulled away from the curb," I announced. The elevator doors opened, and we got on.

Ms. Stocky turned toward me. "Did anybody ever tell you, you were a pain in the ass?"

I gritted my teeth. "You bozos came looking for me." The doors closed. The elevator started up. "And, as you know, kidnapping's a federal offense. You do every day of federal time. You get twenty years, you *do* twenty years."

Neither said anything.

"And if somebody steals my car while I'm held up here, I'm holding you two idiots personally responsible."

They snickered.

I glared at them. "Yeah, keep it up."

The doors opened on Allen's place, and I was shoved off into her spectacular entryway. "I hear the federal penitentiary is lovely this time of year. You will remember me fondly when you're bumming smokes in the yard, won't you?"

Isabella stood there in her crisp uniform. She looked surprised to see me.

"Package delivered," Mr. Stocky told Isabella. "See ya, motormouth."

"You'll see me, all right. This isn't over."

They both chuckled, then Ms. Stocky said, "Yeah, it is."

It took a lot to rile me. It took even more for me to forget myself, but Allen's wild ride had propelled me dangerously close to my breaking point. Isabella gestured for me to follow her, and I tucked in behind her as we walked down the hall toward my meet with the great lady.

The hall was lined with all kinds of expensive doodads and artwork. Allen was such a pretentious woman. With every step, I fought the childish impulse to take my shoe off and hurl it at the most expensive-looking thing. I could feel heat rise under my collar, but I kept my eyes on Isabella's back, using it as my focal point, until we stopped at a door that was slightly ajar. Isabella turned, smiled, and then politely knocked, and Allen's voice called back.

"I'll let you know when I'm ready for her, Isabella. Have her wait in the great room."

I wasn't sure I'd heard right, so I asked, "What'd she say?"

Isabella looked like she didn't want to answer. I gave the door a death stare you wouldn't believe. If I'd had lasers for eyeballs, there would have been a burned hole in the middle of the door, outlined by a ring of desperate fire. I breathed. I bargained with Jesus. I then turned calmly to Isabella.

"Would you mind stepping back, Isabella?"

She gulped, her eyes wide, and then moved slowly away from the door. I squared my shoulders, counted to five, and then kicked Allen's door in.

Chapter 36

When the door banged back against the wall, Allen shot up from behind her desk, a desk, mind you, that was almost a carbon copy of the one in her magazine office. Her mouth hung open. I'd startled her, then angered her. She looked at me as though I were a marauder storming the walls of the citadel. "What do you think you're doing?"

I rushed toward her. She stopped talking and fell back into her chair. That was when Jesus came through and stopped me before I reached her. I pointed a warning finger at her. "Not another word." I was just a few arm lengths from her, a good safe distance. "One syllable. You so much as clear your throat . . ."

Her mouth clamped shut, but I could see she was livid. She squared her shoulders and tried to look unfazed, as though I hadn't scared her. I bobbed around in a tight circle, wound up, working off adrenaline. The nerve of the woman.

"Your suing me is bad enough, but this. *This* . . ." I took a step toward her but caught myself again. "Big mistake. *Big.*"

A small smile flickered across her face. How swiftly she transitioned from off guard to right back at it. She stood, realigned the diamond necklace around her neck, then glided calmly over to the couch and sat, as though she were entertaining a guest for tea. "You wanted to talk. I cleared the time. If you don't want to . . ."

I walked to her desk and picked up her phone. It was one of those frilly little gilded numbers that looked like it belonged in the home of a New Orleans madam.

"What are you doing?"

"Calling the police. Don't get up. They can cuff you from there."

"You think I'm afraid of being arrested?" She said it almost as if I'd amused her, like this was some kind of joke.

"Not the arrest," I said, dialing. "The perp walk. Think of what that's going to do to your brand."

Only a second or two went by. "What do you want?"

I kept dialing. "What I want would get me life in prison. Stop talking to me."

"Fine! I'll answer your questions." She spoke as if she had to force the words out of her mouth. "Sit." I glared at her. "*Please*, sit."

I put the phone down. She gestured to a chair across from where she sat, but instead, I took the seat behind her desk. I did it just to aggravate her, but it looked like it did more than that. I waited until I had her full attention.

"I want to know about Chandler," I said. "Who is she? *What* is she? What hold she has on you. I know you two came from the same projects. That's where you met her, isn't it?" I searched her face. "Why would she kill for you?"

"Kill for me? What are you talking about?" I took a moment, cycling through all I'd learned. "The letters, the flowers, the deaths. All close. All personal. Who's closer to you?"

"The police arrested Rogers. He's . . ."

I shook my head. "It's not him. He's accounted for, for Sewell and Hewitt, besides he had no reason to go after them. He had no idea who you were until a couple months ago, so the Peetses and Dontell are out, too." Allen began to shift in her seat, nervously. "And, of course, he couldn't have known your mother."

Allen looked as though I'd Tased her. "My mother? What's she got to do with this? No, you're trying to run some kind of game, but I'm not playing along. The police told me personally that he sent letters, flowers. Hell, he had a knife on him! He meant to kill me just like he killed them!"

"One letter, never mailed," I said calmly "One bouquet sent, one brought along with him. Nothing else. He says he just wanted to meet the woman who gave birth to him. And he couldn't have shot Chandler, because he was in custody by then. Think for a moment. You see the problem?"

She shot up from the couch. "You're ridiculous. You expect me to believe Kaye is responsible for everything? How can she be? She's right now lying in a hospital bed, lucky to be alive. Kaye may be . . ." She stopped.

"What?" I asked.

"Nothing."

"You mentioned luck. I don't think it was luck at all. Hewitt and Sewell were shot in the head point-blank. Whoever killed them made sure they ended up dead. Chandler's wound? Non–life-threatening. She even had enough time to get to the phone and call for help. It's inconsistent. And it's telling that she can't seem to recall a single helpful detail about who *might* have done it. After everything I've learned about her from people who should know, why couldn't it be her?"

Allen began to pace around the office, furious. "You're insane. I'm calling the police myself." She stopped, turned. "And get the hell out of my chair!"

I swiveled a bit, my arms on the armrests, letting her stew. Granted, this meet hadn't been my idea, but now that I was here and had access to her, it was a good thing. I could work things through in my head and watch her face to see if I'd nailed it. She didn't seem to be her usual ice-queen self. She looked jittery, off her beam. Was it because she didn't have

Chandler here to make sense of things, boil it all down and feed it to her in small bites, or was it because she knew deep down that I was right?

"You don't like problems. You told me so yourself. But you're not the one who deals with them, are you? That's Chandler. She runs your office. She runs your business. She runs you."

Allen's eyes fired, and defiance lifted her regal chin. "*I* run me."

I looked around Allen's glamorous digs. "I don't think so. You're haughty, and you're cutthroat, but she got you here. You razzle-dazzle them, and she makes sure you rise, that every box gets ticked. She handles the messes, like the Peetses, Dontell, Hewitt, Sewell . . . and, again, your mother. You're her pet project. Have been for years."

"My mother wasn't a problem."

"I think she was. She wanted you to become a doctor and was steering you hard toward medical school, where you didn't want to be. Problem. The Peetses had lost their lawsuit, but they weren't going down quietly, and you needed them to shut up and go away. Problem. Dontell Adkins was about to blast your prima-donna ways all over the internet, right at a time when you were trying to get your magazine established. Problem. And Hewitt and Sewell, two flies in the ointment that Chandler wanted out of her own hair, but their removal helped you, too. Problem." Allen looked sick. "Is there any reason she might consider *you* a problem?"

"Why would she? She'd have nothing if it weren't for me."

"You two argued weeks ago. About what?"

She began to rub her hands, as though they were cold. "You have no proof of anything you're saying."

"No, not yet, not indisputable proof, but I'm not giving up. Maybe the proof we need is down at the bottom of a sewer hole." I stood up, relinquishing her chair. I liked my office chair better, anyhow. Allen quickly reclaimed the seat. "The person who did this to you hates you, resents you, wants to see you suffer and agonize, and then, I think, they want to see you die."

She pushed a button on her desk. "That's enough. I'm not listening to another word." The busted door swung open on half its hinges, and Isabella entered. "Ms. Raines is leaving."

"No I'm not, Isabella." My eyes held Allen's. "You asked for me, you got me. Why's Chandler so attached to you?"

Allen's eyes were molten globs of fire. A subtle head flick in Isabella's direction, and the woman was gone again. "You forget what I can do to you."

I reached into my bag and pulled out the balled-up legal paper Lenny Vine had shoved in my hands. I sat the ball on her desk, smoothed it out so she could see what it was. "This is all you can do. If you could do anything else, besides grab me off the street like a Hefty bag, you would have done it already. She won't be in that hospital forever. She'll come right back here."

Allen got up, started to pace again. I could tell that I'd finally gotten through, that I'd worried her enough to truly listen to what I was saying. "No, he had a knife. He called the office, sent flowers." She turned to face me. "Kaye wouldn't kill me. I'm her meal ticket."

"Tell me what you two argued about." Allen hesitated, holding on to the last of her resistance.

I sighed. "C'mon. We're past all that now."

Allen sat again. "The new show. We argued about the new show. I'm transitioning all my efforts over to that. Closing down the magazine."

"And she doesn't want to give it up," I said.

"She considers it her crowning achievement, her success."

"But you're making her an executive producer. Wouldn't that be just as big an achievement?"

Allen looked shocked. "I told her that just to appease her. I have no intention of taking Kaye with me when the show starts."

"When did she find out you were lying to her?"

Allen faced me. "She didn't. She hasn't. I planned a meeting with my advisors and my legal team this week. I was going to tell her there would be a very generous severance package for her." Allen turned to stare out the window. "I needed to distance myself from her."

Every part of me believed that Chandler had caught on to Allen's deception. She basically ran Allen's entire life. How difficult would it have been for her not to catch wind of a meeting convened for the sole purpose of giving Chandler her walking papers?

"You told her about closing down right about the time the letters started, didn't you? Then you faked her out with the offer of the new job, so she figured she was still on the team. That's when she started cleaning things up before the big move—Hewitt, Sewell. Somewhere along the line she found out it was all a lie."

Allen lowered her head. "And now she wants to kill me."

She turned, scanned her office mournfully, as if letting it all go. I'd have sworn that as I watched, Vonda Allen magically melted away and I was meeting Benita Ramsey for the first time.

Chapter 37

"You're right. She's from the neighborhood," Allen said. "We lived a building apart at Robert Taylor. I don't remember how we met, just that one day she was there. Everywhere I would go, there she'd be, so we started running together. My family was poor, but hers was poorer. The breaks never seemed to go her way. I had a chance at college. She never got close, but she was smart, resourceful. She always made things happen for herself."

"Your mother?"

"She worked in the neighborhood, managing a dry cleaners. She was killed my senior year. She did push medical school, not maliciously, but I wanted this."

"Chandler knew what your mother wanted?"

She nodded. "Kaye worked part-time at that same cleaners with my mother. After she was killed, I was free to go into whatever I wanted. Eventually, Kaye earned enough to go to community college and earn an associate's degree. Things changed when I became pregnant. I withdrew from everyone—that included her. I moved. I cut all contact. I had the baby, considered keeping it, then didn't. I came back, but not to Northwestern. I picked up where I left off. Kaye just popped up one day at my place. I don't know how she found me, but I couldn't shake her. When I got the job with Halliwell, she begged to work there, too. She was relentless. I was forced to put her name through. I was miserable the entire time."

"And when you left to work with Devin?"

"I thought I could just go, leave her behind, but there she was again. As the years went on, I resented her more and more, and she held on tighter and tighter."

"You could have ended it by going to the police," I said.

Allen shook her head. "You don't know Kaye."

I thought of Chandler's visit to my office the day of Sewell's murder. It had seemed odd at the time, her wanting to hire me. But what if it'd been about something else? She'd been with me when Sewell's body was discovered. Had she planned on me being her alibi? I remembered something else, too.

"She came to my office the day Sewell was killed. She told me you'd received another letter."

Allen looked exhausted, deflated. "I haven't gotten anything. I thought I could slowly, steadily push her away, assert myself. I thought that would make the break, when it came, much easier. Now you think because I lied, because I was breaking away, she's coming after me next?"

"Unless she comes after me first. I'm the problem you have now, aren't I? I'm the one digging up your secrets. Does she own a gun?"

"I have no idea."

"Do you?"

Allen nodded. "For personal protection. It's in my safe."

"May I see it?"

She appeared to brace herself. This was the diva, the game-player, the invented persona brought low, but this time she was alone. "Why do you need to see it?"

"I mentioned the gun down the sewer hole? That hole's in

the park, not far from where Chandler was found. I don't think she would have tossed her own gun down there, do you? You're taking the magazine from her. You lied to her and were planning on dropping her, ruining her. Maybe she planned on ruining you first? The great Vonda Allen, a victim of murder . . . or a suspect in a string of them. Would you mind checking?"

She looked like she was running through everything in her head, every time Chandler had come to the rescue or things had just "happened" to work out for her. She knew. Deep down, she had to.

I thought Allen's days were numbered the second Chandler found out she'd planned on closing down *Strive*. That had to be when Chandler started terrorizing her. She wanted Allen to suffer, to fear for her life. Then Allen dangled a job in front of her, a job she must have found out didn't exist. No more letters or flowers. Something else was coming. I could feel it. I think Allen could feel it, too.

Allen walked over to a framed oil painting of an old man in African garb and swung it open to reveal a wall safe with an electronic keypad. Her back to me, she blocked the pad before tapping in the code and opening the safe. She rummaged inside, moving things right, left, checking. Then turned around.

"It's gone."

"A Glock seventeen?"

"Registered to me. It's been here in the same spot. I don't . . ."

"Chandler has access to that safe?"

"It and everything else." She closed the safe, swung the painting back. "All this time, all these years, she's been standing right behind me, wanting to take my place, then plotting to kill me?"

"Or frame you for attempted murder. She doesn't necessarily have to kill you to destroy you."

Allen looked like she was in a daze, on overload. "All those people. My *mother*. She's, she's . . ."

"Yeah, she is." I picked up the phone and called Tanaka.

*   *   *

I sat in Allen's pristine kitchen, with Isabella watching me, smiling. Tanaka and another detective, named Grainger, were in with Allen and her lawyers. I was out here wasting time. No sign of the Stockys, naturally, but I wasn't done with those two.

I drummed my fingers on the countertop, eyed my watch. They'd been in there now for over an hour, likely getting the same stunned stupidity that I'd gotten. I was supposed to stay put until they all got to me. That was how Tanaka had said it. "Stay put." It'd rankled an hour ago, and it still did.

I grinned at Isabella; she grinned back. I peered down the long hallway toward Allen's office, heard murmurs coming from inside the room, nothing more. It was times like these that I regretted not having a badge.

"Agh, this is crap." I stood, waved good-bye to Isabella, and booked it. Tanaka knew where to find me if she needed me. I wanted to talk to Chandler while she was still a captive audience, before the police took their shot, before she figured everyone was onto her, and decided to run. I had a good feeling she had seized on Rogers's desperation for contact and then, hoping to stir things up, had pointed him in Allen's direction, which had almost taken Ben out, so we had personal business to settle.

But when I got to the hospital, Chandler wasn't there. She'd checked herself out, and no one could tell me when, why, or how. I drove to her apartment, but I had a feeling I might already be too late. If she'd been desperate to leave the hospital with a fresh bullet wound in her side, she likely hadn't gone home to take a nap. She could be halfway to Timbuktu by now, ahead of the law, beyond anyone's reach.

I knocked at her door, but there was no answer. I tried the knob, expecting the door to be locked, and was surprised to find that it wasn't. I pushed the door open, then stood there, listening. The apartment was dark, eerily quiet, and the air was so still I could almost hear my heart pounding. It felt empty, but I was still in the hall, not in Chandler's living room. She could be hiding inside the apartment or dead inside it. I had no way of knowing. I looked up and down the hall. No nosy neighbors. Either I went in, or I didn't.

"Chandler?" I called.

No answer.

"Great." I could lose my license. I should really call Tanaka or even 911. Why didn't I? Why was I standing here? Ben. I had to see this through to the end. I checked the hall again, then tiptoed in, leaving the lights off, listening out for anything I needed to worry about.

I crept down the foyer, and ended up in the front room, where I stopped, gaped. "Oh no."

The room was a carbon copy of Allen's living room, the same color scheme, the same plants, the same paintings on the walls, the same doodads scattered around. This place was much smaller than Allen's opulent aerie, but everything appeared to be here, only on a smaller scale. I eased farther in, then stopped when I heard a bell tinkling and spotted in a corner a white cat with green eyes, just like the cat Allen had.

A hall led to the back of the apartment. It was dark, and there was no one in it, but I could see doors on either side, rooms I'd need to check. I moved forward, keeping to the edges of the hall, left side, until I came to the first door. I turned the knob, pushed the door back. Bathroom. Empty. I closed the door, moved on. Next door, across the hall. Bedroom. It was a frilly explosion of white and purple, everything from the duvet to the elaborate bedspread and curtains. Did this mirror Allen's place, too? I'd never made it to Allen's bedroom, so I had no way of knowing. I checked everything, drawers, closet, under the bed, but found nothing but Chandler's neatly folded clothes, shoes, and an expensive set of luggage. Maybe she hadn't gone far? Or maybe she had more than one set?

The drapes were open; the sun was setting. I'd soon lose the light. I crept out of the bedroom, kept moving toward the back of the apartment. The kitchen was next. It was neat, looked barely used, everything in its place, no dirty dishes, nothing left on the counters. It was as if Chandler had been a ghost in her own home, barely leaving a mark behind.

I headed back up the hall, passed a small utility room full of mops and cleaners neatly lined on orderly shelves. There was just one more door to check, but when I turned the knob, it was locked. I stopped, stepped back. Who had a locked door in their house? What was that smell? Sickly sweet. Slightly off. Musty. It wasn't the smell of death, which I was familiar with, but something I couldn't quite distinguish.

I checked around me. Still the same quiet, the same emptiness. The place was clear, except for this one room, the room with the locked door. I inhaled, tried the knob again, shouldered it, felt a little give, stepped back to think it through. I'd wandered off the path of the righteous back at the front door. I was on shaky ground here anyway you cut it. I inspected the door. It wasn't as thick as Allen's. Tanaka was going to put me under the jail, and Marcus would be happy to visit me there, just to gloat. *Whatever.* I peddled back, took a running start, and rammed the door. The first hit appeared to loosen the lock and twist the hinges. The second one busted the door open. And there it was, Chandler's shrine to Allen, the woman she had shadowed and harassed for years.

There were dozens of photographs and small personal items that were obviously Allen's displayed carefully on a long table— a compact with the initials V A spelled out in diamonds, a monogrammed handkerchief with the same letters on it, and a pair of old eyeglasses. I turned around in a slow circle to take it all in, before my eyes fell at last on a shelf of dying flowers in glass vases. Allen's flowers: the flowers Chandler had sent her, the ones Allen had ordered her to destroy. They were all there, dying by degrees. That was the smell I'd noticed—organic decay. And against a far wall, on a shelf lined in red velveteen, sat a scuffed purse, a man's watch, a framed photograph of Deton and Henry Peets, and a couple of old billfolds. I found Philip Hewitt's driver's license, credit cards, and money inside the first billfold. The second held only two items—an ID card to *StreetWise*, a newspaper published by the homeless, and an expired meal ticket to one of the local missions, both for a Lyndon Barnes Jr.

"Who's Lyndon Barnes?"

I thought I'd ID'd all of Chandler's victims, but there were obviously others. *How many more?* I picked up a folded piece of paper that looked like it had been trampled on, but I knew what it had to be before I even opened it up. Dontell Adkins's letter of recommendation. Dontell's grandmother had taken comfort in knowing a kind woman had stopped to hold his hand while he lay dying. Safe bet that woman had been Chandler. She hadn't been there to ease Dontell's fears in his final moments. She had been there to get that letter back.

These were Chandler's trophies, her prizes.

The purse belonged to Linda Sewell; her wallet and keys were inside. The woman's wallet belonged to Chandler herself. Was this her idea of a joke? A stack of white paper and a handful of red fine-point markers lined up like pickets in a fence sat on a writing table. The letters had come from here. I rushed out of the room, pulling my cell phone out of my pocket as I went. I dialed Tanaka's number.

"Where the hell are you? I told you to stay put."

"Chandler checked herself out of the hospital." I moved fast for the front door. "She isn't at her apartment, but she's built a shrine to Allen, complete with items she took from each of her victims—Hewitt, Sewell, Adkins, even a guy I'd never heard of, Lyndon Barnes Jr. Try running the name. See if it matches any unsolved homicides."

"Slow down. What? Where are you?"

I closed Chandler's front door so that it was back the way I'd found it. "Are you still at Allen's?"

"No. I'm on my way to the hospital to talk to Chandler. Wait. Did you just say she checked herself out?"

"Yes. You're too late. She's long gone. She's not home, either. There are no signs that she's even been back here. The place looks like a tomb. She's running."

"What are you doing there?"

"Don't worry about it. She's got no reason to come back here, but she could be heading for Allen."

"Then that's a no go. We left her with her lawyers and her security team."

Chandler would be hard pressed to get past all that, I thought, especially in her condition. Maybe she had decided to just cut her losses and go. If so, she had a healthy head start.

"You need to see her place," I said. "And then you need to find her."

Tanaka said, "I need to talk to you first. Will you just stop and . . . Oh, screw it."

The line went dead.

Chapter 38

The cops couldn't find Chandler anywhere. Neither could I. She hadn't booked a plane ticket or run for the train or bus. She'd just poofed. A day went by. The trail was not only cold but arctic.

"She's not just going to give up." I turned to Tanaka, who was sitting in my client chair, glaring at me. "She has to be somewhere. Did you ask Allen if she had any ideas?"

"I'm done with you questioning my capabilities, you know that? I know what the hell I'm doing. I ought to arrest *you* right now. Your fingerprints have been all over this case since day one."

"And you know why."

"Don't care why."

"You saw that room. The trophies."

"Yeah, you walked all over that, too. A good lawyer could argue you planted it all or at least tampered with it."

"Don't be stupid."

Tanaka's expression hardened. "I'm beginning to not like you."

"I don't care."

She stood. "You don't work well with others. Anybody ever tell you that?"

"Yeah, everybody who I didn't work well with. You got something to say, say it."

"I just did."

We gave each other the cop stare. It was more frustration than anything else, I thought. Chandler was out there somewhere. Time was ticking away. Allen was out there, too, going about her business, making herself a perfect target. No one, not even her Titan handlers, could convince her to lay low until Chandler had been found. She was lethal and on the loose, and no one had a clue as to where she was.

"Lyndon Barnes," I said. "Or am I not allowed to ask?"

Tanaka paced. "You don't quit, do you?" She faced me, resigned, it appeared. "DUI two years ago. Alcohol levels through the roof. He hit a pole, took a header into a swampy ditch. It took four hours for someone to find him. DOA at the hospital. And he had no connection to either Allen *or* Chandler, so there's your theory down the tubes."

"There is a connection, or else his ID wouldn't be on her trophy shelf. She killed him, somehow. Question is, Why would she need to? Why was he a complication for her? She shot most of the others, except for Adkins and the Peetses. Why switch MOs?"

"MOs don't usually," Tanaka said. "You find something that works, you tend to stick with it, unless you can't."

"Dontell. She couldn't run him down and be there to scoop up that letter she didn't want anyone to find. She'd needed a hit-and-run driver. And she couldn't have been there to run the Peetses off the road, again, into a ditch, because that was the night of that damned gala, and she needed to be seen with Allen."

"So you're saying she hired Barnes, then got him, too?"

"Tidying up," I said. "I'll bet you anything that's who he is. That's how he connects."

Tanaka turned to leave. "Well, when we find her, I'll make sure to ask her about it."

"But Allen's covered, you said?"

She frowned. "You do not give up."

"That was rhetorical, right?"

"You can't interfere from a cell."

"I won't lie. That would slow me down."

She left. I turned toward the window, watched as Tanaka exited the building, got into her car, and drove away. I had a feeling, a bad one, that Chandler wasn't long gone. Her work wasn't finished. You didn't do everything she'd done and then give up when the prize was close enough to taste.

Ben wasn't in his room the next morning, when I stopped by the hospital. His nurse told me he was down in therapy and still doing well, which was great. I had wanted to talk things through with him, see if he saw an angle I'd missed, but I wasn't used to feeling weird about it. What Carole told me was still fresh in my mind, and I wanted to ask him about it and get it all out in the open. I had even brought him another greasy sandwich hoping to make it easier to get things started. When I found the room empty, though, I saw an easy out and decided not to wait for him to get back. I left the bag on the table by his bed and went home.

I didn't hear anything from Tanaka all morning. No more visits from Farraday or Marcus, thankfully. Allen was still, well, Allen. Maybe Chandler was dead somewhere, no longer a threat, or maybe not. I felt as though I was waiting for the other shoe to drop.

That afternoon I spread everything out on my dining-room table, files, newspaper clippings, Dontell's things, and went over again what I thought I'd been able to piece together. Allen had said she knew Chandler from the old neighborhood, that one day she was just there and never left. There was still no ID on the gun Chandler had used. The make and model matched, but was the gun Allen's? Hers was missing from the safe, but make and model didn't mean much until the analysis could be completed. What if it wasn't Allen's, and it couldn't be traced to Chandler?

After walking the apartment all day, turning details this way and that, coming up with interesting scenarios I couldn't prove, I grabbed my keys and bag and went to Allen's, even though it was after eight and well past the time to pay a visit. Isabella buzzed me up and met me at the door. I knew instantly from the look on her face that something was wrong.

"Ms. Allen went out hours ago. She didn't say where."

"With Titan Security?"

Isabella shook her head. "She sent them away. She said she didn't need them anymore. Mr. Elliott drove her."

"Have you called the police?"

"Ms. Allen wouldn't like me to call them."

If she'd gone to her office or even to Chandler's, the police would have spotted her. Where else would she go? And why alone, with just her driver, knowing Chandler was out there somewhere? "Did she have any visitors? Receive any calls?"

"Yes, a call. Then she went."

I asked for a pen and paper and wrote Tanaka's number down. "Call Detective Tanaka. Tell her what you just told me. Stay by the phone, in case Allen calls." I dug in my bag, pulled out one of my cards. "My number. If you hear from her, if she comes back, call me."

I sat in the car, no idea in which direction to point it. She'd gone alone, Elliott driving. Where? Had the call she had received been from Chandler? If so, why would Allen leave knowing the woman was gunning for her? What was Allen up to? I wracked my brain. They could be anywhere. No, not anywhere. Somewhere significant, somewhere familiar to both of them. It couldn't be the Homes. They were no longer there.

The Peetses and Dontell; Sewell, Hewitt, Lyndon Barnes.

The secret room, the trophies, the shelf. The scuffed purse. There'd been nothing inside of it to identify its owner, but the only victim not immortalized, the one I believed Chandler had also had a hand in killing, was Allen's mother—shot to death outside the dry cleaners she managed.

I pulled out of Allen's garage, headed for the West Side.

Chapter 39

The faded sign in front of the deserted storefront read BRIL-
LIANT CLEANERS, MAKING YOUR WORLD BRIGHTER, ONE SHIRT
AT A TIME. The place looked like it had been out of business for
a generation or more, the windows boarded up, a rusted security gate across the door, weathered ad bills and flyers trapped
between the bars. The rest of the block looked much the
same—shuttered stores, with handmade signs tacked to them,
hawking everything from authentic Memphis barbecue to
human hair, all now defunct, abandoned, left to rot at what felt
like the end of the world, where even light refused to come.

There was an overgrown lot next to Brilliant with weeds and
nettles almost as tall as me. It was likely overrun by vermin,
which the city couldn't keep on top of. There were hundreds of
lots just like this all over town. I eyed the sign, the boards, the
lot, and shuddered, recalling the last lot and the shoes I'd ruined.

No sign of Allen or Elliott or the limo. No Chandler, either.
What if I'd guessed wrong? Miscalculated? What if Allen was
just out here somewhere living her life, minding her business?
What if Chandler had run and eluded Tanaka and the others?

I dug my flashlight out of the glove box, got out, locked up. There was a rusted Master lock securing the banged-up security gate. I tugged at it. Solid. The gate, too. The entrance between gate and door was strewn with yellowed newspapers and garbage that had blown in on a gritty gust and gotten stuck. The cheap plywood over the windows had been inexpertly nailed up, and there were gaps between the rough planks. I peeked through but couldn't see anything inside. Somewhere a dog barked, then howled, but I didn't see anything out on the street that could have riled him up.

I hit the high-beam button on the flashlight and started around the side, sweeping the light across the snaggy weeds at me feet and ankles. There were bars over the glass-block windows running along the foundation—a basement or storeroom. I stopped every third or fourth step, just to get a bead. The rustling from the weeds wasn't coming from my footfalls. *Rats.* I picked up my pace, practically ran the last few yards, then whipped around the corner and came face to fender with Allen's limo, parked at the back door.

For a moment, I stood there staring at it, as though it were some figment of my imagination. But if the car was here, that meant Allen was here. I placed a hand on the hood, found it cold. It'd been here awhile.

The limo doors were open; the keys, still in the ignition. *Bad sign.* I opened all four doors, checked the car, then popped the trunk, hoping I didn't find Allen's body stuffed in it or Elliott's. I approached the back of the limo, took a breath, then slowly lifted the trunk and peered inside. No bodies, just the spare tire and an emergency roadside kit. I let out the breath I'd been holding.

The dog down the street began to bark again. I went back to the ignition and pulled the keys out, stuck them in my pocket, then headed for the back door. The security gate was open, and the back door, cheap pressed wood, was held ajar by a chunk of concrete block, which acted as a makeshift doorstop. I pushed the door in with my foot, and it creaked back, the beam of my flash catching skittering vermin, whose beady eyes reflected in the light. I shuddered. *Rats.* This looked like a job for the cops. I dug my phone out of my pocket to call Tanaka.

"Help!"

It was a man's voice coming from inside. *Elliott?* The dog stopped barking. I watched the rats scurry around inside. How many were there?

"Help!"

I took a breath, pushed through the door, hoping I didn't come to regret it.

Must, funk, and urine, mixed with the smell of cleaning solvent, crawled up my nose as I stepped lightly over a blanket of broken glass, dirt, used hypodermic needles, and discarded bits of desiccated clothing. I could see just enough from the light of the open doorway to register the disaster that Brilliant had become. The gang graffiti scrawled over the walls testified to its current use. The length of each side was pocked with fist- and foot-size holes deep enough to reveal wood and plaster underneath. This was a flop, a drug den. I could hear the rats running along the walls, and I jumped and hopped, letting out a desperate shriek at one point, when a few of them raced across my shoe tops.

I moved farther in, keeping to the center, pausing every few steps, checking my feet, before starting again. It looked like someone, or several someones, had taken a wrecking ball to the counter. The center of it had caved in, and the sides stuck out like bat wings, splintered shards of plastic and Formica studded with bent nails. I stared up at the clothes carousel, frozen midlap. No clothes hung from the hooks, ready for pickup, just a few wire hangers inside dusty cleaning bags. The bags, tattered and suspended haint-like, swayed spookily whenever the filthy air shifted.

I kept moving at a fast clip back toward the rear. When I spotted an interior door about thirty feet in front of me, a sliver of light peeking out from underneath, I stopped. This place had been abandoned for years. Why was there light anywhere in here? I backed up, checked for a light switch, and found one back the way I'd come. I flicked it up. Nothing happened. No electricity, but light coming from under a door. Yeah, that ain't happening. I backed up, turned for the back door. I'd call Tanaka from outside and let her get nibbled on by rats. I was not too proud to tap out. Not that I was a chicken or anything, but light where there shouldn't be light, a killer on the loose? *Nope.* I reached the door, had one foot over the threshold.

"Help."

It was a woman's voice that had called out this time. *Allen?* I could feel fresh air on the back of my neck, hear the night—the dog barking, the rats running in the weeds. My car was parked at the curb, waiting for me. One more step and I was home free. I'd call the cops; they'd come. *Sure,* my inner idiot said. *But will it be in time?*

"Help!"

Dammit. I flicked a look of longing at the limo, the outside. Then turned and went back. Gun up, flashlight on and up, moving fast, past the wrecked counter, the rats, the ghostly carousel to the door. I turned off my flashlight, slid it into my pocket, then yanked the door open. Worn wooden steps led down to what appeared to be a basement. The source of the light was at the bottom of the stairs. I didn't take time to over-think it, or think about it at all. I'd already committed myself. I took a deep breath, tightened my grip on my gun and started down the steps, quickly, alert eyes adjusting to the dim light, mouth dry, my jaw clenched.

Allen was not my favorite person. By rights, I should have strangled her myself days ago, but I did not want to be the one to find her lifeless body at the bottom of these stairs. And I didn't want to die here, either. I wanted to grow old enough to play strip poker at the retirement home. I had a Labor Day cookout planned at my place tomorrow, and I did not want to have it turned into an impromptu wake. *You will not die in this skeezy basement*, I promised myself. *You will not die in this skeezy, rat-infested hellhole of a basement. You will not die . . .*

I was halfway down, just getting a good look at the room. Wasn't much to it. It looked like there'd been some kind of laundry operation down here at one point: a line of outlets and dangling connectors ran along a niche against the back wall, the machines long gone. A couple of long tables had been over-turned, half the legs missing. No sign of Elliott or Allen. Two doors off to the side. Storage? Only place anyone could be. I resumed my descent, heading there. *I will not die in this skeezy basement with beady-eyed rats crawling all over me. I will not die . . .*

I felt something grab me by the ankles from under the stairs. I had just enough time to register that the something was a pair of human hands before I lost my footing, tumbled the rest of the way down, and crashed to the concrete floor. The back of my head made a sickening sound when it hit the floor, and all I saw for a fraction of a second was blinding light dancing behind my eyelids. The basement had gone dark.

Shock quickly gave way to alarm, alarm to panic, and panic to a desperate desire for survival. I scrambled to my feet, afraid of the rats, my head pounding. Thankfully, I had managed to hold onto my gun as I fell, and I aimed it now into the dark, eyes peeled, waiting for whoever was standing in the shadows to come at me, but not even the rats made a sound.

Chapter 40

All of a sudden, a light flicked on, and there stood Allen, next to a cheap camping lantern that sat on an upturned fifty-gallon drum. There was a .22 next to the lantern. Allen didn't look worried or scared or even surprised to see me. Instead, she appeared oddly calm, determined, which worried me more. My eyes slowly swept the room and landed on Elliott and Chandler tied to folding chairs, both looking as though they'd been harassed to death. Elliott was pale; his hair and uniform were mussed. Chandler's face was bruised, and there was dried blood on her shirt, as though her surgical stitches had come undone and she'd begun to bleed. Their hands were bound behind their backs.

I pedaled back quickly out of the light and plastered my back to the wall. The light from the lantern reached only so far. I was sure Allen couldn't see me, but I could see her. She started toward me.

I called out, "Far enough." My head hurt. My vision was a little blurred though it was quickly clearing. I just needed a minute.

She stopped, squinted in the direction where she thought I

was. She didn't look right. Something was off. It was in her eyes.

"Why are you here?" she asked. "This is between me and her."

She didn't come any closer. I eyed the drum, the gun sitting on it.

I slid my free hand into my pocket for the flashlight, then quietly moved a few steps to the left. "What about Elliott there?" I kept my eyes on Allen. "How you doing there, Elliott?"

He grunted, struggling against the ties. "Been better."

Allen flicked him a look. "He wanted to call the police. I wasn't ready for that yet. First, I have to make her pay for everything she did to me."

Chandler laughed. "Everything I did to *you*? Benita, you don't have what it takes. You never did. If you had, you wouldn't have needed me. You'd have been able to do it all yourself. But you didn't, and you couldn't, and you still can't. *I* did it. I did it all."

Allen ran up to Chandler and slapped her face hard. "You shut your mouth!"

Chandler looked up at Allen and chuckled. "Not good enough. Why don't you try shooting me?" She cocked her head toward the .22. "Go on. Pick it up. Shoot me."

Allen backed up, grabbed the gun off the drum. I froze in place. "This gun?" Allen said. "The one you intended to shoot me with?"

Chandler only smiled. Allen turned toward where she thought I was hiding, but I was already several steps farther to the left, making my way behind her, closer to the drum, closer to the chairs, closer to her. Elliott stopped struggling, his eyes on the gun in Allen's hand. This whole thing had nothing to do with him, yet here he was right in the middle of it all. "The only way to end this is to put a bullet in her head. If I don't, she'll keep coming. She won't rest until I'm dead. You see it, don't you? What choice do I have?" I kept quiet, moved left. "She killed my mother!"

Chandler smiled. "Now, Benita, don't be angry. I did it all for you. She would have held you back. There would have been no magazine, no television show, no fame. We were on our way, but then you tried to cut me out, didn't you? You lied to me and you were going to just throw me out with some half-baked severance package?" She shook her head, frowned. "No. Not after all it took to get you here. Not after everything I've done."

It was Allen's turn to laugh. "Jokes on you then, Kaytina. I wasn't going to give you any severance package. I was just going to throw you out. I don't need you. I never did. How's that feel? How's it feel knowing I'm the one with all the control now? You leech!"

Chandler glared at Allen. I moved again, got closer. "I regret now not killing you," Chandler said. "I could have, you know. There were opportunities, but I thought I could mold you into something useful, and I did for a while. Then you got too big, and you started believing you were enough. You're a fool. Always were." She sat back in the chair. "So, what now, Benita? What are you going to do *now*?"

Elliott struggled to untie himself, squinting into the dark. "Aren't you going to stop them? Do something? Help!"

Allen pointed the gun at Elliott. "You keep quiet!"

"You're losing it, Benita," Chandler taunted. "You can't be a killer without a cool head. You've got to think. You've got to plan and strategize, then act. You haven't got the temperament for it or the head. That's my job. Untie me. Let's talk this thing out."

Allen turned away from Chandler, peered into the shadows. "I haven't forgotten you're there." The way she said it, detached, cold, sent a shiver up my spine. "I just haven't figured out what I need to do with you and with Elliott. I'm going to kill her, but I'm not sure yet if the two of you have to die with her."

"You'll have to kill us all," Chandler said. "There's no other way."

Allen turned back to her. "I'm done taking orders from you."

I moved again. This was no place for gun play. The basement was confined, dark, too many things could go wrong and people could die. But if I could just get close enough to her . . .

Chandler kept needling Allen. "Always the martyr. Always the hero, you ungrateful *bitch*. You barely noticed they were gone, did you? Linda and Philip? They were impediments, so I eliminated them . . . *for you*. The others, too, they stood in your way and, more importantly, my way. You're no killer, Benita. I'm the killer." Chandler wrestled with the ties at her wrists. "I'm going to get out of this chair, Benita, and when I do, I'm going to kill you."

What was Chandler doing? Trying to get herself killed?

Allen's hands shook. "The only place you're going is prison or the graveyard. I'll let you choose."

Chandler cackled. "Prison? No, no. I'm not going to prison, darling."

Elliott rocked his chair, trying to free himself, the legs of the chair scraping against the concrete floor.

Chandler looked up at Allen. "I really enjoyed killing Devin. A little something in his coffee. Well, maybe more than a little. I found it on the black market at great expense. Your expense, Benita, not mine. So you could say that you helped me kill him. Hey, you should count that as your first kill."

"Oh, God," Elliott murmured.

Allen stilled, raised the .22. I moved again. Chandler stared into the gun barrel.

"Do it," Chandler said.

Allen didn't move.

"Do it, I said. Do it. Do it. Do *something*, Benita, without my having to reason it out for you. Pull the damn trigger and blow my head off!"

I eased my gun into my tuck holster, and then tightened my grip on the flashlight. I'd only get one shot. "Hey!" I yelled. Allen reeled around and I flew out of the corner. Crouched low, I slashed down on her arm with the heavy end of the flashlight, knocking the gun from her hand, then arced up, slamming her in the chin. I watched as she stumbled back, fell against the drum, toppling the lantern, which rolled along the floor sending light dancing along the walls.

Surprisingly, Allen roared back, her arms outstretched, murder in her eyes. I slashed the flashlight down on her right forearm and heard a crack, then swung up and whacked her across the bridge of her nose. Blood gushed out of her nostrils like water out of a running faucet and she went down like a felled redwood, unconscious before she hit the floor. I picked up the .22 and pocketed it, checked that she was still breathing, and then reached for my cell phone to call the police.

"Yeah!" Elliott screamed. "Now untie me! Get me out of here!"

Chandler stared at me her head angled. "You should have killed her. How else would she have learned?"

I glared at her, said nothing, made the call.

I kept it sketchy with Tanaka, just the address, Chandler, yada yada. She could get the rest when she got here. She sounded a little miffed, but, hey, I'd deal with that later, too. When I hung up, I untied Elliott.

"Go to the car," I said. "Lock the doors. Wait for the police. They're on their way."

He flew up the stairs without looking back. I left Chandler sitting there. She was a murderer many times over, and she *was* going to prison. She didn't bother trying to get into my head like she had with Allen. I thought my flashlight ballet had dissuaded her. So, I leaned against the drum and waited for the cops.

Chapter 41

As I figured, Tanaka was not happy to see me. She was less happy to see Allen laid out like a big X, blood all over her face.

"You're shitting me, right?" Tanaka said.

"She had a gun. Would you rather I shot her?"

"Do you have any idea how this is going to look? Chicago's media darling tied up in all this mess?"

"Well, first of all, you're going to have to come off that 'Chicago's media darling' business. And look to who?" I ran my fingers over the goose egg on the back of my head. "I want to watch you interview Chandler. She's in a confessin' kind of mood."

Tanaka stared at me. "You're . . . you're . . ."

I smiled. "I know, right? I think the words you're looking for are *utterly adorable*."

She walked away from me, mad.

"So? Yea or nay on the interview?"

Nothing.

"Don't be like that, Tanaka. I just bagged you a bona fide psychopath and also handed you the great Vonda Allen, knocked out and practically lying on a silver platter. It couldn't be more of a gift if I'd wrapped them both in Christmas paper."

She kept walking but flipped me the bird on her way.

"Crude and crass, Tanaka. Crude *and* crass."

It was Eli who got me back in the room with the two-way mirror. Allen had been taken to the hospital. At last report, I'd broken her nose and her wrist, and she was threatening to have me charged with attempted murder, as if. Right now I wanted to find out what Chandler's deal was. Why Allen?

It was after 2:00 AM, but Chandler still looked calm and collected. No lawyer. She had turned down representation, and she was talking a blue streak. She was a cop's dream. I glanced over at Eli, who stood next to me, his arms folded across his chest.

"Do you believe this?" he said.

I stared through the glass at Chandler, who was sitting at the table, sipping a can of Diet Coke someone had brought her. It was as if she didn't care who knew what at this point. "It's like it's Tanaka's birthday, and Chandler's the best present ever." I was filthy, tired, and could swear I heard rats skittering around the walls.

"Who's Lyndon Barnes?" Tanaka asked Chandler.

"I found him strung out in front of a shelter. I needed someone who'd do anything for money, and he fit the bill. He stole a car, used it for what I needed him to use it for, and then I paid him in crack. When I needed him again, he was glad to do it. Only this time, I loaded him up on crack and then set him off. The end was inevitable." She chuckled. "It was easy."

"The hit-and-runs?" Marcus asked.

She nodded. "The Peetses and Dontell, but I'm sure she's told you all this already."

Marcus frowned. "She?"

Chandler flicked a look at the mirror. "Her. Detective Raines.

She's much smarter than Benita." She looked up at Marcus, grinned devilishly. "She's probably smarter than you, too." Tanaka glowered at me through the glass. She was still mad at me. I turned to Eli. "She really needs to get over it," I said. "Were we or were we not cooperating?"

"Maybe she thinks you cooperated too much?"

"Whatever. But for the record, I'm not the only one who doesn't know how to get along."

"It's my own mistake," Chandler said. "I made things too easy for her. I thought we were partners, *equal* partners, though she had to be seen to act otherwise. It had to do with the image I created for her. But she started to believe in the lie. She became dismissive . . . of me. She forgot the truth of it. After I'd done so much, killed so many, she was just going to leave me behind. I should never have trusted her." She shrugged. "I built it. It was mine. I intended to keep it. But all that's behind me now."

Tanaka leaned over the table, looking straight at Chandler. "Sewell, Hewitt, Henry Peets, Barnes, Devin, Adkins. Anyone else?"

"Do dogs count?" She laughed. "I did what needed doing." Her cadence had slowed and she began to slur her words. "No regrets."

I drew closer to the glass, watched Chandler closely. "Eli."

Chandler's head began to loll to the side. "That's it. You have everything . . . you need."

"Eli!" I began banging on the glass, trying to get Tanaka's attention, but she had noticed the change in Chandler, too, and was reaching for her over the table.

"What're you doing?" Eli asked.

"Look at her. She's taken something." I banged again. Chandler's eyes rolled back in her head. Tanaka tilted Chandler's head back and slapped her cheeks to try and rouse her.

"Jones, get the paramedics," Tanaka said.

"All . . . you . . . need," Chandler said.

Her head fell to the table. Marcus swept out of the room to get help. Tanaka lifted Chandler out of the chair, laid her flat on the floor, started CPR.

We watched as the room next door erupted in a frenzy of alarm. Cops rushed in, rushed out. Finally, the paramedics came, administered to Chandler on the floor, but she was gone. She'd been right. She wasn't going to prison. She'd decided to go to the graveyard instead.

Chapter 42

After they removed Chandler's body from the interview room, I sat out in the squad, waiting for Eli, who was in with Tanaka and the others. It was over, at least, though it wasn't exactly justice for Dontell and the others. It was just an ending. Now Allen could play it any way she wanted to, could revel in her victimhood, play to every camera placed in front of her. She'd be more insufferable than usual, but she'd be without Chandler, so whatever she did from this point forward would be all her. Let's hope she could handle it. I stood when Eli walked up.

"Don't see that every day. She poisoned herself," he said.

"She likely did it before she even walked into that basement. She knew how much time she had and used it efficiently."

He tossed his legal pad on the desk. "Well, this one's a wrap."

"Was the gun in the park Allen's?"

"Yeah. Chandler's prints weren't on it, but they were on the inside of the glove they found with it. Allen will probably walk. Chandler *was* after her. The housekeeper can say she got that call, and her driver confirms Chandler had a gun on her when they got there. Allen was lucky enough to get it from her, given Chandler was right out of the hospital and weak. All that works in her favor."

"That and Chandler's creepy 'special' room. She didn't exactly try to cover her tracks. I think she was trying to get Allen to kill her down there. Whatever she ingested was just a backup. She knew either way, she had an out."

"Good thing you had that flashlight, or we wouldn't have gotten the full story. How's the head?"

"Still attached."

Eli stood watching, a slight smile on his face. "That was me asking on a personal level."

"A little sore, bruised, like the rest of me. Thanks for asking . . . on a personal level."

"Notice how I didn't swoop in and try to handle any of that for you?"

I smiled. "I did. You're a quick study."

He rocked on his heels. "When properly motivated." He leaned over to whisper in my ear. "I can kiss it and make it all better, you know."

I pulled back. "Not here you can't."

He laughed. "So, you're good?"

I squeezed his arm. "Yep." I moved past him. "I'll see you later. I'm going to get some sleep. The cookout starts around one. Come ready to eat."

"Don't I always? Hey, I talked to Mickerson earlier. He's getting sprung and wants to talk to you. You haven't been around, he said."

"He's coming to the house later. I'll see him then."

"Everything okay with you two?"

"Sure. Why?"

"Nothing. Oh, he wanted me to tell you he's got a line on some security job for this guy he knows. He says the work's minimal and the pay's good. He . . ."

I walked away on the rest of it. From behind me, I could hear Eli chuckling.

After a few hours' sleep, I got showered and dressed and drove out to the Adkinses. I had Dontell's box in the backseat of my car, its contents neatly arranged, just like I'd found them. I drove with all my windows down, too. After the rats, I couldn't seem to get enough fresh air.

I parked, carried Dontell's things all the way to the front door, and rang the bell. Chandler had hired a desperate man to run their baby down in the street, and now she was dead, too. And what for? Some kinked-up facsimile of devotion? For fame and success? It was done, or as done as it was going to be, but Dontell was still gone, as were the others, and all the Adkinses had to carry on with was the box in my arms and the memories they held. Small comfort. Inadequate, but all there was and ever would be.

Mr. Adkins answered the door, looked at me, at the box.

"I've brought Dontell's things back."

He called his wife, let me in. I placed the box carefully on the coffee table as the Adkinses held hands, drew strength from one another, braced themselves for whatever news I had.

"You find out what happened to our boy?" Mrs. Adkins asked, a slight tremor in her voice.

"Yes, ma'am."

She eased herself down on the couch, and Mr. Adkins, too, their hands still entwined. I kept standing, my hand on the box, hoping to steal some strength from the strength Dontell had had. He'd refused to be undervalued and played for a fool. He had stood up for himself and had demanded respect. I drew in a breath, then told the Adkinses about Allen and Chandler, about the craven way Chandler had chosen for Dontell to die. How Chandler's end was a conclusion, but not justice. When I was done, Mrs. Adkins cried. So did Mr. Adkins. I stood there and witnessed the grief, my hand on the box.

Chapter 43

Labor Day had bloomed like a rock star. The last blast of summer did not disappoint. Sunny, mideighties, birds chirping their little hearts out. It was gorgeous. I put on the music, got out the ice chest, and stuffed it with beer and pop and cold water. Whip and Eli had the grills going in the backyard, and the smell of hickory smoke filled my yard and the yards on either side of me, both of which had their own grills going strong. Chips? Check. Buns? Check. Mustard, relish? Check, check.

I had set the loungers and folding chairs out early and had covered the picnic table with gingham cloth and arranged the citronella candles. Everything was ready to go. I stood on the back porch, taking everything in, glad the weather was good, glad I had those who mattered the most to me here. I'd invited my father, Sylvia, and Whitford, as an experiment, I guessed, to see how it'd go. Whit had quickly attached himself to Eli, wanting to be regaled with cop stories.

Mrs. Vincent had made the potato salad and other sides, along with a couple of her famous coconut cream pies, which were chilling in her fridge. Hank Gray had brought very good beer and a couple of fireman buddies. And Ben was here, sipping pale ale, trading sports stories with, surprisingly, Whip as he babied the ribs with a pair of meat tongs. I thought we were okay, Ben and me. It felt like we were okay. I was going to leave it there.

Barb and Mrs. Vincent fussed over the table, putting out plastic forks, napkins, cups.

"Cass? Look there in my Frigidaire and bring out the fruit salad, will you?" Mrs. Vincent asked. "We're about ready to get this party started."

"Oh, and the other bottle of mustard," Barb added. "It's on the table."

I gave them a thumbs-up and slipped inside. *Frigidaire*. I clocked the mustard on the table, then reached into the *Frigidaire*, found the salad, and pulled it out. When I turned back, Ben was standing there, leaning on the cane he needed temporarily to steady his steps.

I said, "Oh, hey."

His eyes narrowed. "Oh, hey? That's all you got? What're you doing?"

I eyed the bowl of fruit in my hands. "Seems obvious, doesn't it?"

"You drop a sandwich and run, then ghost me? What are we? Acquaintances?"

"I didn't ghost you. I—"

He held up a hand. "Zip it. I got it out of Carole. She never could hold up to interrogation. First, she doesn't know a damn thing about partners, okay? Two, she knows even less about relationships, seeing as she's had a string of no-account losers dating back to junior high school, and there is absolutely no evidence that her losing streak is going to let up anytime soon. Don't get me wrong. I love her, but she's no authority on anything. Just putting that out there. Three, I got something to say to you, I'll say it myself."

I put the salad down. This was it. The talk. "You said you needed to talk, then things happened. Let's do that now."

He nodded. "All right."

"All right."

"This is it," he said. "I'm going to put it all out here on the table, along with the mustard."

"Okay," I said.

He looked at me, but didn't say anything for a time.

"Ben?"

"Yeah?"

"The salad's getting old."

"Right. I'm just going to put it all out there."

"With the mustard," I said.

"It was about your chucking the job. I got it, but I was a little pissed, too, mostly for me, having to team up with some other rube while you were out there with nobody watching your back. There was that dust-up a couple months ago, remember? That's what fueled it. Since then I've been able to get my head around it. I'm good now in that regard. I could tell you were worried about how I was getting along, maybe feeling like you were responsible. Don't. You did what you had to do. It was the right decision. We never really talked about it, but that's where I'm at. That's what I wanted to say. You with me so far?"

I nodded. "I am."

He cleared his throat nervously. "Also, this. We've been through a lot, not all of it easy. But we trust each other. Good partners become almost one person after awhile. One zigs, and the other zigs. They zag, and you zag. Same direction, is what I'm saying. We're not the same . . . We're different, but where it counts, we're . . ."

"Zigging in the same direction," I said.

"Exactly. Carole? Clueless. You took a bullet for me, kept

me from bleeding to death, and I'd walk through fire for you."
He smiled. "So what you let a potential murder suspect flee a
crime scene. Nobody's perfect, that's what I'm saying."

"You don't have to keep bringing that last part up," I said.

"My point is we're family. Doesn't mean I want to date you.
Truthfully, it'd be like me going out with Carole, and that isn't
even legal in this state."

I sighed. Relieved. I hadn't been wrong. I hadn't missed anything. Ben and I were as I thought we were, and nothing had to
change or get weird or end. I smiled, practically giddy, high on
friendship and hickory smoke and a perfect summer day with
fruit salad and cold beer.

"Something else Carole said."

Ben rolled his eyes. "What is it with her? I'm in the OR
bleedin' half to death and she's out in the waiting room flapping
her gums? Give it to me. C'mon. What else did she say?"

"That you went looking for Farraday after . . . you know.
That you left your star behind." He took a moment, watched
me. "My partner had just gotten shot because of his fuckup.
Would you have done anything different?"

I let a beat pass. "Absolutely not."

"So, we good?" Ben asked.

I grinned. "We're great."

"Good."

I picked up the salad.

"One more thing," Ben said.

I put the salad down again. "Ben, frankly, I don't think I can
take one more thing."

He waved me quiet. "What's with the tree trunk out there?"

"What?"

"Hank Gray? The firefighter. You couldn't go CPD? You
had to go CFD?"

I groaned, and then picked up the salad again. "Not you, too."

Ben grabbed the mustard off the table on our way out the

back door. "I'm feeling encroached upon, crowded," he said. "We're like mortal enemies, in a professional kinda way. What got into you? When'd you go red?"

"He's a very nice man."

"Not the point. The point is you've acquired some very radical viewpoints lately. A smoke eater living right under your roof? I just don't know where to begin with this."

"You're drinking his beer."

"No shit? Well, I'm not going to lie. It's good beer. Doesn't change anything, though."

"Ben?"

"Yeah?"

"Drink your beer, eat a hot dog, and *evolve*, for God's sake."